MW01243858

Dayflower

By: Cameron Vail

Nightflower Journals Vol. 2

ISBN-13:978-1496124173
ISBN-10:1496124170

Cover Photo provided by Jamie Shirley of Nefalhim Photography

Dayflower

Acknowledgments:
My wife Terra for her support.
Chistina for the help and guidance.
And always, Mom.
Not to mention the support of my friends through this journey.

Prologue
Watching

He sat in the old van watching the girl walk down the street. It was a nice residential neighborhood and the rusted old cargo van was a sharp contrast to the nice SUVs and minivans lining either side of the street surrounding it. Only the weather beaten ladders bungee tied to the roof and the faded "Roger's Plumbing" stenciled on the side kept him from being too conspicuous.

The girl looked to be in her early to mid teens. He had never seen her before, but he had several good pictures. There was no doubt in his mind that this was the girl he had been looking for. She was short, maybe five feet tall, and very slight. Her straight black hair cascading down her back almost to her waist stood out starkly against her china-white skin. With her jogging pants and tee-shirt she could be any teenage girl, but he knew better. She walked with a sense of purpose no teen he had ever seen possessed. That and she showed no fear even this late at night.

He lifted the cell phone off of the console between the seats. Dialing the number he had been given, he waited as the phone rang several times before being answered.

"Hello?" the voice one the other end of the line answered.

"I have her. Give the word and I can take her right now."

"No. You need to wait for the others to arrive."

"What? She's just a girl. You don't think I can handle one teenage girl?" he knew he had failed at keeping his irritation out of his voice. The man on the other end of the line wasn't even trying.

"I said NO! I don't care what the old man has been telling people, I'm not buying it. I don't care what she looks like, she's dangerous. She killed Anton. Don't EVER forget that. Are we clear?"

"Yeah, man, we're clear," he muttered into the phone.

Dayflower

"Good. As soon as the others arrive then you can take her. Until then just make sure you keep an eye on her," the tone of his voice left no doubt that he would be obeyed.

Not even bothering to answer he slapped the phone closed and tossed it onto the dash. Spending another week or two watching soccer moms shuttle their kids home from practice was the last thing he wanted to do. But if things worked out like he had been promised it would all be worthwhile. Smiling coldly he started the van and pulled onto the street in a cloud of smoke. He had been by her house and knew where she was going so he didn't see the need to watch her the whole way home. Since he had time on his hands he decided he may as well go get something to eat. She paused briefly as he started the van and watched him drive by. He didn't even look.

Chapter 1
A New Life

Her feet were pounding the ground in a distance eating stride. Pushing herself as hard as she could irritation pricked at the edges of her mind. As fast as she was going she knew she could go faster. The speed was there, she could feel it, but she just couldn't reach it. With a growl she pushed harder. Her arms pumped as her feet flew beneath her in rhythm to her pounding heart. There was a crowd ahead of her and she knew she was almost done. A small roar engulfed her as she ran past them slowing to a jog before finally stopping. An older man walked up and clapped a hand on her shoulder.

"Fifty-three point four three. Not bad Miller. Do that at a meet and we'll go to State."

"That sucked, Coach," Vanessa said shaking her head.

"Miller, you do that in a meet and you'll break the school record for the four-hundred. I'm not going to complain if you can pull a better time, but I will if you hurt yourself trying to be Wonder Woman. Go ahead and take off."

"Thanks Coach," she replied. Heading back to the locker room to get her things she had already caught her breath and knew her heart rate was back to normal. By this point it didn't surprise her but it did make her think from time to time. Other runners were beginning to filter in from the track and she fell in beside another sophomore.

"A few of us are going out for pizza. You want to come?" the other girl asked her.

"Thanks, Cari, but I have my self defense class in about half an hour."

"Are you nuts?" Cari sputtered, "You're going to go to that after practice?"

Dayflower

Vanessa shrugged, "I guess. I'll go another time, though. Okay?"

"Sure," Cari shot back before heading off to her locker.

Looking at her watch Vanessa knew she didn't have time to take a shower before heading out. She would need one after class anyhow, she decided. Throwing her things in her backpack she slung it over her shoulder and left the locker room. Once she was clear of the building she hit the parking lot at a jog. Her class was on the other side of town and she would have to run to get there in time.

As she ran she let her mind wander to the last year. She had been living with Lilah for almost six months. In that time their relationship had slowly changed. At first she treated Vanessa with a friendly distance. Like a niece she had just met. Over time Lilah had begun to treat her more like a mother would. Being mothered drove her crazy and overjoyed her at the same time. If she tried she could slip into the illusion and forget the life she had left behind. And however annoying Lilah's mother hen routine was, it was a far cry better than the foster homes she had been forced into. The first one had been nice enough people but they were convinced that she needed "saved." Shortly after a fight over her refusal to attend church she had been shuffled into a different home with a lecherous man she would have gladly killed a few months before.

That one she had run away from. And the next half dozen she had been sent to. After the last one she had lived on the streets for a few weeks before they found her and put her in a juvenile home. She had been stuck there until Lilah found her. Or to be more accurate Cyrus found her and Lilah had come to claim her. It was obvious that Cyrus had pulled heavily on a lot of strings to make everything go so smoothly and quickly. The entire matter was settled before most adoption cases manage to go before a judge. She had been terribly impatient to see Cyrus after that, but he refused. The first time she had talked to him on the phone he told her that she needed to get settled in her new life instead of dwelling on the past.

She knew what his real reason was. He was hesitant to face her after her last visit. It was obvious that he wasn't prepared to kill her for what she had done but he was not one to let his principles relax so easily. But the time had come soon enough. Seeing him again had been like coming home for her. More so

4

than she had ever remembered he had seemed like a rock when they embraced.

"How are you my Little Flower?" he asked.

"Happy." She hadn't needed to say more. As she stood there laying her head on his chest clear bright tears ran down her cheeks. Lifting her face with his thumb on her chin he kissed first one cheek then the other, wiping her tears away as he did so.

"I am glad that you have found your peace at last, Little One. Come, let us talk of pleasant things. I want to hear all about your new life."

They talked for hours that night while Lilah read from one of Cyrus's books. At some point Cyrus had gotten them drinks, pouring her a glass of blood out of habit. Lost in the moment she had drunk it without thought. Neither of them had realized it until Lilah's shocked voice cut through their conversation.

"Is that *blood*?" she almost shouted in shock.

Vanessa had looked at the nearly empty glass in her hand and felt the world rushing away. Somehow she managed not to black out, but the experience had terrified her. Nothing more was said about it that night but Vanessa worried over it for days. She told herself that she had spent over three hundred and fifty years as a vampire so drinking blood without thinking about it wasn't a big deal. No matter how much she told herself that, she couldn't get the incident out of her mind. On her last visit to Cyrus's he had turned in for the morning and she decided to pick up before going home. One of many new habits Lilah had relentlessly driven into her. As she gathered everything she found a glass of blood he hadn't finished. She stood in the kitchen and guiltily finished it like a child with her father's wine.

For several moments she examined her feelings. Other than feeling ashamed for having done it at all there was none of the warmth or vitality she remembered from the act. At the same time she was puzzled at not feeling anything ill either. She would have thought that a normal teenager would have felt *something* drinking almost half a tumbler of blood. Shaking her head she was disappointed that the experiment hadn't really shown her anything.

Snapping out of her reflections she came to a stop in front of the gym. Sheepishly she slipped into the door well aware she was several minutes late. She slid her backpack into the cubbyhole with her name taped to it. Silently she slipped her shoes off and eased into the training room. It was dimly lit and smelled of old canvas and stale sweat. A large black man with a nose like a flat potato stood in front of four other people. The teacher had been a boxer and had tried MMA fighting briefly. After that he had begun teaching this class. Unlike the karate and tae kwon do classes she had tried before ending up here, Miles taught *real* self defense. Instead of forms he taught a smaller weaker person to use dirty tricks to hurt their assailant and get away.

"You're late Miller," he barked at her.

"Sorry, Sir. I had track practice and had to run over here," she mumbled with her head down.

"That's your problem. Don't think I'll go easy on you because you're tired. A mugger won't wait for you to be fresh as a daisy will he?"

"No, Sir."

"That's right. Since you were late you can drag out the heavy bag," he commanded, pointing to a battered canvas bag in the corner.

Vanessa walked over towards the heavy bag glad the chastising hadn't been worse. The last time she had been late he had made her do fifty pushups before starting. She had gone perhaps five steps before she was hit from behind. An arm like a steel bar went across her throat. Instinctively she turned her chin towards the elbow and shoved her hand against her jaw along the side of her neck. Kicking back she caught his shin just below the knee, her heel skating down it to impact the top of his foot. Before she had even completed the kick she went slack, the force of her kick getting her the space she needed to slip through her assailant's grip. Hitting the floor on one knee she pushed herself back up driving her elbow up and behind her, catching him squarely in the groin as she leaped into a run to the other end of the room.

"Good, Miller! But you pulled the elbow, why?" Miles called out.

"I thought Kevin might want to have kids some day," she shot back, smiling at the blond twenty-something limping back into line.

"That's a bad habit to get into. You practice pulling punches, you'll do it when it counts. Kevin had better be wearing his cup and needs to be able to deal with nut shot if he's going to learn to fight too. Now get that bag over here."

Dayflower

The rest of the class was grueling. She had the sneaking suspicion that Miles was extra hard on her for being late, but she didn't back down from it. Even though she was nowhere near as fast as she had once been she was still much faster than he was. As it was when he managed to get a hold of her she felt like a small child. Even at the peak of her strength she was sure he would have been stronger. As it was now he could manhandle her with ease. Anger, not at him but at how weak she was, bubbled up inside of her and she fought all the more viciously for it. By the end of the class they were both winded and bleeding from a handful of scratches and scrapes.

Her classmates had paired off, working on the moves he had demonstrated before she had arrived. By the end they had stopped to watch the brawl developing in the middle of the ratty old gym. Vanessa and Miles stopped and smiled at one another, breathing heavily.

"We have fifteen minutes left," Miles panted, "Anyone else want to give Vanessa here a workout before we call it a night."

"I don't think so, Sir," Kevin answered, "She might kick my ass."

"That's the point," Miles barked, "Don't get cocky or you'll get your ass handed to you. By the same token don't back down because he's bigger than you. That's enough for today." He paused, exchanging words with each of the students as they walked into the night. As Vanessa passed by he stopped her.

"You've come a long way in the last few weeks. You've got a lot left to learn, but I doubt you need to be afraid of whatever brought you in here anymore. And I better not hear about this from your Mother," he concluded touching a deep scratch on her forehead.

"Don't worry, Sir, you won't. I will, but you won't. And thanks."

Walking home slowly she watched the shadows out of the corner of her eyes. She didn't let it show but she was a little afraid of the dark these days. Pondering Miles' statement she added it to her earlier musings. She wondered if he was right. Somehow she doubted it. The irony of the situation wasn't lost on her. For centuries she had lived by night, fearing the sun. Now every shadow made her heart stop. Cyrus assured her that no one would be hunting for her. He had declared Lilah and herself as Familiar Blood protecting them from harm. That he had gone to Court to

7

claim that right surprised her. In her memory he had never dealt with the Night Courts. But no matter what he or Miles said she was certain she would never be safe.

Pushing the melancholy thoughts aside, she smiled anticipating Lilah's face when she got home. She wasn't disappointed either. Tossing her backpack on the couch as she walked in the door she took in the sights and smells of the house. A modest split level it was no mansion, but she loved it. The smell of whatever Lilah was cooking for dinner mingled with the scent of the countless books lining the walls throughout the house. The furniture was somewhat worn but it was comfortable and clean. Everything in the house was that way. In just a few short months this had become home to her more than anyplace since Cyrus' house. Maybe even more, she thought as she popped into the kitchen.

"Hey Vee," Lilah chirped, still stirring the skillet.

"Hi Mom," Vanessa answered. The word came to her naturally and she embraced it. She hadn't got to finish growing up with her own mother. Now that Lilah was willing to give that to her she wasn't going to resist. Lilah looked up as Vanessa walked over to her.

"My God! What happened to your face?" she shrieked.

"We got a little rough in class tonight. It's nothing. I bet it'll be gone in the morning," Vanessa shrugged. Lilah reached out and ran her thumb across the scratch.

"You need to be careful, Vanessa. You aren't indestructible anymore." She had to drive on over Vanessa's protests, "I understand why you feel like you need to take that class. I really do. But you already have offers for music scholarships. Don't risk that for this class."

"I'm fine. Do I have time to shower before dinner?"

"Dear Lord, yes," Lilah sniffed, stepping back, "But hurry."

Hopping up the short staircase she ducked into her bedroom. Somehow she had ended up making it almost identical to her room at Cyrus' house. The large windows overlooking the back yard being a major difference. A quick glance at her clock told her it would be a short night tonight. She had a lot of homework to finish by tomorrow. As she showered she pushed down the bit of panic she felt contemplating her assignments. That was the hardest part of her new life. Time suddenly had meaning again. For as long as she could remember the passing of days or even years were meaningless to her. It had been nothing for her to spend weeks at a time without even moving from where she was. Now there were things expected of her every day and places she had to go. At times it was almost more than she could handle. But it was part of growing up and that was what she wanted more than anything in the world. If she had to spend a few years being rushed through every minute of the day she could deal with it. What was another two or six years to her anyhow? In the back of her mind she knew that she didn't have forever before her anymore but somehow that didn't seem real.

Lilah was waiting for her at the dining room table when she came back down. As she sat down she dished herself enough to avoid the disapproving look Lilah apparently had trademarked. She knew she needed to eat but she just wasn't ever hungry. Picking at her food she waited for the first question.

"How was your day?" Lilah asked right on cue.

"Fine," Vanessa answered, playing her best angst ridden teenager.

"Did you have that math test today?" Lilah continued. "How did you do?"

"I think I did Okay," Vanessa mumbled, never looking up. "I know I passed."

"You should do better than passing, Vee. You're getting A-s in everything else."

"Well, algebra isn't like everything else. I didn't spend a couple hundred years doing equations like I did reading. And the history and government classes are jokes," her voice was heated. This subject had gotten old for her long before tonight. Gritting her teeth it was an effort not to lose her temper. Just as she was on the verge of boiling over Lilah changed her tone.

"I'm sorry. I know this is hard for you, Vee. It's just that with everything I know about you I can't help but expect you to be exceptional. Sometimes I forget you're just a fourteen year old girl with all the baggage that goes with it now. Did track practice go okay?"

The change in tone, and the apology, diffused Vanessa's temper.

"It was okay," she sighed," "Coach seems happy with my times, but I know I can do better."

"Vee, You are an amazing girl," Lilah offered, "but you have to stop comparing what you can do now to what you could do then. Try, God I beg you to try, and realize how much you are capable of now. What I wouldn't give for just a little of your stamina." The last said more to herself than to Vanessa.

The rest of the meal was spent in pleasant chatter. Once everything was cleared away and the dishes were done Vanessa settled down to do her homework. She didn't let herself get irritated over it. This weekend was her weekend at Cyrus's. As long as she kept that in mind none of the rest of it bothered her. He only let her stay there on rare occasions and she relished each visit. By the time she had plowed through the mountain of schoolwork her head ached. The clock told her it was almost midnight. With a sigh she rolled off the bed and began putting her books away. She knew she would be awake as soon as the sun crested the horizon no matter how little sleep she had gotten.

Chapter 2
Shades of the Past

Vanessa rolled out of bed as the first light tinted the sky. With a weary sigh she trudged to the bathroom and began to clean herself up. Scrubbing her face she looked into the mirror and smiled. While the scratch on her forehead wasn't entirely gone as she had expected, it was simply a light pink line. As she dressed she growled as her alarm clock beeped once before she silenced it with a savage slap. It had been a year and only in the depths of winter had she managed to sleep until the cursed thing went off.

Easing her way through the house she tried not to wake Lilah. As she sat on the couch and tied her shoes she was grateful to see a clear morning through the window. She would have still gone running if it had been raining, but there wouldn't have been any joy in it for her. Slipping through the door she stood for a moment and simply took in the neighborhood around her. This was the only time of day that she felt at ease here.

Most of her existence had been spent avoiding places like this or moving through them in the dead of night. Dark windows shuttered in silence were the normal way of things to her. The constant hectic activity of the neighborhood was more than she could handle most of the time. It was hard enough for her to get through the day at school without feeling overwhelmed. After centuries of spending time alone the constant press of people made her feel panicked.

She dove off of the steps at an easy run. The calm quiet of the early morning and the bright sunlight peeking over the horizon brought her earlier smile back to her face. As much as she hated to admit it, Lilah was right. There were times when it was overwhelmingly frustrating to her that she wasn't as strong or fast as she had once been, but all things considered she decided she should count herself lucky. She was still faster than anyone else

11

she knew, and while she wasn't a powerhouse she was certainly strong for her size. So while she had lost a lot of power she was still ahead of the game. Looking at the sun dappled sidewalk ahead of her as she ran and thinking of how it would have made her feel a handful of months earlier it certainly seemed a worthwhile trade.

Lilah was up and had breakfast ready by the time she was back from her run. Stopping in the kitchen on her way to the shower she peeked in the pot in the stove. With a wrinkle of her nose and a derisive snort she let the lid fall back into place.

"What?" Lilah asked with a hint of exasperation.

"You put that stuff in it again."

"That 'stuff' is called flax seed and it's good for you."

"Whatever," Vanessa sighed, walking towards the hall. "Don't know what's wrong with peaches and cream every once and a while."

She couldn't hear Lilah's retort, but it didn't matter. She didn't really care what they had for breakfast, it was just fun to poke at Lilah's buttons from time to time. It made her feel *normal* somehow too.

After that the day moved much faster. The mad rush to get to school on time followed by the crazy scramble through one class after another left Vanessa feeling like her head was swimming. It was the same as every other day had been since she had started this new life, but for some reason it left her feeling overwhelmed. Ducking into an empty doorway she slid to the floor and put her head between her knees trying desperately to shut out everything around her. Centuries of listening to every sound, watching every movement for danger came crashing in around her in one deafening moment.

"You alright, Miller?" one harsh, commanding voice cut through the din.

Looking up Vanessa saw the track coach standing over her with a slightly less stern than usual look on his face. Fighting to keep her breathing under control, the lie that she was fine died on her lips.

"Not really, Coach."

He reached past her to unlock the door to the vacant classroom she crouched in front of and waived her inside.

12

"What seems to be the problem?" he asked once they were inside.

"I spent a lot of time on my own avoiding people. Sometimes it's all a bit too much," she admitted.

The coach leaned against a desk and crossed his arms. Looking at her thoughtfully he paused long enough that Vanessa began to grow uncomfortable under the scrutiny.

"Tell me about it," he said at last.

Vanessa drew a deep sigh and stared at the floor between her feet. It took her several moments to gather her thoughts. She respected the coach and felt like she owed him as much truth as she could manage. He waited in silence giving her the time she needed.

"I've been on my own a long time," she began picking her truth carefully. "A lot of that time I had people after me. And I don't mean police or social services. I was hunted. Almost died when one of them caught me." She paused, trying to decide how much she wanted to share.

"How about now?" he asked more gently than she had ever heard him speak.

"Things are fine now. Lilah's a great mom, but it's hard sometimes." She tapered off, unable to find the right words for what she wanted to say.

"What's your next class?" he asked before she could continue.

"American History."

"How are you doing in it?"

"Setting the curve in the class, actually," she said with a small smile.

He looked at her again as if he were weighing something. Finally he nodded to himself and stood up.

"Out in the equipment shed the hurdles just got thrown in a heap after last practice. Would you mind sorting that all out for me? I'll talk to Mr. Croft."

"Thanks Coach," she sighed.

"Don't thank me before you've seen the mess. And don't think this means you're going to get out of helping load for the meet Thursday," he shot back as he walked out of the room.

Vanessa made her way through the suddenly empty halls towards the sports complex to start working on her project, grateful for the hundredth time how fortunate she was. The work in the storage shed was hard and dirty, but it was solitary. As she untangled the hurdles and stacked them in rows she tried to push the panic she had been feeling away. A little time to herself was all she needed so that she could center herself and recover from the assault on her senses. By the time she made her way back inside she had regained her composure and was able to get through the rest of the day.

Walking out to the parking lot after practice she wondered if Lilah would be home when she got there or if she would be working late again tonight. She pulled her cell phone out and turned it on, surprised to find herself annoyed at the necessity. Just a few short months ago Lilah was having to chide her about never remembering to turn it on; now she was annoyed at the school's requirement that she turn it off. She frowned at the text icon lighting up already sure it was Lilah saying she would be late tonight.

"Hey Vanessa!" Cari called out from behind.

"Yeah?" Vanessa replied, turning to wait on the other girl.

"We're going out to eat again. You up for it?"

Glancing at the text again Vanessa hesitated for just a moment.

"Sure, why not," she shrugged, texting Lilah back as she fell in step beside Cari.

"Really?" Cari asked with a surprised tone.

"Yeah really. Why?"

"Well, you never go," Cari said with a shrug, "We kinda figured you had a bad case of hover mom."

Vanessa shot Cari a look before she caught herself and took on a disinterested air. Glad that the other girl hadn't noticed her look she waved her hand dismissively and shook her head.

"Nah, she's alright. I just have a lot going on."

The two girls continued to chat as they walked to the local pizza place near the school. As they walked through the doors they were enveloped in a roar that rolled over them like something solid. Vanessa blinked as she tried to take it all in. Instinctively she fell into her hunting mindset. Her eyes darted from face to face as she skimmed the crowd. The noise faded away and only certain sounds came through to her. A voice here, a bang there when a pan hit the floor. In moments she knew exactly which parents were likely to notice if something were amiss, knew that the man by the counter was an off duty police officer, and a thousand other details of the room full of people. All of her natural reactions were shoved aside as the mannerisms she had relied on to hunt for so many years took over. Feeling a hand on her arm she turned calmly to see Cari looking at her strangely.

"You okay?" Cari yelled over the din.

Only then did Vanessa realize that Cari had been trying to talk to her.

"I'm fine," she nodded, "It's just loud."

"The rest of the guys are over there," Cari said loudly, pointing across the room.

Vanessa simply nodded and let herself be led to the rest of the group. Panic tried to well up again as she realized what she had done. As she followed Cari she realized that she had seen the rest of the team waving at her, but hadn't recognized them. The part of her that had seen them hadn't ever been part of a group. Just as she hadn't heard Cari because she wasn't prey, she hadn't seen them waving. Knowing that was still a part of who she was made her stomach turn.

By the time they reached the table she had decided that however much she hated that part of herself, it was the only way she could deal with the situation. Sitting there she joked and smiled with her teammates, appearing at her ease. A well practiced act performed flawlessly hid her interior struggle to focus on the conversation instead of searching the crowd. She berated herself every time she caught herself measuring someone as a potential target. Finally she realized that she needed a break. Excusing herself from the group she slipped to the bathroom. Relief flooded her as the noise outside dropped to a low hum as she closed the door.

Ducking into a stall she closed her eyes until she could think clearly again. On impulse she checked her phone and saw that she had missed a message from Lilah. She couldn't help but smile at the simple message. A smiley face followed by an exclamation point with nothing more. After that it didn't take her long to regain her bearings and feel up to going back out.

Somehow the noise didn't seem as oppressive when she walked back out into the dining area. She wasn't sure if it actually had calmed down some or if she was just better prepared to deal with it now. Either way she was glad she didn't feel as claustrophobic now. Working her way through the crowd she was startled when every instinct she had screamed at once. Her face calm, firmly in the act, she glanced around seeking the source of her alarm.

He was obvious the moment she laid eyes on him. It was clear to her that he was much older than the early twenties that he looked. Without even being close she could feel the demon in him singing for blood. Not giving him more than a passing glance she continued back to the table. The urge to watch him was strong, but she didn't do any more than keep track of where he was. It was a huge relief when everyone decided that they were ready to go.

As they filtered out into the evening Vanessa was surprised at how long they had been in the restaurant. The sodium lights of the parking lot cut a harsh contrast to darkness beyond. She realized it would be night out, but it seemed darker, more ominous, knowing that there was a vampire inside. She could still feel his presence even through the walls.

The group broke up; small knots of them each going their separate ways. Cari and a few others walked along with her as one of the older boys got into his car. Vanessa contemplated asking for a ride, but decided against it. The rest of her teammates were walking too. She wouldn't be able to live with herself if something happened to them while she had gone without them. At least she was aware of the danger.

They had gone less than a block when Vanessa realized that she could still feel the presence from behind her. With a sigh she closed her eyes and reached out. It was an old familiar exercise she had tried before and felt nothing. She had assumed that the ability was gone along with her other vampiric traits. Now she wondered if it was simply that there had been nothing for her to feel before. His presence was as tangible to her as the breeze on her face. Her shoulders slumped slightly at the realization he was following them.

"Hey guys, hold on. I forgot something," she growled with real irritation.

"You want us to wait for you?" Cari offered.

"Nah, I'll catch up. Could you take this though?" she asked, holding out her backpack.

"Sure," one of the other girls replied as she took the pack.

Vanessa took off back towards the restaurant at a quick jog. She wanted the others to be far enough ahead that they wouldn't be able to hear anything when she met him. Fear gripped her as she ran back to face the predator. Gritting her teeth, she shoved the feeling down and kept going. It wasn't long before she saw him ahead. He was standing there leaning against a tree with a satisfied look on his face. Now that she was really looking at him Vanessa realized that she could still tell how old he was. It was a relief to see that he was young, turned no more than five or six years.

"Well look at this," he laughed as she slowed to a stop several feet short of him. "I go looking for a bite and a tasty morsel comes to me."

"Wow you suck at this," she scoffed, "Have you been watching bad movies or what?"

The smirk slid off his face to be replaced by a scowl as he shoved away from the tree. Stepping closer he moved around her with a menacing air. Vanessa turned casually keeping him on the defensive line Miles had taught her. While she refused to show it, she was acutely aware of the range between them.

"Mouthy little brat aren't you," he sneered, "You don't know what you're dealing with."

"So I'm not dealing with a near infant vampire hunting in a restricted territory?" she shot back. She had to stifle a smile as his threatening demeanor wilted slightly. It was still a dangerous game she was playing, but at least he had given her the opening she had hoped for.

"Oh, you didn't know," she continued, "Have you even been to Court here? Know who the magistrate is?" She paused to see if that was enough to make him rethink his plans. He looked slightly confused, but he hadn't changed his bearing towards her.

"So you picked up a tidbit here and there. You think I won't kill you just because you know about us?" he said as he stepped in closer.

Going against everything she had been taught, all of her instincts screaming for her to run she stepped in as well. She could feel the demon pushing him on. If he was intent on hurting her she knew there was nothing she would be able to do about it. With a lot more confidence than she truly felt she stared him down.

"Listen moron, even you should know about the law. Look at me and tell me you can't see the mark. I'm Familiar Blood. You don't want to cross my protector."

Dayflower

She could see the understanding dawn on him. Now that he was looking for it the protection laid on her would be clear. Without saying a word she simply waited to see what he would do. While she had heard of vampires violating Familiar Blood it was a rare thing and nothing that was done simply for a hunt. As she watched she saw his expression change. It was a look she had seen before. Anytime a young vampire able to read age saw Cyrus they had the same look in their eyes that he had now.

"What the..." he muttered before turning and walking away, shaking his head as he went.

She had to fight the impulse to go after him, to make him tell her what he had seen, but she knew that would be foolish. Deciding it would be wise to take the victory she had and run she turned to catch up with her friends. She knew she shouldn't be surprised if her true age showed through. It was just one more connection to her old life she didn't really want.

It didn't take her any time to catch up to the group. As she came up behind them everyone stopped to wait for her.

"Everything okay?" one of them asked as she slowed to walk the last few steps.

"Yeah," she replied, realizing that she was still scowling. "Some creep tried to follow me, nothing big."

The girls resumed their conversation, Cari bringing her up to speed as they walked. One by one they each dropped off to go their own way home until Vanessa was left alone. The outing had been a good time other than how it had ended and checking the time she saw that she would still beat Lilah home by at least a little bit. Now that she was free to do so she let her thoughts drift back to her encounter with the vampire. There was no doubt that what she had done was foolish, but if he had gone after one of the other girls she wouldn't have been able to live with herself.

She tried not to think about the other implications of what had happened. It was just one more thing reminding her she wasn't normal. For a moment she considered talking to Lilah about it, but decided that it was a bad idea. There was no way Lilah would take hearing what she had done calmly. It bothered her to do so, but she decided she would just keep it to herself. Once home she got out her violin and practiced until Lilah got home.

18

Chapter 3
To Cyrus's

Lilah knew that the week was going slowly for Vanessa. Every time she looked Vanessa was checking her watch. The girl's impatience was endearing and a little amusing. She was at least glad to find that Vanessa had gotten a B on her algebra test. Lilah was pleased at the news and Vanessa was grateful to have avoided another lecture. On Friday evening Vanessa ran home as soon as track practice was over and hurriedly packed her bag before she even took a shower. Lilah had dinner ready by the time Vanessa had showered and changed. With a wry smile she watched as the girl wolfed down her meal. She smiled as Vanessa set upon cleaning up the kitchen like a woman possessed. As soon as the last dish had been stored away in its cupboard Vanessa sprinted upstairs to her bedroom and grabbed her bag.

"C'mon let's go!" she squealed, bouncing on the balls of her feet.

"Give me a minute. Can't a girl at least sit for a minute after dinner?" Lilah teased.

Vanessa went ahead and tossed her bag into the back seat of the car. Impatiently pacing between the car and the house while Lilah leisurely changed her shoes and got ready to go. Vanessa knew Lilah was doing it to torment her which made it that much more infuriating.

"Come on!" she screamed, gripping her hands before her in a begging gesture. Lilah laughed at the little display and relented.

"Okay. If you're that worked up over it, let's go."

Before she had even finished the sentence Vanessa was out the door and bounding into the car. The fact that she still couldn't drive was still a sore spot for her. So many things were, Lilah reminded herself. She tried to imagine what it would be like to have been on her own for as long as Vanessa had been and suddenly have to live like a teenager again. She couldn't do it, she decided with a shake of her head.

They worked their way slowly through the maze of houses in their neighborhood. As they passed a white cargo van they had noticed around lately Vanessa tensed.

"What's wrong," Lilah asked.

"Nothing," Vanessa lied, "I just had a chill."

Her unease was obvious. Out of the corner of her eye Lilah could see her looking in the mirror back to where the van had been. She had never seen Vanessa act like this before and it worried her. After what Cyrus had told her, she hadn't gotten by for as long as she had without good instincts. Making a mental note she decided to keep an eye out for that van from now on and call the police if she saw it again.

After that the drive to Cyrus' house was uneventful. Both of them knew every turn of it by heart. Lilah had been making it for years before Vanessa came into her life. Even though she didn't come as often as she once had, she still loved Cyrus' gentle ways and his apparently inexhaustible pool of wisdom. She decided that she wouldn't stay too long, however. It was obvious how much this time meant to Vanessa and she didn't want to detract from that. Now that she was responsible for the girl it surprised her how much Vanessa's happiness meant to her.

At first she had taken in Vanessa as a favor to Cyrus. The man had done a lot for her over the years. Aside from the invaluable resource his library had been while she was in school he had simply been a friend. When her father died he was there for her. Unable to cope, she had been forced to take some time off from school to deal with her grief. That had made her lose her scholarship too. She couldn't prove it, but she was certain he was the mysterious benefactor that had paid for her tuition after that.

It had been hard for her, at first, to accept what he was. She had been young then, though, and a teenager's fantasies of vampires were still strong in her mind. For quite a while she had foolish notions of him making her like he was and being able to live forever. After a few years she had abandoned that and realized he was quite serious about his pledge not to create another of his kind. In time that came to be one more thing she loved about him.

She had begun to offer her blood to him out of some foolish romantic notion that he wouldn't be able to resist her after all. By the time she realized that was never going to happen, she was old enough to appreciate his resolve. There was also a certain amount of pride in offering him freely something he needed but refused to take otherwise. Now she was much older and he hadn't changed at all. In the back of her mind she felt like that should bother her. She had a crisp mirror reflecting her mortality back at her that most people didn't. Surprisingly enough it had the opposite effect on her. Lilah was grateful to have a constant in her life the likes of which no one else did. Cyrus was a friend that she knew she would always be able to count on. *Always.* He would never grow old on her, he would never die. Whatever else in her life changed he didn't. That fact was profoundly calming to her.

Looking at the young seeming girl in the seat beside her she was also glad for the chance to be a mother that she would never have had otherwise. She had never had time for relationships in college. After that her job had taken too much of her time. She wasn't some high power attorney but she found her legal work rewarding. Unfortunately it showed her a lot of the worst people had to offer. At every turn she found a reason to end every relationship she stumbled into. In the end she realized that she was creeping up on fifty and alone. Like so many other things in her life, Cyrus had managed to fix that for her too.

She loved Vanessa, that much she knew. She was certainly difficult at times, but then what teenager wasn't? Typical teenage and school problems aside, Vanessa wasn't like any other girl. It was hard to remember looking at her and Lilah had to keep reminding herself that Vanessa was far older than she looked. The girl had lived a life she could hardly fathom and for all practical purposes come back from the dead. That seemed to be her constant. Cyrus had told her much of Vanessa's history before she agreed to adopt her. At every turn she did the impossible and did it without a second thought.

That made raising her very difficult. In a lot of ways she was more worldly and seasoned than Lilah thought she would ever be. In others she was more innocent and helpless than other kids her age. If that comparison was even applicable. Lilah tried to imagine being thirteen forever. That Vanessa, in her heart, was still the teenager she had once been was clear. Glancing over at her Lilah felt a lump in her throat at the way she watched the scenery roll by wide-eyed and excited. She had often cursed her vanished youth and wished she could have been young forever but

Dayflower

Vanessa made her think about what that would really mean. Looking at the fine wrinkles just starting to form on the backs of her hands, she decided growing old wasn't really so bad after all.

~~~~

Vanessa felt the anticipation build as they neared Cyrus' house. By the time they got there she was fighting the urge to bounce up and down in her seat like a child. Hardly waiting for the car to stop she jumped out and ran up to the door. Her heart sank to find the door locked. She had a key, but the rule for all of her existence had been that if the door was open then visitors were welcome, if it was locked they were not. Had he forgotten? Dispirited thoughts raced through her mind as Lilah strolled sedately up the walk behind her, Vanessa's backpack in hand. Halfway to the porch she stopped and lifted a rose blossom from the arbor to her nose. When she reached the step the wistful smile slid from her face when she saw Vanessa's crestfallen look.

"The door's locked," Vanessa said weakly.

"We're here early," Lilah countered, "Maybe he just hasn't gotten around to opening it yet. Let's go in and see."

Vanessa looked back at the door hesitantly. It was plain that she wanted to go in, but was afraid to do so. Her relationship with Cyrus had been much longer and more complex than Lilah's had been. They both had keys to the house, given with assurances of being welcome any time, but Lilah knew as well as Vanessa did the customs surrounding that lock. Vanessa stood there paralyzed, one hand on the latch, memories of even Alaric turning back at finding that door locked. Suddenly the door pulled away from her hand. Cyrus stood there in the doorway a brilliant smile lighting his face.

"Good, you are here already. I did not want an uninvited guest to intrude upon your visit."

Stepping back into the room, he gestured them in with a sweep of his arm. The two women eased past him into the main room. Both paused to take in the room with a sweeping look. In the thirty years Lilah had been coming here nothing had changed. Every detail, from the massive limestone table in the center of the room to the low shelves of books radiating out from it, remained exactly the same. Vanessa, in her time, had watched the oil lamps replaced with electric ones and the hearth fall into disuse in favor of a Franklin stove and then later a furnace. Cyrus closed the door behind them and turned the latch.

"Please, make yourselves comfortable. Would anyone like a drink or a respite?"

"No, thank you," they murmured in unison.

Vanessa took her backpack from Lilah and thundered down the stairs to her room. Throwing the door open, she turned on the light and tossed the bag on the bed. Everything was just as she had left it. Even during the time she had been gone for more than fifty years he had changed precious little here and then it had been assumed she would never return. Turning she ran her fingers lovingly down the heavy lexan of the case holding her violin. The instrument was a Stradivarius that Cyrus had commissioned for her during the craftsman's lifetime. She couldn't begin to imagine what it would be worth today. Not that she would part with it for the world. Cyrus had offered to let her take it to her home with Lilah, but she had refused. The chance that it would come to harm was too great outside of this house. Instead she made due with another piece Cyrus had bought her. She was sure it too was worth a small fortune but it lacked the clarity and feel her own treasure had.

She lingered over putting her things away. Lilah and Cyrus would want some time together and she respected that. Lilah had been here for him when she hadn't. A tiny part of her resented that, but she squashed it firmly. Whatever pain she felt over her exile she knew she deserved tenfold. Her only solace was that the creature responsible for it was gone. Anton's death at her hands had gone a long way towards repairing the damage she had caused in creating him. Even if that creation had been accidental, she was still responsible for the atrocities her had committed. But that was all behind her now. Cyrus assured her that now that she was human and living a normal life that she was beyond the purview of the Night Courts of vampire society. Even if she still had her doubts.

~~~~

"There is a matter of great urgency I must attend to," Cyrus said, pulling Lilah to sit opposite him in the great leather chairs he had brought near the table. Still grasping her hands he leaned forward slightly. His voice was pitched low for her ears only. Lilah couldn't remember ever having seen him so serious and it frightened her slightly.

"I will not go into the details with you. It is not a matter for those not of the Blood. Suffice it to say it is of great enough weight to cause me to get involved."

If Lilah had been a little frightened before she was terrified now. Cyrus had given her only the smallest of hints about the workings of the vampire Courts. She was aware of the Magistrates even if their names escaped her. And Cyrus's disdain for them came through crisp and clear when he spoke of them. She knew she shouldn't be concerned with the squabbles of the vampires amongst themselves, but she was always afraid that Vanessa's past would come back to haunt them both someday. She was sure that was the only thing that would concern Cyrus enough to become involved.

Reaching into his jacket Cyrus pulled out an envelope and held it out to Lilah. The paper was heavy and rich, almost more like linen than paper. As she turned it over in her hands she saw the crimson wax that formed the seal. Of course Cyrus would still seal his letters, she thought to herself. The heavy script on the front told her that it was for Vanessa. The envelope had a peculiar weight in her hands. She was sure it felt heavier to her than it truly was, his gravity adding to its weight.

"I am going to leave for a time. There is some business I am required to attend to that I would normally resolve from here. I am going to tell Vanessa of that before you return for her, but not for the real purpose of my trip. Alaric has been deposed over the *incident*," he continued. Lilah didn't have to ask what incident. The details of Vanessa's last visit here we well known to her.

"But what does this mean?" she asked

"For now there is an interim Magistrate. As long as she follows the Laws it should mean nothing to you. Or to her."

"As long as?" she sputtered, "What do you mean as long as?"

"Alaric should never have been charged. He was within the letter of the law he upheld. There is something happening I do not like in the Court. Lilah," he breathed, his voice almost a whisper, "There is a Blood Price on Vanessa's head. That only held as long as she was a vampire. Now that she is not one any longer she should be safe."

Lilah's head was reeling. So much of what he was telling her was beyond her understanding. He was trying to reassure her, she knew, but she could hear the warning in his words too.

"You said should. That means there is a chance we aren't?" As hard as she tried she couldn't keep the edge of panic out of her voice.

"I will admit that there is a small group in the Court that denies she is a vampire no longer. If any of the Magistrates agree with them she could be in danger. You are not one of us and protected by Familiar Blood so you are safe."

"Then what is this for?" she asked. Nothing he said lessened the terror she was feeling. There were too many "ifs" in what he was telling her.

"I am going to argue this case before our Senate. That is my real business abroad. The other matters are genuine, but they are not the true reason for my trip. An associate of mine, Meri, will see to my affairs here while I am gone. If she contacts you give that to Vanessa so that she may know what is happening. I do not want Vanessa burdened by all of this unless it turns out I am unable to stop it."

Lilah was numb. Looking into Cyrus' eyes she couldn't read him. She felt like the stone she had built her foundations on was cracking. She knew Cyrus was wrong in thinking she was safe. If Vanessa was in danger then that threat included her as well. For a painful moment she regretted taking Vanessa in before she brushed the feeling aside. The warmth of her love for the girl flooded back in and she knew it was worth the risk. Even if things went worse than Cyrus thought they would she wouldn't trade being a mother to the girl for anything.

"I can do that," she murmured at last. "I guess I should get going and let you two have your time." Rising slowly she looked at the letter one more time before slipping it carefully into her purse. Cyrus escorted her to the door, his regular smile on his face. At the door they embraced warmly. Lilah held him tight, biting back her tears.

"You be careful," she whispered into his ear.

"Oh do not waste your fears on me. I will be quite safe. Have a nice journey home and we will see each other again Sunday."

Stepping away from him Lilah slipped out the door into the night. She drove home in a daze and spent the rest of the night holding the letter he had given her. Eventually she found herself in Vanessa's room sitting on the bed. Turning the matter over in her head she decided to leave the letter on Vanessa's dresser. She knew Cyrus didn't want her to know what it said right now, but she had decided he was wrong. That, as much as any of the rest of the affair, was what bothered her. Never, in the thirty years she had known him, had she ever doubted Cyrus in anything. She understood his reasoning, even if she didn't agree with it, but that wasn't what mattered. Vanessa trusted her and she wasn't willing to endanger that trust. If there was someone out there that wanted to hurt her, she had the right to know about it. Lilah decided that there was too much risk of something happening to Vanessa if she didn't know the danger was there. The fact that Cyrus wanted to keep that from the girl bothered her as much, if not more than anything he had said.

Chapter 4
Like Old Times

Vanessa heard the front door close and went upstairs. Cyrus was walking back from the door when she reached the top of the stairs and Vanessa felt a little disappointed that Lilah hadn't waited to say goodbye to her. Something about the way Cyrus was moving made her pause. She had seen that look about him before and didn't like what it meant. There was obviously something bothering him that he was trying to hide. She knew that there was no point in trying to get it out of him. If he wanted to share it with her he would, and nothing she did would make him if he chose to keep it to himself.

"She go home?" Vanessa asked.

"Yes," he answered simply. He stood there staring into the case holding his clay tablets, thumb pressed to his chin in thought. Vanessa was sure that whatever thoughts were occupying him must be really serious. Hesitant to disturb him, she eased into one of the chairs and curled up to wait for him. It was several minutes before he spoke again.

"I am sorry I am so distracted, Little Flower. There is some business I must attend to that will require me to be away for some time. It is pressing…"

"It's because of me isn't it," Vanessa interrupted.

"No, Flower. First of all I must return these tablets to Belfast. After that there are a few other things I need to take care of while I am in Europe." Vanessa gave him a flat stare.

"Cyrus. You haven't left the territory since I've known you. The last time I saw you acting like this was when Alaric came and talked to you about if the Senate was going to order me destroyed. What's going on?" Cyrus let out an explosive sigh and lowered himself into the chair opposite her.

Dayflower

"Alaric has been deposed. I am going to argue his case before the Senate. Since you are no longer one of the Blood I didn't want to bother you with it.

Vanessa was sure there was more to it but she knew better than to try and push the issue too hard. Their time together was short enough as it was without spending it dragging up issues neither of them enjoyed. There was nothing she could do about any of it in any case.

"So how are your studies, Little One?"

"They're okay," she answered with a shrug, "Math sucks but everything else is going alright. History was rough until I figured out that they wanted their cute little stories quoted back to them instead of what really happened."

Cyrus smiled, well aware of the discrepancies between history as it was recorded and how it had happened.

"So you are coming to terms with the new mathematics they use these days." he asked hesitantly.

Vanessa's response was much less polite than she would have been willing to give if Lilah had been present. Cyrus smiled as she complained about her classes and the teachers. Each grievance reminding him of similar words coming from Lilah during her visits years ago.

They continued talking as the night wore on. At first Vanessa worried that the endless stream of questions Cyrus asked was out of politeness. After a while it became clear that he was genuinely interested in her new life. The details were painfully boring to her, but Cyrus seemed fascinated by them all. It highlighted how much she missed having him be a regular part of her life. These visits were nice, but she could feel the distance between them. A part of her wanted to believe that it was just the time they spent apart but she knew that it was the different lives they lived that was really what was changing things. Even returning after her fifty year exile, it had been like time hadn't passed to them. Now each day took her farther from him. As painful as that was, it had to be weighed against her new life with Lilah. She gave Vanessa the mother that Cyrus never could.

Talking in turns they discussed every detail of her life. Cyrus seemed particularly interested in the fact that she was learning to fight. "So my Flower is growing thorns," he laughed. In return he told her about the latest books he had acquired and his latest translation project.

Dayflower

"I wonder what some of these museums or universities would say if they knew where you learned those languages," Vanessa mused during a pause in the conversation.

"Oh there are a couple that do," Cyrus responded. "I have let a few in on the secret. If I say so myself, I am the most valuable secret a few curators posses. They pass the knowledge down with the office."

"Isn't that dangerous?" Vanessa gasped.

"However could that be dangerous?"

"What if they told someone? It could ruin everything! Hunters-"

"Hush!" Cyrus commanded lightly, "If one of them has not done so after these many, many years I do not think one will do so now. Besides, Little Flower, these are intelligent men. Do you think they would risk their reputation or esteem with talk of *vampires*? Not only that, they know that they would lose me as a resource if they did so. Do not fear, Flower, I am quite safe there."

Vanessa mulled over his reassurances. While she was uneasy with the revelation she was forced to add it to the growing list of things she couldn't do anything about. Their talk continued until the early morning when Cyrus looked over to see that Vanessa had fallen asleep in her chair. Smiling to himself, he stood silently and walked over to her. With the slow deliberateness that marked everything he did, he gently lifted her from the chair and took her downstairs. Somehow he managed to carry her into her room and slip her into her bed with the same dignity he did everything else. Once he had removed her shoes and tucked her in her kissed her forehead.

"Sleep well, my Flower," he whispered.

At the top of the stairs he was met by a small woman with a thick red braid hanging down her back and a stern look on her face.

"You're not going to tell her are you?" she demanded.

"Tell her what, Meri? That there is a Blood Price on her head? She is no longer one of the Blood. Even if that ruling still applied to her what purpose would it serve?"

"Bullshit!" she spat. "And you know damn good and well that wasn't what I meant." She stood there, the top of her head reaching just shy of his nose but still seeming to loom over him somehow. "She deserves to know the truth."

Dayflower

Cyrus straightened himself and fixed her with his iciest stare. They stood there for a few moments, eyes locked. After a few minutes of giving her a look that magistrates had withered under in their own Courts Meri met him glare for glare unfazed. Finally Cyrus heaved a tired sigh and relented.

"And what is this 'truth' you would have me tell her?"

"Well, warning her that there is a price on her head would be a good start. Don't you think that may be useful information to have? But you know what I'm getting at. The girl needs to know she isn't what she thinks she is!" Cyrus sat heavily in his chair, the bridge of his nose pinched between his thumb and forefinger.

"She is under my direct protection. I hope there are not any foolish enough to test the sanctity of that. You say she is not what she seems. What would you have me tell her then? She sleeps, she eats, and she goes to school. All of this in the bright shining sun if I must remind you. Do you say she is still like us then? I do not think so."

"Fine, she isn't one of us but she isn't some all-American teenage girl either. I can feel her from here Cyrus!"

"Meri, we are done. Did you arrange my flight?"

There was a long pause as Meri fought the urge to continue the argument. Her lips pressed into a tight line, she glared at Cyrus in a way few would have braved. The silent battle of wills continued for a few short moments. *The man could outwait a glacier,* she thought to herself before relaxing.

"Yes. I put everything in your valise. Be careful while you're over there. Things have changed."

"I would not have expected any less. Thank you. Will you return before my departure?"

"Probably not. I haven't finished the rest of your list yet. Let me know when you get there." She stepped forward and gave him a tight hug that he returned somewhat awkwardly before heading to the door. It was several hours before Cyrus was able to concentrate on his work.

Vanessa woke with a start. Looking around the room her natural sense of time failed her. For a few brief seconds she was terrified that everything had been a dream. With a trembling hand she reached up and felt her throat for a pulse, only calming down when she felt her heartbeat hammering beneath her fingertips. She swung her feet to the floor and was puzzled to find herself still

30

dressed. Groggy and confused, she pulled out her cell phone and saw that it was early morning. It surprised her that she had slept through the dawn, but she had been up much later than normal too. As she came awake she figured out what must have happened. Guilt pricked at her as she changed into her running clothes. She knew Cyrus wouldn't have been upset but she felt bad nonetheless.

She had barely slept, but she tried to keep to her normal routine. While she didn't really feel like going for a jog she braced herself to at least make an attempt at it. Without much enthusiasm she made her way upstairs. The main room was bathed in the twilight state Cyrus kept it in when he wasn't working there. She thought it was odd that a creature of the night would keep things lit like he always did. But that was just one of the things she had come to accept about Cyrus.

Vanessa didn't bother to look around, she simply slipped out the front door after making sure she had her key. The morning was far too bright for her liking and for once running seemed like nothing but a chore. Before long she gave up on it all together and simply began wandering around the neighborhood. Not really thinking about anything, she was too tired to really think about much, she just reflected on how much things had changed. Not just in the neighborhood, but in her life as well. All she wished for now was that things stop changing for a while. With a sigh she decided to go back to Cyrus's.

Easing her way in much as she had left she gave the room a much closer look than she had before. Seeing that the room was empty she crossed the room and stood before the great limestone table that had stood there since near the time of her birth. She wasn't sure exactly when Cyrus had come over from Europe but knew it had been in the very beginning much like her parents. A glass of dark red liquid still sat where he had left it.

Picking it up Vanessa discovered that it was still warm. He must have been up until recently she decided. Taking it to the kitchen she intended to dump it out and rinse out the glass. She didn't remember making the decision to drink it. One instant she was standing over the sink ready to pour it out, the next she was holding the empty glass, the taste of blood on her tongue. Looking at the empty glass in her hand she felt the world rush away from her. As hard as she fought, she knew she was going to pass out. It seemed to take forever for her to reach the floor. While she fell she wondered distantly what was happening.

Dayflower

When she woke she knew instantly that the sun had just set. For a heart stopping moment her fear from that afternoon returned until she felt her heart racing. The blood was dried and sour on her lips and as she stood her entire body was stiff and sore. Cold too, she added as she pulled herself to her feet. She wasn't surprised, having lain on the tile floor in the kitchen for several hours. Leaning on the edge of the sink she rinsed her mouth out and puzzled over what had happened. She could hear Cyrus coming up the stairs as she watched the last of the dried blood spiral down the drain.

"What have you been up to, Flower?" he asked as he came into the kitchen.

"Nothing. I found this glass out there and was going to rinse it out."

Even though what she had said was the truth she felt like she was lying to him. The way he paused made her sure he knew that there was more to it than that, but thankfully he didn't question her any further.

"I have a few things that I must complete tonight," he said wrapping his arm around her shoulder. "I would like it very much if you would play for me while I do so. If it is not too much of a bother, that is."

Vanessa was thrilled. Without answering him she darted down the stairs into her room and grabbed her music stand and book all of her earlier fears forgotten. In a second trip she gingerly carried her violin upstairs. She relished every opportunity to play the instrument, but usually felt obligated to spend as much time with Cyrus as she could. He waited patiently as she arranged herself and began to play. With a small smile he noticed that she had carefully set up her stand and book but never opened it before playing. Before long the strains of songs they both knew by heart filled every corner of the house.

Cyrus donned cotton gloves and began to carefully pack the ancient clay tablets from the display into a heavy case. Vanessa was only half aware of what he was doing as she played. His sense of calm and peace was so strong that she could feel it as she played. Grasping his calm she pulled it into herself and used it to smother the fears she had been fighting herself. She wasn't sure how long she had been playing when she realized he was standing before her again. As she let the last note die, she lowered her arms and realized how tired they were.

"I fear I must leave before the morning, Flower. Lilah is going to be here to get you soon."

"Oh," she answered crestfallen. Gently she placed the violin on the table and walked slowly to Cyrus, embracing him. "I miss you," she whispered.

Cyrus held her for a moment, stroking her hair as he did so. "I know, Flower. But it is not healthy for a young girl to associate with those like myself."

Vanessa snorted to herself. She would have made some sort of retort but she was afraid she would start to cry if she talked. Cyrus's discomfort at the length of her hug was almost tangible to her but he indulged her nonetheless. When she was ready she stepped away, taking his hand as she did so.

"Be careful," she implored. There was so much more she wanted to say but she wasn't sure if she even knew what words would fit.

"Oh do not worry for me, Little One. I will be well. You just keep up on your studies and take care of Lilah."

"I will," she promised and turned away.

Vanessa set about putting things away and gathering what she had brought with her. She could hear Cyrus moving around upstairs as she packed her clothes in her backpack. Sitting on the bed she thought about the day. A heavy sensation had been sitting in the pit of her stomach since she woke tonight. For a blissful few hours she had lost herself in the music and it was like no time had passed. Part of her wondered at that. Now that she had what she had always wanted she missed parts of her old life so much that she could hardly breathe. She knew it wasn't fair to want both, but she did. Cyrus was holding her at arm's length. That much she had figured out and it pained her. He hadn't come out and told her that, but he had done everything short of explained why to her tonight. The fact that he saw her as a young girl was almost enough to make her laugh. Although compared to how old she knew he must be she knew she was young by comparison. Before things had changed she had always been able to feel about how old another vampire was. When she reached out to Cyrus that way, all she had felt was an endless abyss.

But that had been another life. Now she had school tomorrow morning. A glance at her watch told her it was going to be a very long day. It was almost five in the morning and she had slept all day the day before. If she was going to sleep tonight she would have to stay up all day too. At least Lilah wouldn't have had to get up too much earlier than normal, she decided. Lilah would be less than charitable with her if she hadn't gotten any sleep herself. Shaking her head she got back to work putting things in order. While she worked she wondered if she would ever be able to stop adding new things to the growing list of things she didn't understand.

By the time she got upstairs Lilah was there. She and Cyrus were standing by the table talking in hushed tones that Vanessa wasn't quite able to make out. The tense look on Lilah's face did nothing to ease Vanessa's concerns about what was going on. As she walked up the conversation died and Lilah brightened.

"Hey there, Vee! How's it going?"

"Okay," she answered giving Lilah a warm hug. "Sorry if I kept you waiting."

"No, you're fine. I was just asking Cyrus how long his trip was going to be. We'll have to put together another visit when you don't have something going on," she said, turning to Cyrus.

"Unfortunately I will not know how long it will take until I know how serious the charges are. I told Vanessa about Alaric," he explained at Lilah's look of surprise.

"Bring me back something Irish," Vanessa told Cyrus before giving him one last goodbye hug.

"You have my word," Cyrus smiled.

The three of them left together, Cyrus locking the door behind him. After they parted ways Vanessa and Lilah walked in silence for a time. Vanessa could feel the tension building in Lilah as they walked.

"You didn't say goodbye," she tried to make it sound like a jest but knew she had failed as the words left her mouth.

"I'm sorry, Vee. Cyrus told me some things that were a bit distracting."

Hearing the seriousness in Lilah's voice made her sorry she had complained about something so trivial.

"Cyrus doesn't want me to tell you what's going on," she continued, "But I think you have a right to know. I'm not going to try and explain it all because I don't really understand it all myself."

Dayflower

The conversation halted as they got in the car and Lilah concentrated on getting them back on the road. Vanessa bit back her impatience as they made their way through the urban streets back towards the highway. Once there Lilah was visibly gathering her thoughts before she resumed speaking.

"Cyrus gave me a letter to give you if something happened while he is away." Holding up her hand she stopped Vanessa before she could interrupt. "That is why I think things are serious enough that you need to know at least what he told me. There is a Blood Price on you. I'm not sure what that means, but I doubt it's good."

"It means that any vampire that can catch me and take me to Court has a get out of jail free card. Or a huge jump in standing. Usually exiles hunt for a Blood Price because if they bring it in all of their crimes are transferred to the bounty."

"Oh," Lilah's face went white as she realized what that would mean. Vampire penalties were not light, she knew. "Well, I hope he explains the rest in the letter. I didn't open it and he already told you about Alaric. He swears that you're safe since you're not, you know, anymore."

"Mmm, hmm," Vanessa mumbled. Her head was spinning. Now she knew what Cyrus was really going to Europe for. They didn't talk the rest of the drive. Vanessa was gripped by a fear that she hadn't felt since Anton was hunting for her. For over three-hundred and fifty years all she had wanted was to be a girl again and to grow up. Now that very thing was in her hands and the past threatened to rip it away from her.

Lilah knew very well the torment Vanessa was fighting. When she had first taken in the otherworldly teen they had spent many nights talking about her life then and now. While the larger part of her concern was for the girl she feared for herself too. Cyrus had tried to keep the workings of vampire society from her, but having been awakened to their world she read the news with new eyes. From time to time a headline would catch her attention and she would ask Cyrus about it. Sometimes he would answer her questions, others he would go silent then change the subject. Between the two she had put together a fair picture of life in the darkness and it wasn't pretty.

Dayflower

The sun had come up by the time they got home and Vanessa was dismayed at how bright it seemed. Half way to the door she stopped and held her hand out in front of herself. She could almost swear that the morning light was burning her. Ever since she had started this new life she had burned easily. If she was in the sun for more than a few minutes without sunscreen on she began to turn pink. As the months passed she stopped worrying about it, other kids at school with fair skin burned quickly too. But this felt different, familiar.

"What's wrong Vee?" Lilah asked, walking up beside her.

"Nothing, I guess." She watched for some change, but didn't see any. Dropping her hand to her side she followed Lilah inside.

When she entered her room she saw the letter instantly. Lilah had propped it up on her dresser. Tossing her backpack on the floor beside the bed she approached the letter like a poisonous snake. With trembling fingers she picked it up and turned it over in her hands. The paper was thick and heavy, almost like cloth more than paper and sealed with a red wax stamp. She smiled to herself. If she knew Cyrus it would have been written with a fountain pen too. He had finally given up on quills in the fifties.

She was glad to see the seal intact too. The fact that Lilah had both told her of the letter and not looked at it herself gave Vanessa a small rush of joy. At times like this she thought it was a shame that Lilah hadn't had children of her own. Dropping onto the bed she cracked the seal and unfolded the letter. Dark heavy strokes in a precise hand she knew all too well filled the page.

My Dearest Little Flower,

If you are reading this then either my trip has not proved as successful as I would have hoped or Lilah did not heed my wishes and has delivered it to you. While the latter is not how I wanted to handle this I will not second guess her as she is your mother now and your welfare is in her care. As I compose this, it is my intention to spare you the anxiety of worrying over any of this that I may. Alaric has been deposed in no small part due to his handling of you during your last visit as one of the Blood. I will not bore you with the legalities of the matter, but this was wrongly done. Even this would not be enough to pull my attentions back to the Court were it not for the added affront of a Blood Price being placed upon you.

Dayflower

While there are a myriad of reasons involved, Anton stands the highest. Your dispatching of him should have prevented such a severe measure even if they felt the need to seek retribution for the rest of your so-called crimes. You no longer being one of the Blood would preclude that penalty in any case. I go now to Europe to argue for the correction of these miscarriages of justice. Should I be unsuccessful I have arranged for a trusted acquaintance to give you warning, and if needed take you into hiding. I fear it would not be safe for me to do so as any wishing to collect the bounty will surely follow me. Her name is Meri and while she can be brash I trust her completely.

I hope you never read these words but if you do remember that I care for you deeply and will do everything in my power to see you safe.

The letter wasn't signed but marked with the odd pattern of triangles that Cyrus used for his signature. Carefully Vanessa folded the letter closed and rolled off the bed. From underneath she pulled out a small wooded chest, its surface dark with oil. After pulling it out and popping the latch Vanessa looked at her hands with a frown.

"I must be imagining things," she muttered to herself.

The box was coated liberally with anointing oil and she swore the palms of her hands felt hot after opening the box. She rubbed her palms on her jeans and looked intently at her hands. Seeing nothing she returned her attention back to the contents of the chest. Inside was a small hand crossbow and wooden darts she had made herself and soaked in oil as well as bottles of holy water. On the other side was a small collection of her greatest treasures saved over the course of centuries. She solemnly added Cyrus's letter to that collection and snapped the lid closed.

Vanessa wondered who this Meri was. She knew he hadn't known her before her exile, and it wasn't like Cyrus to trust someone so quickly for him to have come to know her since her rebirth. That meant she had to have met him after he had kicked Vanessa out. If she was a trusted friend of Cyrus's then Vanessa would have to trust her if the time came. The other question was what made her an outcast. She didn't have any doubt that Cyrus wouldn't have befriended her if she were a hanger-on at Court. That meant she had to be at least on the fringe of vampire society. Vanessa couldn't help but think she would be interesting to meet.

Chapter 5
Nightmares

Worry ate at Vanessa all day. She knew that there was nothing she could do about whatever problems Cyrus was dealing with, but somehow that made things even worse. Lilah was on edge too and she felt guilty for that as well. Being tired wasn't helping her mood either. By mid afternoon she surrendered and went to her room for a quick nap. Her sleep was haunted by dreams of frightening things moving in the dark. After a couple hours of restless tossing and turning she gave up on napping. With a sigh she rolled off of her bed and shuffled down the hall. If anything she felt worse than she had before.

"Dinner's almost ready!" Lilah called.

"Okay," Vanessa answered. She walked into the dining room and dropped heavily into her chair. Lilah had already set everything out and was beginning to fix her own plate. With a start Vanessa realized she hadn't eaten since dinner Friday night.

"You okay Vee?" Lilah asked with a concerned look on her face.

"Yeah," Vanessa shrugged, "I stayed up all night last night and took a nap this afternoon. Now I feel all crummy." Lilah made a sour face but didn't comment.

There was little conversation during dinner and Vanessa decided to go to bed as soon as the dishes were done. As she was settling down for the night Lilah came in and sat down on the edge of the bed.

"He's going to take care of things, he always does."

"I know. But he shouldn't have to," Vanessa replied, sitting down next to Lilah. "Maybe Alaric was right. Maybe everyone would be better off if they had destroyed me after Clarius died like they wanted to."

Dayflower

"Don't ever say that!" Lilah scolded. She reached over and pulled Vanessa to her. Letting herself be pulled in Vanessa sat there with her head on Lilah's shoulder trying to fight back her tears. The woman that had become a mother to her smoothed her hair while searching for the right words to say and the tears came despite her.

"Do you think Cyrus feels the same?" she asked at last. Unable to speak Vanessa just shook her head. "Do you think I feel that way?" Lilah continued.

"You may before this is all over."

Lilah lifted Vanessa's chin with her finger until the two were eye to eye.

"Vanessa Elizabeth Miller I do not want to hear talk like that from you. I love you, and you need to remember that. I knew full well what the score was before you ever knew who I was. Cyrus told me all about your past and the things that haunt you before I agreed to take you in. I knew it could be dangerous. So you can set the weight of the world down for a minute. Cyrus knew what he was getting into all those years ago. I knew what I was doing last year. I think the only one that has forgotten that is you." She pulled Vanessa into a tight hug and held her there, "I love you Vee. Never forget that."

Vanessa cried, letting all the fatigue and fear flow out of her at once. Before too long Lilah realized that Vanessa was asleep in her arms and eased her into bed. She spent the rest of the evening pacing the house, her mind alternating between concern for the girl she cared for and fear at what this whole affair may be bringing to her doorstep.

~~~

Vanessa's feet pounded the sidewalk at a frantic pace. Looking behind her she was relieved to see nothing but an empty street. A cold misty drizzle drifted through the air keeping most people off of the streets tonight. It was just enough to keep her from being able to run full out. The wide tear in her jeans that was letting the cold water run down her leg reminded her of how well that had gone when she tried it earlier.

She knew that there were two of them. The one that had tried to grab her outside of the restaurant had to be trying to herd her to his partner.

"Stupid," she chided herself under her breath.

Dayflower

She had almost gotten in his truck on her own. He pulled up beside her as she walked down the sidewalk and offered her a ride. There was something vaguely predatory about him that had given her pause, but at the same time she thought it would be better if he picked her up than some other girl. She had opened the door and had her foot on the running board of the truck before she had recognized him. He was shaved now and his hair was shorter, but there was no mistaking the cold eyes and tattered army jacket. The thin scar running up from under his collar to his ear was fairly distinctive as well. They had tried to grab her several months earlier.

He saw the look on her face and dove towards her. Gripping the sleeve of her coat he tried to force her into the cab of the truck. Acting on instinct she slammed the truck door on his arm. For a moment he held his grip, but he released her as she went to slam the door again. Sprinting at full speed, she tried to outdistance the truck. The resulting spill left her with a knee that was still creaking as she ran and a pair of tattered jeans.

More irritated than scared, she wondered how they had found her again. Spinning to check behind her again she cursed as her wet hair covered her face. With long hair currently in fashion she had let hers return to its natural length. Not for the first time she longed for the shorter styles she had enjoyed in the Twenties and Thirties. With a shake of her head she began to run again.

"God, why does this keep happening?" she growled as she rounded a corner.

She was answered by a sharp blow to the side of her head. Reeling she fell back against the store window behind her. Construction paper turkeys smiled down on her as she slid to the pavement, stars clouding her vision. Confused, she tried to figure out how he had gotten ahead of her. The raspy voice she heard told her that he hadn't, but his partner had.

"Why does it keep happening? Because you keep slipping away," he replied casually as he swung the pipe he had hit her with once again.

The pipe caught her in the center of the chest with a telling crunch, driving all the air from her lungs. Doubled over by the blow, she dropped to her hands and knees only to catch another blow to the back. Unable to scream she tried to roll away from him. If only she could get to her feet she could get away.

Dayflower

"You're the Holy Grail, girl. Didn't you know that?" he asked, pausing to hit her again. "The vampire no hunter can take. Hell, you're a legend."

With an underhand swing he caught her in the face, throwing her backwards. As she tried to roll away he pinned her to the brick of the storefront with a boot on her shoulder. Cocking the pipe back he swung again. This time Vanessa caught the pipe. Pushing back against him, she tried to force him to drop his foot from her shoulder. When he didn't she shoved harder. She wasn't strong enough to push him away, but it was enough to make him lock his back leg to resist her. As soon as his knee went straight she kicked for all she was worth. The blow was far from perfect, but it was enough that he yelled and staggered back from her.

Not wasting a second, she rolled to her side and scrambled to her feet. Staggering around the corner into the alley she tried to find some way out. In desperation she tried the flap to an old coal chute into the store basement. With relief she managed to pry it open and slide inside. Rust held the door up making her jump back up and force it as closed as she could get it from the inside. Looking around she was disheartened by the lack of anything useful in sight. The basement was mostly empty. Cooler cases covered with rust lined one wall accompanied in the dark by some water damaged boxes. There was nothing she could use as a weapon and no hiding places that wouldn't be immediately noticed. Creeping along towards the door she just had to hope that they didn't see where she had gone. The coarse whine of the coal chute's hinges quickly stole that hope from her.

"I've seen your kind kill more of my buddies than I could stomach," the man that had beat her yelled into the opening.

Vanessa felt utterly exposed in the center of the empty space, but she knew he couldn't see her. Not even her vision fully penetrated the utter dark around her. Closing her eyes she strained to listen. Shutting out his rambling was hard, but she knew he was just trying to distract her. The other hunter had to be close; probably making his way to the door to block her escape. Faint footsteps told her he was in the store above her making her wonder how he had gotten in without her having heard. Barely able to make out where the door was she began to inch towards it. The slow pace was agonizing, but she was certain that the man behind her was armed with more than a pipe.

"If it wasn't bullets, it was you vermin. It wouldn't have been so bad if they'd just taken the enemy or been gooks themselves, but no. I watched a lot of good men die with their throats torn out. Landmines my ass," he continued, his voice rising in pitch as he went.

Vanessa had heard about things like he described. Cyrus called them vultures with disgust thick in his voice; vampires who went to war zones so that they could hunt with impunity. He told her they were gluttonous monsters that simply enjoyed the kill.

A single beep from somewhere outside ended the man's tirade. Vanessa froze for a few moments listening to the silence until a clank and a low hiss took its place. Turning, she saw a canister rolling towards the center of the basement emitting a thick smoke that crawled across the floor towards her. As it filled the space she continued to move forward, slightly faster now that she had some cover. The first tendrils of the smoke reached her and she was grateful that she still couldn't breathe after her beating. It burned her nose and throat without her even taking a breath. Her eyes felt scorched as it billowed around her. In moments the blood tinged tears it drew had totally ruined her ability to see. *One hell of a neutralizer,* she thought to herself as she realized that her advantage in the dark was gone.

Finally at the stairs she had to feel her way to the door at the top slowly, only managing to ease herself up one stair at a time. Once there she pressed her hands against the door. Out of reflex she went to take a deep breath, meaning to smell for any signs of the other hunter. The dual fires of her broken ribs and burning nose from the smoke made her fight not to cry out. Frustrated, she put her head against the door, wincing at the bruises there as well.

She extended her senses what she was able, but the pain and exhaustion she felt overwhelmed anything she might have been able to pick up. The blows to the head had left her dizzy and struggling to think clearly. With a sinking feeling in her stomach she decided that there was no answer other than to go ahead and risk the door.

The instant it opened she heard a telltale click and threw herself forward and to the side. Her battered body protested the abuse as she rolled through the doorway. Before she had even completed her roll a deafening roar shook the room. Slowed as she was she couldn't completely dodge the blast and a handful of shot still found its way into her side. Springing to her feet with a growl that was equal parts pain and anger she could at least feel the hunter before her.

She lunged forward and grabbed him, her hands scrambling up his chest to meet something rubbery over his face. He rabbit punched her in the ribs forcing a strangled whimper out of her, but not making her release her hold. Throwing herself back with all of her strength she drug him along until they were tumbling down the stairs. In the melee she managed to force the mask from his face leaving him to choke and gag in the clouds of gas.

Tossing the mask to the far side of the basement she once again forced her way up the stairs only to scream in agony as a deluge of holy water poured over her face. The combination of her injuries, exhaustion, and hunger brought the demon out more than normal and the holy water scalded her like steam. She dove forward hoping to grab the other man. Brushing him with her hand, she spun as he stepped away.

~~~~

"VANESSA!" the yell cut through everything.

Blinking she realized it was light. Reflexively she struggled against the hands gripping her shoulder until her vision and head cleared enough to look around. Her heart was pounding and she could feel her cheeks were wet with tears. Pulling away she curled in on herself and tried to make sense of everything.

"Vanessa, you're fine. Everything's okay. You were just having a nightmare," the voice soothed as a hand stroked her hair.

It took her a moment to realize it was Lilah. Confusion rushed in as the memories of a night long ago finally started to recede. She let out breath she hadn't realized she was holding and struggled to control herself. Seeing that she had stopped fighting Lilah scooted closer and held Vaness close.

"It's alright," she whispered as she held Vanessa, rocking her gently as she shook. "Do you want to talk about it?" she asked once things seemed to have calmed down.

"What happened?" Vanessa asked, sitting up unsteadily.

"Well, I heard you scream and ran in here to find you thrashing around. You scared me to death!" Lilah replied.

Vanessa took a deep breath, half wincing at remembered pain, and looked around the room. A part of her struggled to reconcile the sight before her and the nightmare she had just left.

"Are you okay?" Lilah prodded gently.

Dayflower

"Yeah," Vanessa sighed heavily, leaning her head against Lilah's shoulder. "I was just dreaming about something that happened a long time ago."

"Oh?"

"Hunters. It was the early Seventies, I forget what year."

"Was it bad?" Lilah asked. The tone of her voice relaying that she already knew it had been.

"Yeah," she breathed with a shiver.

"You don't have to worry about that anymore," Lilah reassured her, "Those days are long behind you now."

Vanessa nodded and let herself be soothed. She couldn't bring herself to explain the truth of the matter to Lilah. It was a worry the woman didn't need. That night had made things clear to Vanessa. All of the times she had encountered hunters hadn't been chance. They were actively looking for her. Not just her as another vampire, but her in particular. The man's words came back to her, *"The vampire no hunter can take. Hell, you're a legend."* If vampire society couldn't accept that she wasn't a vampire any longer would the hunters be any different? She shuddered again thinking about how things would turn out if she were to meet a pair like that now.

Eventually she managed to shoo Lilah back to her own room, and tried to go back to sleep herself. As she sat there in the dark images of the ugly brawl that followed and the days it had taken her to recover, even with her unnatural healing, kept coming back to her. She tried to put it all behind her, but sleep simply wasn't coming.

She couldn't decide if she was just worried about being forced to repay the debts of her past or if there was something more to it than that. Unease ate at her as she thought back to her time at Cyrus's. That was the first time she could remember since she got out of the hospital that she hadn't awakened with the dawn. Ever since she had begun her new life she had found herself as tied to the rising of the sun as she had been to its setting before. The fact that she had slept through the day along with being sure she was feeling old sensations was bad enough. If she tried hard enough she could convince herself that it was simply a return to old habits from being with Cyrus. But all of that and finding out that there was a Blood Price on her too just didn't seem like coincidence.

Chapter 6
Night Visits

Cyrus watched the girls walk to Lilah's car before leaving the steps himself. By the time he reached the street his own transportation had arrived. The young man driving hopped out and quickly held the door open for Cyrus. With a nod of thanks he slid into the back seat and made sure he had everything he would need. He smiled as the driver waited his signal before pulling away from the curb. Meri was nothing if not a marvelous planner. The young vampire driving could not be more than five years turned. From his skittish manner Cyrus guessed he was one lucky enough to be able to read the age of their kind. He had no doubt that she had chosen him for that very reason. He had learned that he was treated much more respectfully by those with that particular talent than he was by those lacking it.

Cyrus had long ago stopped trying to discern what caused the wide divergence in abilities his kind had developed over the years. Most of them seemed to run in bloodlines but not all. He had a strong suspicion that it had as much to do with the nature of the person turned as it did with the demon that possessed them. Some abilities he had seen seemed almost unique. Meri's ability to read objects was a prime example of that. Perhaps it was a new ability manifesting in their kind he mused.

A quick glance at the clock on the dash of the car told him that he was well within schedule. While the flight wouldn't leave until after dawn he would be in the airport and his driver gone long before sunrise. He was not all that concerned about a little sun himself, but he was sure his driver did not feel the same. Checking the tickets he was glad to see that it would be after dark when he landed in London and late at night by the time he reached Dublin. Hopefully the driver there was as conscientious this young man. Meri's note assured him that she could have gotten him a flight directly to Belfast at the expense of another half a day of travel or going entirely during the day. Most of what she said in the letter was lost on him, never having traveled by air before. A short drive across Ireland at night didn't bother him nearly as much as it apparently did Meri.

Crossing the ocean in one evening was still a bit of a wonder to him, he had to admit. While he had read volumes on the science of flight he couldn't get past the speeds achieved by such large machines. Not for the first time he sympathized with the scores of elders that had decided that they could not abide the changes time wrought on their world and had taken to the earth to sleep. But with a smile he knew that as long as there were books and knowledge in the world he would walk upon it.

The trip through the airport was taxing. More than once he was forced to dominate the security personnel to get his case holding the tablets through unmolested. By the time he was seated on the plane he was glad he had never attempted this before. He tried not to think about the fact that he would have to make a return trip as well. The flight was long and he had plenty of time to think about what would happen once he was in Ireland. His story to Vanessa about returning the tablets was true enough. Normally he would have arranged a courier instead of taking them himself, but with the need for travel already present he had decided to take the opportunity to examine the rest of the collection.

His real business, however, was the meeting with the Senate. It had been centuries since he had allowed himself to get involved in the Night Courts. The petty positioning and political games ate at him ceaselessly. There came a time when he couldn't trust anyone whom he had called a friend because every interaction was seen as part of the great game they all played. He was certain that the passage of time had not improved that any. Using ancient forms he had called for a meeting two nights from now. As an elder and a former member of the Senate such was his right. If he was going to be honest with himself he guessed he wasn't a former member at all. Other than the seats held by the Magistrates, inclusion in the Senate was for life. Any of the sleeping ancients could awaken and take part if they so desired. Despite his self imposed exile he was still connected to it all.

Even though he didn't participate in the Senate any longer, Cyrus paid attention to what was happening in his world. Alaric's deposition was the first since the time of the inquisition. Something was changing behind the scenes if his alleged crimes were considered sufficient reason for that. Cyrus only hoped that he would be able to save Alaric. He had not heard of an execution so he was sure there was still time to spare the man's life even if he didn't manage to restore his station. Then there was the matter of the Blood Price on Vanessa. He knew it was going to be a challenge, but he was determined to see that overturned. It was doubtful that he could make the problem go away entirely, but if he could convince them that she was no longer of the blood then she would be safe from reprisal. At least as long as no one turned her once more.

Cyrus knew he should spend his time aboard the plane getting what sleep he could. He had a long night ahead of him when he arrived as it was, but he couldn't find any rest. His mind turned time and time again to the problems before him. The legal facts did not concern him. The letter of the law was on his side and he knew it. But so would the senators and any Magistrates that may be there. The fact that Alaric had been deposed in spite of the law was the true issue. That spoke of a shift in power Cyrus cared little for. That, in truth, was what brought him here. He had no doubt that he could protect Vanessa at home better than he could by standing before the court. But if things had changed so much in the Senate then he was compelled to act. He spent the rest of the flight working on the problem. By the time he had arrived in Dublin he had a basic plan of attack prepared.

He was a bit surprised to find a human driver waiting for him when he exited the terminal. The driver's crisp uniform and equally crisp Mercedes were obviously from a service. Cyrus entered the car and ran his thumb across his chin in thought. If Meri had selected a service that meant she had been unable to find someone she trusted here. His opinion of the situation was not improving as the trip continued. He wanted to take care of the business with the museum immediately, but with it being after ten o'clock now and would be almost one in the morning by the time they got there he wasn't sure it would be possible. During the drive he managed to catch a couple hours of rest before being awakened by the driver at the hotel.

"Can you wait here for a moment?" he asked the driver.

"Well, Sir, we are already well into after hour rates. I can wait, but it will be quite costly."

"I am not concerned with that." Cyrus answered mildly. Leaving the car he went inside and checked into the hotel before making a few calls. The curator was less than enthusiastic about being disturbed in the middle of the night, but finally agreed to meeting at the museum when he learned what it was about. Returning to the car he found the driver waiting impatiently.

"Take me to the Ulster," he commanded.

"Yes Sir," the driver sighed.

It was a short drive to the museum and Cyrus was pleased to find that security had been foretold of his arrival. As he walked through the museum shadowed by his escort he wished that all of the lights were on. Taking in the artistic treasures and cultural displays, unimpeded by the press of humanity he knew would be here during the day, made the trip worthwhile in itself. He knew he had been receding from the world but this trip was already showing him the extent. As he entered the Mesopotamian collection a smile crept onto his lips. Walking past the cases he glanced across the selection of tablets and cylinders presented.

"You have a couple of these dated incorrectly," he observed, sensing someone approach him.

"What do you mean?" a mild voice asked.

"These were made at least two hundred years later than the dates you give on the plaques," he answered when he recognized the voice as belonging to the curator of the exhibit. "That character did not come into use until, how is it you say it, thirty-three hundred BCE." The curator stared at him perplexed.

"Dating ancient artifacts is far from an exact science I know, but how is it you can so cavalierly claim our experts are wrong?" Cyrus smiled and shook his head.

"Please forgive me, it is a matter no consequence. I thought that you would like to take possession of these yourself," he said patting the side of the case holding the tablets, "The translations are inside as well. I made some notes about the dating if you are interested."

"Are those the tablets?"

"Precisely." The curator suddenly looked more alert. Reaching out he took the case gingerly from Cyrus. Leading him to another part of the museum, they went back beyond the displays to an area Cyrus presumed was used to clean and inspect the treasures as they needed it. The curator placed the case on a table and opened it.

"Wonderful," he breathed as he examined the tablets. "And the translations are complete?"

"Of course."

"Please pass our appreciation on to Mr. Cyrus." The curator paused at Cyrus's chuckle. Only then did he connect the voice of the man he was speaking to with the one he had dealt with on the telephone. The astonishment on his face deepened Cyrus's amusement and he gave the man a small bow as he realized whom he was speaking with.

"I'm sorry Sir," the man stammered, "I was lead to believe that we would always be dealing with an intermediary."

"Do not concern yourself. This is a singular event, I assure you. I am glad to have finally seen your fine establishment after all these years."

"Sir, if it isn't too impertinent, I was told a great deal of fantastic things about you when I assumed this position. Given the opportunity, I must ask if you are the same Cyrus we have been dealing all these years. You certainly don't appear to be over a hundred years old." Cyrus's laugh cut the man off as he spoke.

"My good man, I am most assuredly much older than that. Believe what you will, but my knowledge of these," he said, taking in the tablets on the table with a gesture, "is from personal experience." The disbelief on the man's face was obvious but Cyrus didn't feel the need to persuade a human of his true nature. "Now since it is well past time for you to be in your bed I will leave you with these and be about my other business here."

The trip out of the museum was a quiet one. He was sure the curator was trying to decide what to make of his visit. Normally he made it a point to avoid talking about his age. At times it was simply because it made him weary to think of the expanse of years behind him, others because of reactions such as he had received tonight. He couldn't say what prompted his revelation to the curator. Perhaps it was the man's umbrage at his assessment of the dates for the tablets on display.

Examining himself he was somewhat ashamed at the thought he had acted so pettily. On the ride back to the hotel he decided that he couldn't allow himself to be distracted by such a minor thing just now. By the time he dismissed his driver and returned to his room the matter was far from his mind.

He knew that he faced a challenge the following night. Even though he had been awake for better than a day he was still unable to relax. Taking to the street he began to walk around the city, lost in thought. He knew things would have changed since he last stood before the Senate. That had been when the Romans still held Britannia. Their numbers were small then, the Romans having been as efficient in their hunting of his kind as they had been in so many other things. There were few from before the Empire to survive its growth.

The inquisitions that began seven hundred years later were equally hard on his kind. He frowned for a moment thinking of the poor innocents taken by fire when the Church soldiers' practice of staking vampires out to be burned by the sun had been misinterpreted by the common folk as burning witches.

The odds of him seeing a familiar face were slim. Whether that was a bane or a boon would remain to be seen. Not knowing the feel of the group both irritated him and made him uneasy. He kept coming back to the fact that the legalities weren't in any doubt. Never since its creation had the Senate failed to uphold at least the letter of the laws they created. That meant he wouldn't just be arguing against an interpretation of the law but against a motive he knew nothing of.

Deep in thought, he didn't realize that the pair approaching him were not humans until they were almost on top of him. In his slowness to recognize them for what they were he didn't have time to react before the taller of the two slammed his arm forward driving a stake into Cyrus's chest. Cyrus's shock at the attack was matched by his attacker's at the failure of the stake to penetrate the chest of the older man. The sharp point penetrated the skin before shattering on the ancient muscle underneath. His assailant's blow struck with enough force to drive him back a step as the stake exploded in the man's hand. Not waiting for either of them to gather their wits Cyrus reached out and grabbed them both. With a cruelly tight grip he drove them both to the ground before him.

"Do either of you realize the magnitude of your error?" he asked even as the look on their faces made it clear they were beginning to understand. "Under our law both of your lives stand forfeit to my will. Do both of you understand this?" He was satisfied to see both of them nod sickly. Fixing the smaller of the two with a stare, he squeezed until he felt the bones of the man's shoulder grate under his grip. "Since you did not strike me I will let you go on your parole. I will never lay eyes upon you again or hear that you have spoke of this either. If you fail in either of these things I will find you, pull your limbs from your body and leave you for the sun to find. Am I perfectly clear?"

"Yes Sir," he whispered, his terror plain on his face.

"Very well, be gone. You, my friend, will come with me. I have a few questions for you to answer," he said turning to the one that had held the stake. Cyrus paused, brushing splinters from his shirt, while the other vampire ran into the night. Roughly he pulled the one he still held to his feet and shoved him against the wall.

"Do you have a name?" Cyrus asked.

"Liam."

"Very well, Liam. Will you walk with me if I release your arm or will I be forced to hobble you?"

"I'll walk."

Cyrus released Liam, prepared to grab him if he tried to run. Apparently not wanting to test Cyrus's claim, Liam stayed with him as they walked down the street. It didn't take Cyrus long to decide what questions to ask and he found the answers very enlightening.

Chapter 7
Fight or Flight

Vanessa woke the next day feeling stiff and sore. She had sat up thinking until falling asleep at some point in the early morning. The dream that woke her was still fresh in her mind while she crawled out of bed and gotten ready for school. Despite what Lilah said she didn't think it was all as far behind her as she and Cyrus kept saying. Long experience had taught her to trust her instincts. Right now they warned her that trouble was coming.

She was disappointed to see Lilah had already left for the office by the time she made it downstairs. Talking to her might have helped ease her mind, or at least that was what she had been hoping. As it was her entire day was spent in distraction. Lilah's talk the night before made her feel better, but the problem still remained. The fact was, until Cyrus could do something about it there was a Blood Price on her head. That meant every outcast and hunted vampire out there would want to take her. She was afraid, but refused to let that fear make her a prisoner. At least tonight she had her self defense class. When she was fighting she was able to let everything else fall away.

By the time school was out her nerves were getting the better of her. She didn't feel like going to track practice and slipped out without anyone from the team seeing her. Her growing sense of unease had bothered her all day. At first she didn't know what it was but eventually it hit her. The old feeling from when Anton had been hunting her had returned. That realization alone was almost enough to make her feel sick. She pushed experimentally in her mind but wasn't able to feel anything outside her own head. As she walked from the school towards the gym she tried to convince herself that she was worrying over nothing.

It was still early for class when she got to the gym. Miles wasn't in sight when she went inside. Dropping her things by the wall she slipped her shoes off and stretched. Heavy footfalls from the ceiling told her that he was in the office upstairs. She decided to try and work off some steam before the rest of the class arrived. The heavy bag lived up to its name as she dragged it to the center of the room. It was all she could do to lift it high enough to hook the chain on the clip in the ceiling. Once it was there she stepped back and smiled at herself. Almost daily she missed the strength and speed she had lost, but she was sure that there were few fourteen year old girls that could have gotten the bag there. And she was certain that there were none her size that could.

By the time Miles came downstairs she had a good sweat worked up. He stood there watching her work over the bag for several minutes. His presence was distracting to her, but she did her best to push him out of her mind. Pushing from the shoulder she rolled her hips forward and threw her whole body into the punches. After a while he dropped his clipboard and walked up beside her.

"Whoa, whoa, whoa," he said, catching the bag. "You're turning into it too late. Your hip's just an afterthought at that point. It needs to be one fluid motion from your heel to your wrist. Like this." He threw a few jabs into the bag. Each punch hit the bag with an authority that was almost insulting to her. "And you're going to break your wrist if you ever hit someone holding it like that. You need to keep this line on impact," he added adjusting her hand. "Try it like that. And remember, stay loose until the second right before impact."

She stepped back up to the bag and tried to find the zone she had been in again. Remembering his advice she threw a punch. The impact jarred her to her teeth.

"Felt that didn't ya?"

"Yeah," she panted.

"Well if you felt it imagine what the other guy felt. Try that a while then cool down for class."

She went back at the bag with a renewed vigor. Carefully she worked at it until she had the timing down right. Using the same tricks Clarius had shown her when he taught her how to hunt she memorized the movements of her body. It was more difficult without heightened senses but she was still able to do it. An evil grin slid onto her face as she worked, able to repeat the motion every time before she stopped. Her blows still fell short of what

Miles had shown her but they were much harder than when she had started.

The rest of the class began to trickle in shortly after that and she stopped to catch her breath. Miles showed them a few new ways to break holds and let them pair off to practice. He relentlessly paced the floor of the gym watching the groups work. From time to time he would stop, moving an elbow here or adjusting someone's grip there. Time after time they went over the moves until he was sure everyone had them down. As keyed up as she still was Vanessa was glad she had the extra workout behind her. By the end of class she had almost forgotten about the troubles from the day before. When she walked out into the night she was smiling. Both from the warm pleasantly tired feeling the class had left her with and the fact that she managed not to jump at the shadows as she walked home.

She barely noticed the sound of the engine starting behind her. Only when the van pulled up beside her and the door slid open did she realize what was happening. Instantly she felt the wrongness of the man that jumped out of the now stopped van. Without hesitation she took off at a dead run. Pushing for every ounce of speed she could muster she sprinted for her life. It wasn't enough. Barely fifty yards down the sidewalk he was on her. She was nearly yanked from her feet as he grabbed her backpack and hauled back on it. Not breaking stride she let the pack slide from her arms and kept running.

The impact of the thrown pack was enough to knock her from her feet. Determined, she went into a combat roll coming up into her sprinter's stance. Before she could take off again he grabbed her hair from behind and jerked back savagely, pulling her over to land on her back. Rolling with the motion she kicked upwards catching him in the face making him stagger back. A hard kick in the side from a second man knocked the wind out of her. The moment's pause while she gasped for breath was all the time they needed to grab her. With a grip like a vice the first one twisted her arms behind her and lifted while the other pinned her legs together. Together they carried her back to the van face down, her weight hanging painfully against her shoulders.

Rage and fear coursed through her. Her side still ached from the kick and spots swam in her vision from the pain in her shoulders. Biting her lip she, she refused to give them the satisfaction of crying out. *Please let someone see this and call the cops,* she prayed. The pair tossed her roughly into the van and climbed in behind her. Before the door was even closed the driver gunned the engine and she felt the van surge forward beneath her.

The inside of the van matched the exterior. Racks to hold plumbing supplies still lined the walls, now empty save for what the previous owner hadn't deemed worth saving. The floor was caked with dried mud and an assortment of fittings and debris. Against the other wall was a duffel bag that obviously didn't fit with the rest of the van's contents. With a sick turn of the stomach Vanessa tried not to imagine what it held.

Desperately she looked for anything she could use to get away. She could feel the same wrongness from these three that she had from the vampire at the restaurant. Now that she knew what was happening the fact oozed through her mind like a sickness. If she was going to get out of this it would have to be while one was still driving. Refusing to give into the despair that was trying to overcome her she scrambled to come up with a plan.

As she thought the second one, a dark haired man, grabbed her and forced her around so that her head was towards the front of the van. The blonde one that had began the attack rummaged in the duffel bag before pulling out several items. Horror filled her as he began to set them side by side on the floor by her head. The utility knife and stake were bad enough; she guessed they thought her still one of them. But the silver thermos and large carafe made her blanch. Tears burning in her eyes she wondered if she would ever be free of being hunted. Her mind went back to a hotel room just over two years before.

Her face a broken mass of bruises Anton's men threw her to the floor of the room. She was certain she felt broken ribs creak together as they forced her arms behind her and handcuffed her to the heating register. A small moan escaped her lips as one of them did something behind her. She tried to see what they were doing but everything was still blurry. Her vision slowly returning, she began to make out the thermos and the knife they were holding. With a moan she dropped her head back to the floor as she realized they were bleeding her.

Somehow these guys had gotten their hands on that thermos. There it was sitting just inches from her face. She could feel the threat it contained like it was a physical thing. It didn't matter that she wasn't a vampire any more. They were going to fix that. For a moment she was transfixed by the impossibility of the situation. She knew Anton and his men had the thermos of her blood, but had never wondered what happened to it after she had killed Anton. That was part of another life that she hadn't wanted to remember. To tell the truth she had never given the men another thought after she had left them battered but alive in the car they had caught her in.

She knew she shouldn't be worrying about how they had it. They did and from the looks of it they intended to use it now. The shock made it hard for her concentrate. Her eyes kept being drawn back to the stainless steel cylinder. Not the knife or the stake, nor any of the other dangerous things scattered around the back of the van worried her nearly as much as that simple thermos did. For a brief second she wondered why they meant to use it at all. If they wanted her to become a vampire wouldn't it be easier to just turn her themselves? But even as she thought it she knew why. Her creator would be accountable for her crimes. If they made her one of them with her own cursed blood everything would be on her head and hers alone.

Suddenly she felt the van jerk to a stop and the driver slid out of his seat to worm his way into the back with her. Despair filled her as she realized she had waited too long. They hadn't been driving very long at all. She was sure they were still in the neighborhood no farther than they had gone. The one at her feet knelt down on her calves, his knees digging into her legs. She growled as the driver forced her arm out flat against the floor of the van and held it there. With the knife in his hand the blonde man drove a knee into her ribs and pried her other arm out straight. He held her wrist above the carafe and cut a deep furrow in her arm with the knife.

Transfixed she watched the bloodied blade fall to the floor. Unable to help herself her eyes followed the stream as her blood trickled into the container. Her anger slowly built up inside her as they casually went about their business.

"I can't believe he thought this was going to a tough job," the blonde man said to the driver.

"Yeah. She's feisty, but so is any kitten you catch," he grinned back. Only the one holding her legs didn't share in the smug joking.

Dayflower

"Well, easy or tough, what Ivan's paying for the package makes it worth it."

At the sound of Ivan's name her rage boiled over. Gritting her teeth she growled and felt her chest tighten. Tossing herself around her struggles were lost on her captors. A burning sensation began to build up inside her. Slowly it crept from her chest through her whole body. Suddenly she felt a strength that hadn't been there before. Still filled with rage she bucked as hard as she could, managing to pull her legs free from the dark haired man. As he sat there shocked she pulled her knees to her chest and kicked her legs out as hard as she could.

The blow caught him square in the chest, the force of the kick drove him back against the rear doors of the van knocking them open. As he tumbled out onto the ground she felt the driver's grip on her left arm loosen just enough. With a violent twist to the side she pulled her arm free and snatched the stake from the floor. He had just turned back to face her, arms extended in a grab for her own, when she slammed the stake into his chest. Paralyzed he toppled sideways, shock written on his face.

Before she could do anything else the blonde man had jumped on top of her. Sitting on her stomach he still held her right arm in an iron grip. He scrambled with his other hand to grab her wrist. Desperately she got her hand on the knife. Waving it wildly she cut his palm and arm several times before she got the angle she wanted. Stiff armed she brought the blade across herself in a wide arc. The blade slashed across his throat peeling it open as easily as it had her arm. A torrent of blood splattered across her chest. Immediately her arms were free again as he groped at his throat in an attempt to stop the blood. Again she bucked, forcing him back far enough she could get a leg free to kick him off of her.

As she scrambled past him to the open doors at the back of the van the dark haired man was beginning to climb back inside. Miles's training took over and she jumped forward. Using the advantage of her higher position she reached out and laced her fingers together behind his head. With a swift jerk she pulled him forward, driving her knee into his face at the same time. A satisfying crunch told her she had at least shattered his nose. He grabbed his face and toppled back to the ground with a gurgled yell as she jumped over him.

Looking around herself she recognized the park they were in. Heedless of the blood still trailing from her fingertips she sprinted across the grass towards the road on the other side. By the time she reached the pavement she was beginning to feel dizzy. Too afraid to stop she kept running, her breath coming in jagged gulps. After zigzagging down a few more streets her vision began to blur and she staggered to a stop. Dropping to her knees she gripped her arm, the blood flow just a weak trickle now. As the lights washed over her she slumped in upon herself, sure it was the van. A small black sport car pulled up beside her, the passenger window gliding down.

"Get in," the woman behind the wheel yelled. Relief washed over Vanessa as she lurched to her feet. It took all of her strength to pull open the door. She collapsed into the seat and leaned back, using her weight to pull the door shut again.

"Thank you so much," she sighed. The car pulled forward smoothly as the woman driving slammed through the gears quickly.

"No problem. You look like hell."

"Yeah," Vanessa answered, unable to come up with anything more. She looked over at the woman for the first time and knew immediately that she was a vampire too.

"Oh God!" she screamed and began scrabbling frantically for the door handle.

Chapter 8
The Senate

The sunset found Cyrus already dressed. Having retired before dawn he woke before the sun had touched the horizon. As he looked in on his guest, still sound asleep, he was grateful for his unusual constitution. Every other elder he had ever encountered felt the press of the sun more every year that passed. Most of them would often go days or weeks without stirring, none of them ever having reached near his age. Cyrus was quite the opposite. The endless march of years had left him less able to find rest even when weary. The demon that polluted his soul still recoiled at the touch of the sun but he had long ago beaten out of it the burning torment it used to try and drive him from the sun.

But Cyrus, the man, often spent long sleepless days toiling at his work. He thought now, as he straightened the lines of his jacket, on the volumes of research he had amassed over the years. No one else that he was aware of had actually made a study of the vampire's condition. He had started with his own mastery of the demon. Millennia ago he had grown weary of the driving torments of the demon's hungers and fears. Finally he had resolved to seek either mastery or oblivion. After decades of study he formulated a plan. He knew that he could not just charge into the daylight for the demon would destroy him itself in an attempt to drive him back into the darkness. Just as a trapped animal will lash out against a trap until it has killed itself in its fury and desperation.

Several years were spent preparing for his fight for control. The room was not remarkable. A small pallet set in the center of the floor and a small stand held a pump to give him water. There was a carefully constructed arc in the ceiling. As the sun passed through its journey each day a band of sunlight worked its way from wall to wall. He had made sure that there was no place in the room he could reach that the sun didn't also. If there had been the demon could have forced him into the deep sleep of their kind and waited for the trial to pass. The door was locked with a complex mechanism that could only be opened through a sequence of carefully completed steps. He had hoped that this was enough of a precaution. He wanted to make sure that the animalistic nature of the demon would be unable to take over and flee the chamber.

Days and then weeks passed as he sat in the room. The line of sunlight was merciless as it seared him each day. Eventually hunger maddened him as well. He kept his intentions fixed in his mind, meditating on self mastery for hours on end. More than once he found himself coming to from a fugue state, his hands bloodied from clawing at the door or pounding on the heavy stone walls. Thinking back over the years he couldn't think of a single instance in which his will had been tested as terribly as it had in that room. But he had been resolute. The demon was going to relinquish its hold on him or he would be destroyed. Like a lion under the whip it began to cringe beneath his will. Slowly one step at a time he forced it back until finally the day came when he was able to sit in meditation as the sun passed slowly over him without burning his skin in its passing.

That evening he opened the door to the chamber with the sun still above the horizon. As he watched the sunset he knew that he had won. It took him nearly a thousand more years to complete his control, but now it was absolute. A broad smile filled his face as he watched the last glow of the sunset fade from the sky. With the sky fully dark his guest still hadn't stirred. Impatient he went into the bathroom where the youth slept. Gripping the front of his jacket he lifted the lifeless body from the floor and tossed it into the shower. Once the cold water began flowing he sputtered to life.

"God I'm up, I'm up!"

"Good. Please get yourself in order. We will be leaving in a few minutes."

Cyrus finished his preparations as his charge dried himself and emerged from the bathroom. At Cyrus's gesture he led the way into the hallway and out to the street. The night was mild and Cyrus was glad for the walk. By convention the Senate was set to meet outside. The approaching sunrise did amazing things to his kindred's willingness to resolve disagreements over petty issues. Tonight's meeting was set to happen in a local park. His threat of destruction still much in place, Cyrus counted on his new companion to guide him there.

He could feel the presence of the other vampires before he even set foot in the park gate. It would be a small session he could tell. With just over three dozen vampires here it was the smallest gathering Cyrus had ever attended. The age of the group shocked him also. Aside from himself he could only feel one other true elder in the group. His earlier expectation proved true in that he hadn't previously met a single member here. He was instantly the focus of the group as he approached. At some unspoken signal almost a third of those present dispersed moving to the entrances of the park. To keep mundane authorities from interfering with their meeting he presumed. Turning to the only elder present he waited for the meeting to be called to order.

"I presume that you are the one that called for this conclave?" she asked icily. She was barely fourteen hundred years old by Cyrus's estimation. Almost as tall as he was she was very pretty, he observed, with fair skin and raven hair. Her eyes were an intense blue, their beauty was marred only by the malice they contained.

"If this is the courtesy shown to elders and members of the Senate than this institution is in a far sorrier state than I could have imagined," Cyrus replied. He matched her stare with impatience. "Yes, I have business to bring before this body."

The group dropped into a rough circle around the pair. Tension was almost tangible in the air. It was clear to him that she was the leader of the pack and the rest of the group waited with anticipation to see if he would wilt before their queen. The spectacle of it all disgusted him deeply. Since she had yet to formally open the session he was content to stand his ground and wait her out. Hands clasped behind his back, he stared her down. His unblinking stare was met by those cold blue eyes for far longer than he expected. She was certainly no shrinking violet, that much was certain.

"Let this session of the great Senate be hereby opened," she began, scorn dripping from each word she uttered. "May all business brought before us this night be resolved by majority or unanimously held for the next dusk or may the sun take us all." With those words they were officially in session. The decisions made from this point forward carried the weight of law backed by

Dayflower

custom older than written history itself. Turning to Cyrus she resumed her cold stare.

"Please, oh great elder, grace us with your name and whatever this business you bring before us may be."

"I am called Cyrus," he answered coldly. His patience for her attitude was already wearing quite thin. "I resume the business of Alaric's deposition and the Blood Price placed upon the head of Vanessa Miller, formerly of the blood."

Her snort was sudden and far from what you could call a laugh. "Do you claim to be *the* Cyrus? Self exiled ancient, writer of the first code of Law?"

"I am he."

"No one has seen him for almost two thousand years! What proof do you offer?"

Cyrus's anger bubbled to the surface and he reached out, grabbing her by the neck. Pulling her roughly to him he stared into her eyes close enough they could almost have kissed. The push was as forceful as it was brief. In seconds he shoved his identity into her mind. A whirlwind blur of centuries passing like the ticks of a clock filled her mind. When he released her she staggered back, one hand held to her head. A number of the other members stepped forward, an aura of menace surrounding them. Holding her other hand up she gestured for them to step back. Cyrus was certain now that few, if any here, could feel the age of their fellows.

"My apologies," she whispered. "We have been led to believe you would never leave your region." The cold steel was still there beneath her newly found civility but Cyrus was willing to accept that. The rest of the pack eased as she changed her tact. "I am Landina."

"Now that we are no longer set to tear at each other like so many jackals, may we address my business?"

"Very well, but the Senate has already ruled on both of these matters. Do not expect to overturn us."

"I will start with the matter of Alaric's deposition. I would like a full list of the charges he was convicted of."

"That is a simple enough matter. He refused to bring a known criminal to justice that was known to be hiding within his territory in direct defiance of a Senate ruling." Her haughty tone had returned in full measure. Cyrus smiled to himself. This was exactly the fight he was expecting on the subject. Turning to sweep the assembly with his gaze he began to recite the speech he had prepared.

"Alaric came to me with word that Vanessa was wanted within the Ohio territory. I informed him at that time that any extradition of her from New York to Ohio was invalid since her claim to Sanctuary had been violated. After that she was under my direct protection and taking her was outside his jurisdiction."

"My dear Cyrus, Vanessa has earned her Blood Price by having created the abomination Anton, not to mention the countless other offenses she has committed over the years, but she is not the criminal in question. You are. By offering her shelter and your direct protection you, who are bonded as creator to her, are hereby accountable for her sins." Cyrus was shocked. More than at the twist of logic used here, he was astounded he hadn't foreseen this possibility. He had even discussed this very topic with Alaric himself. While at the time he hadn't taken the suggestion seriously it was clearly serious now.

"Very well," he answered. "Is my protection of Vanessa the only charge leveled at me?"

"No." So far no one else in the group had even attempted to speak up. Landina must have been building her power here for quite some time, he decided. "There is one other matter that was brought before this body. You are also held responsible for the destruction of one of the Blood without right or provocation," she continued. Suddenly he knew about how long she had been in control of the Senate. His destruction of Gordon over two hundred years ago was coming home to roost now.

"Gordon."

"Yes, Gordon. How do you answer this charge?"

"You were his creator."

For the first time he saw the connection. As he looked around the circle he could see the bloodlines. Only two of the others in the circle were of her blood, but the rest were still connected. Long ages of practice combined with a natural talent had left him with the ability to see the lineage imprinted on his kind. He stood now alone before the branches of a single family line. The plot Gordon had come to him with all those years ago had matured despite his absence. A complete takeover of the Senate had nearly been achieved. Only the magistrates in the New World stood separate, judging from what he saw here. And unless he was terribly wrong, the newest Magistrate would stand side by side with her brothers here.

"How do you answer?" she demanded.

"He kicked in the door to my home and accosted me. It was my right to destroy him for that affront. Just as it is my right to take your younger son for attempting to stake me last evening."

"Liam was simply attempting to collect the bounty on you. His life is safe from you. As to Gordon, Do you have any proof of this attack?" Cyrus threw back his head and laughed.

"Do we need to find one of the truth stones for my testimony? I challenge you to find a single soul in all of creation, damned or otherwise, that can swear to a single deception I have committed." Landina paused. She was obviously loath to lose this point, having penning him in so well until now. He could see her mind working as she sought to find a way to force him to concede this as well.

"Do you consent to a reading by the Senate?" She asked smoothly.

"Of course," he replied without hesitation. He could not remember the last time this had been done. In all honesty he was surprised that she knew how to perform such an arcane rite. One by one the members linked hands forming a spiral from the outer edge curling in until Lanina held the end of the line. With her free hand she reached up and touched a finger to the center of Cyrus's forehead.

"Open to me and let your mind go back to that day." Cyrus did as she bid and the memories floated to the surface of his mind.

Gordon came pounding on the door demanding to be seen. Cyrus refused to answer it and continued his work. Finally Gordon kicked the door in.

"What have you been telling them old man?" he screamed.

Cyrus carefully put his quill back in its stand and rose, turning to face his junior.

"I have told no one anything, Gordon," he replied calmly, "I will ask you now to leave and never return."

Gordon crossed the room and stood before Cyrus, towering over him. Jabbing his finger into Cyrus' chest he continued his rampage.

"Alaric is holding a hearing on this tomorrow and someone has been telling those fools what I was doing. Other than my men and you no one else knew!"

Dayflower

"I swear on my blood and that of my Little Flower here that no one here is telling your secrets Gordon. Your men are a bunch of loudmouth braggarts. Look for your betrayer there. Now it is almost dawn and I have a door to repair. Leave and never return, Gordon."

Cyrus moved as if to return to his work but Gordon grabbed him. Cyrus spun and grabbed the younger man. Twisting Gordon's arm behind him he lifted the man off of the floor and carried him out into the predawn light. As the sun continued to brighten the sky he continued walking to the water's edge.

Just then Cyrus felt a subtle push in his mind. Landina was trying to exert influence over him. Backed as she was by the circle it was a powerful force. His anger renewed he pushed back, closing his mind to her. For an instant she battered at his mind, trying to use the collective strength behind her to force her way back into his mind. The attack recoiled feebly from Cyrus's fury. He lashed out making her stagger and breaking the contact. When she met his eyes he could see the surprise behind the calm facade.

"Very well," she sighed at last, "Gordon's death was justified." With a nod Cyrus accepted the concession in silence. "You are still accountable for the crimes of your little pet."

"Very well. Then I will move on to my other order of business. If you are holding me accountable for her crimes then you must lift the Blood Price on her."

Landina smiled coldly. "Nice try, Cyrus. If the crimes are serious enough both the guilty and her creator can be held to account. Considering the bloody swath Anton tore through our numbers I doubt you will argue that the severity is lacking."

"I will not argue the severity of the crime. But those deaths were on his hands. And while you can hold her accountable as his creator you cannot claim his creation alone as a crime. In any case, not only did she destroy him herself, she is no longer one of us."

"Bullshit!" A dark skinned man exclaimed. "Do you honestly expect us to believe she found some way to stop being a vampire?"

Cyrus turned and looked at him.

"I would allow a reading to prove the truth of my words if the last one had not ended in an attack on my will." He fixed Landina with a cold stare with the last words.

"That isn't a matter for us to discuss at this point," she interjected. "The fact of the matter is that you still sheltered her and having done so protected her from this assembly."

"My protection was only required because her claim to Sanctuary was violated. My actions were a correction of Ivan's violation of the laws of this Senate. While he was banished for it, she was still denied protection to which she was entitled. Tell me Landina, if someone threatened your offspring with destruction by taking away shelter to which they were entitled would you stand by or would you restore that security to them?"

They argued back and forth for the rest of the night. Each point was argued tirelessly by both sides. Occasionally one of the other Senators would step timidly into the fight only to have their arguments quickly cut down. By the time the sky was beginning to lighten in the east they were arguing over minutiae of the wording of the laws. A part of him was enjoying the exchange. Her mind was a sharp one and she forced him to think much quicker than he had grown accustomed to. Here he didn't have years or decades to work the problem over until he had dissected it completely. Finally Cyrus had endured all he could take.

"By all of the stars in the heavens, do not dare presume to tell me what the meaning of the law is. I wrote a great portion of it myself!" The outburst brought back to mind just how far he stood above her in rank. With a bitter look to the east she gauged the growing light and sighed.

"Fine. Where does this body stand on the charges against Cyrus? Are they to be upheld or withdrawn?"

One by one they stepped forward and answered the call. Other than a few exceptions they muttered "Withdrawn" in response. By the time the circle had been completed there was no need to count the votes. Cyrus was unable to find joy in his victory. He not only felt as though he was watching a wonderfully staged performance, all he had done was to extract himself from a situation he hadn't expected. To make the situation worse he had managed to place the entire burden completely on Vanessa.

Wearily he made his way through the streets back to his hotel. The situation was much worse than he had originally feared. The fact that Gordon had been a tiny part of the overall machinations troubled him greatly. By his own inaction he had allowed this travesty to occur. One step at a time, he decided. Tomorrow night would be just as long. For the first time he could remember he was exhausted. Lying on the bed he wondered in passing how Vanessa was doing.

Chapter 9
Meri

"Good Lord will you stop that!" the woman barked. Vanessa paused warily and pressed herself against the door as if she could sink through it get and away from this new vampire. The woman kept driving without looking over at her, for which she was grateful. Glancing down at herself she felt a little faint. Everything from her neck to her waist was covered in blood. As it dried it made her shirt stick to her and pull uncomfortably. Where her skin showed through the gore it was too white. Beyond even her normal paleness it was almost gray in the queasy blue light from the streetlamps.

Her thoughts were still sluggish and disjointed. She knew she had lost too much blood. Almost as an afterthought she looked down at her wrist. Her own blood, now drying black, coated her lower arm and hand. It had stopped bleeding somehow and she giggled a little hysterically as she flexed her fingers. As she turned back to look at the woman driving she almost vomited. Everything swam in her vision and her ears were ringing. The feeling of her head hitting the window jarred her back alert and she realized the woman was talking to her.

"What?" she mumbled.

"I said you can calm down. I'm not going to hurt you. Cyrus sent me. My name's Meri."

"What?" She heard the words but nothing made sense. The name meant something to her if she could just remember what.

"Boy they did a number on you didn't they. Can you grab that case on the back seat?"

Vanessa leaned into the gap between the seats and spotted a small leather day planner lying on the back seat. As she reached for it the sudden motion got to her and she felt sick. Black spots swam in her vision and she managed not to wretch or pass out. After taking a few deep breaths she regained control.

"Sorry I'm getting blood all over your car," she muttered thickly.

"I couldn't care less about the car."

She went back to retrieving the case and saw a business suit, still in a dry cleaner's bag, folded neatly on the other side of the seat. Suddenly she was sure she knew why Meri didn't care about the car. She was sure the owner wouldn't be offering any complaints either. Deliberately she reached out and grasped the case, pulling it to her. As she slid back into her seat she held it before her in trembling fingers.

"Open it," Meri ordered. She struggled to get the zipper open. Her fingers felt cold, almost numb but she did manage to get it open. Aside from the standard calendar and notepad she saw three small vials, each not much larger than her thumb. A crimson liquid, so dark it was almost black, rolled around inside. Pulling one from its sleeve she held it up before her. She wasn't sure how she knew, but she was certain that they contained Cyrus's blood.

"He left those in case you needed them," Meri offered. "I think now qualifies."

Vanessa tried to pull the cork but was too weak to get it out. Almost dropping the vial she stopped. When she looked up Meri had her hand extended. Without a word she took the vial, pulled the cork and handed it back. The only other time Vanessa had ever taken Cyrus's blood had been when he bonded her as his progeny and she had been much different then. Trembling slightly she brought the vial to her lips and downed its contents. It felt as though liquid light was running through her core. Her head whipped back as she felt it race through her body like an electric current. A searing line tore its way down her arm as the cut healed instantly. All of the bruises and scratches left from her attack disappeared and she was left breathless and shaking. Sudden drowsiness threatened to overwhelm her as she recovered from the onslaught.

"Oh God," she gasped as her head lolled against the window.

"What's wrong?" Meri asked, obviously confused. Glancing over at her companion Vanessa was startled to realize that she could feel Meri, much as she had before her return to humanity.

Dayflower

"You're only what, thirty? You've not seen what vampire blood does to a human have you?" Meri's face took on a pinched look as the turned back to the road.

"My age is none of your business girl, but no I haven't."

"It heals any wounds or damage to the body all at once. Or at least as much as is possible depending on a lot of things."

"I knew that," Meri interjected.

"But it can't cure diseases," Vanessa continued, "Or replenish blood loss. In fact it uses your own reserves to do it." She sat there for a long minute looking as though she were searching for words. "I'm going to pass out," she murmured and slid down in her seat.

"Shit!" Meri spat as she slid the car to a stop in the road. She reached over and pulled Vanessa back up into her seat. Reaching across she fastened the seat belt and checked to make sure Vanessa was still breathing. By the time she went to take off again Vanessa was beginning to stir.

"Is it me or is everything flashing?" she asked.

Meri looked up to see a police car coming to a stop behind her. Slamming her hand against the wheel she let out a low animalistic growl.

"You're bad luck. That's all there is to it!" she hissed.

Jumping out of the car she stormed back towards the patrol car.

"Miss, I'm going to have to ask you to return to your vehicle," the officer commanded as he stepped out of his cruiser, hand on his pistol. Meri never slowed stride, grabbing him as he stepped around the car door. In a single quick motion she lifted him from the ground and slammed him into the side of the car. She stood over him as he slid to the pavement radiating menace.

"You are going to get back into your car and pretend you never saw us," she hissed.

"But," the officer began to protest. Not waiting for him to finish Meri yanked him to his feet and pulled his face close to hers. Slowly she let her fangs drop. The policeman's face went white as she pulled him closer. Her eyes went inky black, the irises glowing a dark red as she stared him down.

"Again. You are going to get in your car and drive away. Aren't you?"

"Y-Y-Yes!" he stammered. With that she released him to fall to the road once more and stalked back to the car.

Dayflower

"What was that all about?" Vanessa asked as she slid behind the wheel.

"Not all of us can do those neat little Jedi mind tricks like you and Cyrus."

"I can't do that. I'm not a vampire anymore!" Vanessa protested.

"Yeah. Okay, we'll go with that."

"What the hell is that supposed to mean?"

Meri half turned to face her as she drove.

"It means you tell me how many of the girls you go to school with that could get away from a vampire bent on hurting them? How about three vampires? Don't try to feed me the same BS Cyrus does about you being a regular fourteen year old now. I'm not buying it." She turned back to the road leaving Vanessa to wonder where the hostility came from.

Having lived with Cyrus for so long she guessed that this was not a new argument between the two. Vanessa could tell that they were going to her house now that her head was beginning to clear. Before long they were pulling into her driveway and Vanessa was glad to see Lilah wasn't home. She normally hated it when Lilah had to work late, but she didn't want to be seen looking like this. As the car came to a stop she got out and walked to the back door. On the second step she staggered, Meri catching her elbow saving her from a fall. Grating against the necessity, she was forced to let Meri guide her into the house.

Once inside she made her way directly to the bathroom. With the bright lights of the vanity shining in her face she saw her reflection for the first time. Blood caked her hair to her chest and arms. Her shirt cracked and flaked as she peeled it off. Even with the powerful healing effects of Cyrus's blood she was sore when she moved. Kicking her ruined clothes into the corner she sat on the edge of the tub, jumping at the first cold touch. The cold water ran over her toes as she waited on the hot to make its way to her. She tried to push off her attack but couldn't. Tears fell one by one into the water at her feet as her adrenaline and the euphoria of Cyrus's blood faded.

The pain and violence she had experienced wasn't what haunted her, she had grown used to pain and violence by now. Her helplessness when they had taken her, however, shook her to the core. Even with everything she had learned they had grabbed her and held her down to drain her life away. Remembered feelings of helplessness suffocated her like a weight on her chest. Shock and fear ate away at her will until she was sobbing into her hands. She wasn't sure how long she sat like that before the water began to run warm over her feet. Shaking herself she stood, almost falling as her knees threatened to buckle on her. Scrubbing her cheeks with her palms she sniffed and straightened herself, letting the water from the shower pour over her face.

The water washed the blood from her to run in swirls down the drain. Hers rusty brown, the vampire's still a vibrant red. She let it carry her pain and fear with it. *I'm getting a lot of practice letting things go lately,* she thought. Warning Lilah was foremost in her mind. Whatever happened to her she couldn't let Lilah come to harm. Gritting her teeth she was taken once more by regret at having brought all of this onto her adoptive mother. She wasn't sure how she was going to reach her either. Her cell phone had been in her backpack and she had no idea what Lilah's office number was. Once she had programmed it into her phone she hadn't thought of it again. She emerged from the bathroom wrapped in a towel to find a very impatient Meri waiting for her.

"Bout fricken time! We need to get a move on, we've only got about fifteen minutes until they are here. And I'm fairly certain I can't keep three of them off of you."

"What?" Vanessa cried.

"I said we need to go. Now!"

There was a clear edge of fear in Meri's voice. Vanessa had no idea how she knew when they would get there but it was clear she was sure it would be soon. Darting into her room Vanessa got dressed in a flurry. Almost at a run she charged into the hallway looking for something to pack clothes in. For the second time in minutes she felt a prick of anger at the loss of her backpack. On the verge of screaming in frustration she rounded the corner into the living room to see her backpack sitting on the couch.

"How the hell?" she gasped. Crossing the room she went to grab the pack and recoiled at the sharp slap Meri laid across the back of her hand.

"That has to stay right there," she said sharply. Rubbing the back of her hand Vanessa shot her a heated stare.

"It's my backpack. How did it get here?"

"I picked it up," Meri answered, "And it *has to stay right there*!"

72

Dayflower

"Can I at least get my cell phone out of it!" Vanessa spat. Meri paused, eyes scrunched as she thought.

"Yeah. I guess so."

Vanessa retrieved her phone and went back to her search. Back in her room she rummaged in the closet, pulling out her leather jacket. Pausing for a second she pulled it in and hugged it. The smell of the leather hit her nose filling her with memories. After placing it on the bed she went back to her hunt, squealing in surprise when she pulled her old pack out of the bottom of the closet. The tattered old knapsack was filthy and smelled like a musty cellar. She couldn't believe it was there. Lilah had unpacked for her and Vanessa had sworn that she had thrown the old pack out. Somehow it had dwelt underneath a layer of other things Vanessa had forgotten at the bottom of the closet.

With a crinkle of her nose she tossed it on the bed and began grabbing the clothes she couldn't live without. As an afterthought she grabbed her phone charger and a few other odds and ends. Then she dropped to her knees and with a sigh pulled the box out from under her bed. She hesitated over it for a second before tucking the whole box under her arm. With a glance to the chest in the corner that held the rest of her treasures she breathed a prayer that she would be able to come back here again.

"Come ON!" Meri screamed from the front of the house.

"Coming MOTHER," Vanessa shot back acidly.

She took off down the hallway at a jog and went to hop down the stairs to the living room. As she hit the floor her legs buckled under her and she pitched headlong towards the floor. Before she could cry out Meri was there to catch her. Another wave of weakness hit her making her lean heavily on Meri who, with an annoyed grunt, tossed Vanessa over her shoulder and carried her to the car. Face burning with embarrassment Vanessa kept silent as she was deposited in the seat of the car. She sat there, knees pulled to her chest while Meri pulled back onto the road and accelerated violently towards the city.

It seemed clear to her that they were heading to Cyrus's. Meri picked turns almost identical to the route Lilah used. The drive usually took at least a couple of hours with Lilah behind the wheel. Vanessa guessed that they would make it in less than half of that with Meri's hard driving. Now that she was still the motion of the car brought back her earlier fatigue in full measure. She dozed lightly as they drove, occasionally jolted awake by an exceptionally hard turn or aggressive acceleration. Her phone slid from her pack on one such turn, catching her eye. With a start she realized she hadn't called Lilah. Reaching down she grabbed the phone and fumbled with it in a panic to find the number. A steady ringing with no answer met her at the other end of the line. Fear gripped her as she tried Lilah's cell phone next. Relief flooded her as Lilah's voice answered on the other end of the line.

"Hey, Vee. Sorry I'm running so late. I'm almost home."

"Don't go home!" Vanessa screamed into the phone.

"Why? What's wrong Vanessa?"

"They tried to take me tonight. I'm okay now but you can't go home! We're going to Cyrus's. Meet us there."

"Who is 'we'?" Lilah asked.

"Cyrus sent help. I'll explain later, just be careful."

"Okay, Vee. You be careful too," she paused, clearly wanting to say something more. Vanessa was beginning to wonder if they had been disconnected when she spoke again. "I love you Vanessa. See you in a little bit."

"Love you too, Mom."

A sick felling settled in her stomach as she put down her phone. Talking to Lilah made it all seem more real, more dangerous somehow. She wondered what it was Lilah hadn't said. The thought turned itself over in her mind until she had exhausted it. There was no way to know she guessed. Head back and eyes closed, she let her mind drift. The sick feeling got stronger until she realized that there was more to it than stress. It was past dinner time and she had eaten anything since lunch. That coupled with what she had been through was taking its toll.

"Can we get something to eat?" Meri gave her an impatient look but softened immediately.

"Hope drive through is okay," she replied.

Vanessa answered with a nod and went back to dozing. Meri prodded her awake at the speaker and she ordered without thought. Back on the road she tore into the food. The burger tasted like ashes on her tongue but she forced it down. In the least the food and drink managed to change the nature of the queasiness she felt. She passed the rest of the trip in a daze and was only half aware of Meri's guidance as they made their way into the house.

She stumbled down the stairs to her room, one shoulder dragging against the wall. The knapsack fell from nerveless fingers as soon as she crossed the threshold to fall by the dresser.

Dayflower

Meri watched impassively as Vanessa collapsed on the bed and was out. For a long moment she stood there not moving, her face a mask of deep thought. Finally she pushed herself into motion and slid the girl's jacket and shoes off, half covering her with the free end of the blanket.

Chapter 10
Memories

Meri took the stairs slowly, pausing at each step as her mind focused more on its own thoughts than on what she was doing at the moment. She felt bad about her sharp way with the girl, but there was a bit of a sore spot there for her. Vanessa's name had met her at every turn since she had entered this new world of darkness. It wasn't really all that new, she admitted to herself. She had now been dead longer than she had been alive anyhow. But time was different now. That constant creep of time slowly pulling her to the grave was gone. Constantly there her entire life, she hadn't even realized she had felt it until it was gone. Old age would never claim her, nor would accident or injury. Ivan had done that already.

She chuckled to herself as she thought of it. She had always been brash; speaking her mind was as natural to her as breathing. It was such a petty thing, really. It was a beautiful spring night and she had gone out to have a drink with some friends. They had gone home while she decided to enjoy the night. The large, obviously Russian man had made a pass at her and she had laughed. "I don't think so, buddy," was all she said before walking away, shaking her head. She knew it was him the instant she was pulled into the alley on her way home in the early hours of the morning. Too scared to scream she watched almost as if from another body as he held her against the wall with one arm, railing against her for her insult. Finally her shoved her head to the side and bit down on her neck. All she could feel was confusion as the world went dark around her.

Three days had passed when she awoke to the darkness of the night. Her entire body was sore and stiff, her limbs felt wooden as she forced herself to her feet. The room was pitch black but she was still able to see. A ravenous hunger consumed her along with a rage she couldn't control.

"So the sleeper awakes," he taunted. The voice made her sick as memory flooded back to her. "You were long in changing. Making me wait. You will have plenty of time to learn respect now, though." His laugh was cold.

Meri looked around the room desperate to find a way out. Ivan rose from the dusty old couch on which he had been reclining. Old furniture and boxes of detritus filled the room. Heavy tapestries covered the walls obscuring any way out. The demon screamed in her mind and she could feel its strength singing in her body. With a feral smile she waited for him to come. He stood before her, looking down at her with satisfaction.

"Kneel," he commanded.

"Go fuck yourself."

His face contorted in rage and he grabbed her face under the jaw and lifted her till their eyes were even. At his touch her eyes went wide in shock. Images filled her mind in a sepia flurry. All at once she knew where they were, the front of the abandoned theater clear in her mind's eye. Other snapshots from the days since she had died came pouring in until she screamed. Ivan smiled at this, wrongly thinking fear of him caused her outcry.

"I said KNEEL!" Meri felt something slide across the edges of her mind. The force was there, pressing in on her until it cut off the torrent of images and brought her back to the present, but it didn't touch her mind. Ivan tossed her to the ground and stood over her with clenched fists. Rage contorted his face and she could feel emotion rolling off of him in waves. Time and time again that strange pressure pounded at the edges of her mind trying to force her to his will. By the time she had staggered to her feet blood had begun to drip from her nose and her eyes felt tight in their sockets. Her own rage grew with each additional onslaught. The blow to the side of her head didn't surprise her in the slightest, but it sent her rage beyond control. As the second blow began to fall she stepped forward and drove her knee into Ivan's crotch. He was less affected than she would have hoped but it was enough to make him pause. Grateful he hadn't searched her she pulled her taser from her jacket and fired it. He went ridged and dropped to his knees as the wires hit him.

Not waiting to see what happened she ran from the place. Conflicting emotions ran through her. Anger sat on every thought like an oily film while hunger gnawed at her maddeningly. She hadn't gone two blocks before bloodlust took her. The man didn't stand a chance as she slammed him against the wall and tore into his throat with abandon. Horrified screams of onlookers rang meaninglessly in her ears as she drank until the blood stopped flowing. Only after she dropped his body to the sidewalk and looked around her did she realize she was in the empty center of a crowd. Wiping his blood from her lips she took off at a run. The realization of what she had become chased her in her flight. Everything she thought she knew about the world threatened to collapse on her as she tried to take it in.

She tried to deny it, to find some footing in her mind that would make sense of it all, but she couldn't. The taste of the man's blood on her tongue and the memory of the power she had felt made denial impossible. Any doubts she had left were burned away when she almost died in the sunrise that morning. The next several days were spent drifting and hiding. Shock, fear and the ever present rage filled her mind until it throbbed in her skull.

It wasn't long before she was captured and hauled before Alaric in Court. Her first kill, witnessed as it was, combined with the ones that followed had put a price on her head. Here was when she had first head Vanessa's name whispered when the others of her kind thought she couldn't hear. Their crimes were compared, her defiant attitude as well. She should stand before the dawn, the whispers said, like the brat should have long ago. Instead Alaric listened to her story and nodded.

"Since her creator failed to handle her properly she shall receive lenience, such as it may be. One month in The Embrace. After that I will take her in hand," he proclaimed.

She had no idea what The Embrace was but she learned soon enough. The Magistrate's men shoved her into a coffin and buried it in sacred ground. Meri went mad in the first night. Claustrophobia drove all reason from her until she clawed at the inside of her prison like an animal. When her bloodied fingers had finally breached the lid dirt sifted in, burning her like coals. The end of the month found her broken and catatonic. Alaric cared for her until she returned to the world and greeted her when she woke again.

"That was a light punishment," he told her, "Remember that when you feed. Find a way to do it without killing. And if you do kill, find a way to hide it. The next time I won't be nearly as forgiving."

Unable to speak, she merely nodded. The thought of returning to the ground sent crimson tears trailing down her face.

"I am going to take you to Cyrus," he continued, "He may be able to help you."

Everything was a blur after that for a while. The trauma of her creation followed by the Embrace was more than she could endure. Cyrus cared for her in a gentle, if distant way until she was herself again. Tired of her cot in the kitchen she discovered the bedroom downstairs. Girl's clothes still littered the floor and the unmade bed. A book sat open on the dresser and other little things giving it the feel of a room just vacated. She knew she had been there for weeks and no one but the two of them and Alaric had set foot in the house.

"That was Vanessa's room," was all he would say when she questioned him on it.

At first he was cold, angry even when she pushed him for more answers until he finally relented and told her everything. That was the first night her rage had been raised over the girl everyone whispered about. She had spent a month buried in the ground for a first offense while *she* walked free without repercussions for a mile long list of crimes! Her anger simmered for a long time after that as Cyrus taught her the rules of her new world. It only faded after they began to explore her abilities.

Every object she touched flooded her with impressions, pictures of its past. Cyrus had never heard of this talent before and was intrigued. Hour after endless hour he worked with her until she could lower her resistance enough for him to touch her mind. That too, he told her, was unique to her. A vampire could resist the compulsion of one weaker than themselves, but she clearly didn't have that ability. Cyrus put her to the test and decided that he could overpower her but at the risk of shattering her mind. After that he was much gentler with her. Countless hours of grueling work taught her how to filter the impressions she received and how to direct her ability. Now she could tune out all but the strongest impressions.

She shook herself out of her reflections to find herself standing before Cyrus's work table. Biting her lip as she laid her hands on its cool stone surface she extended her senses trying to see through time. Now that she had decades of practice she had discovered that she could see more than just the past. Everything she touched was a window into what might be as well. Only strong tipping points came through to her. And most frustrating to her, nothing from her own path was visible. Almost as bad was her inability to see exactly why things happened, just how they could unfold.

Moving silently she made her way back downstairs to Vanessa. Kneeling by the bed she steeled herself and grasped the girl's leather jacket. The force of the impressions was painful. When she had caught Vanessa as the girl had stumbled on the stairs it had taken everything she had not to stagger herself under the unexpected onslaught. Feeling the terror and pain pouring out of the jacket, seeing a bit of her path, Meri had tempered her attitude towards the girl. She would have helped her anyhow. Her word to Cyrus guaranteed that, but she let go some of the resentment she had felt.

The old leather was rough in her hands. Its painful past made it hard for her to see through to anything else, but she focused on a half seen image she had caught earlier. Desperate, she was looking for anything that would make her path clearer. She had already passed the first tipping point tonight. Another dozen sat before her in the nights ahead. Each possible path was like a rope being pulled through her fingers. She would have to let one go to hold onto another. The backpack had been the first junction. When she found it she knew where she would have to go for Vanessa. If she had failed then not only would Vanessa have died, but a darkness she couldn't understand covered everything after that. Then at the house she *had* to leave the pack there. Otherwise Lilah would have died before dawn. *She may still,* Meri reminded herself. But the odds had changed.

With a grimace she thought of Cyrus. He would be in the heart of his trial tonight. That much she had seen. As much as it pained her she couldn't warn him either. That would have sent everything she saw skittering away like dust. Glancing at her watch she decided it would actually all be over by now.

Cyrus's house was the perfect center for her. He had acted as a sage to Alaric's territory for so long anyone of note had come here at one time or another. And everyone she knew was tied to whatever was happening had been here enough for her to get a good picture. Even Ivan, her stomach clenching at just the thought of him, had been here. There was a particular book he had always held that gave her glimpses of him. Enough to know he was behind what was happening here. At least on the surface. That there were other powers at work she never doubted. She just couldn't see them. If only they had been here or touched something she could get her hands on. Her blindness there frustrated her to the point of screaming.

A deep sigh escaped her lips as she closed her eyes and concentrated on the jacket. The sheer volume of violence that saturated Vanessa's jacket made her head spin. In her talks with Alaric and Cyrus she had been made aware of how deadly drawing the attention of hunters could be.

"Of all the vampires in our entire history there have been precious few that have faced more than four or five hunters in their day and lived to tell the tale. And there is only one alive today that has faced as many," Alaric told her with a gravity that gave her chills to this day.

Sitting there crouched at the foot of the girl's bed she cradled the jacket in her lap and gasped as visions of hunter after hunter rolled through her mind. She knew who that one was now. The girl seemed to draw them like moths to a flame. Meri wasn't sure how many hunters Vanessa had faced, the images rolled by too fast for her to count. It made her want to laugh at Alaric's estimation.

Finally Meri managed to push through the pain of the past that wrapped the jacket so thickly. She tried to feel the possibilities it held. The ropes slid through the fingers of her mind as she felt for what she sought. What was she supposed to do next?

There it was! A small snippet caught in her mind like a sliver. It quivered and jumped in her mind as the details changed and then changed back again. That moment was inescapable now. She was certain of that, but what she saw in the changing details made her sick. The first thing that made her recoil was her own lifeless form staring glassy eyed at the ceiling. Vanessa stood over her, changing faster than she could think. Before it became too much for her she shoved the jacket away.

Shaking, she made her way upstairs and tried to think. Nothing about what she saw made her feel better about how things were going. But, she had to admit, what she saw wasn't always what it looked like either.

"Gods, why is this all up to me anyhow!" she growled at the darkness. At first she had embraced her power as a gift. Being able to see how things were likely to unfold had given her a feeling of power even greater than that of her new found immortality. But the delicacy and ever changing nature of her visions combined with the fact that her own future was barred to her caused more frustration than anything else for her. Everything she tried to change invariably spun a dozen other things off in directions she hadn't foreseen. On top of everything else seeing what was going to happen made her feel responsible for it. It wasn't a burden she wanted to bear.

More than anything else that confused her. She had always been a person of conscience that much she knew, but it was different after she had been changed. The thought of the lives she had taken didn't bother her. Neither did countless other things she did as part of her new existence that would have horrified her before. She was aware of the change, but couldn't find it in herself to be concerned about it. But no matter how hard she tried she couldn't walk away from the things she saw.

Hours passed as she drifted around the dark house, so empty without Cyrus here to give it life. It felt like she should do something, but there was nothing more she could do. The next night held more tipping points for her to navigate. As it all started to take shape everything felt like it was closing in on her. She didn't like her options, but the alternatives were all much worse. Finally, with a determined scowl, she made her way downstairs to try and find some rest during the day. As long as the girl didn't do anything too stupid she might be able to get them out of this.

Chapter 11
A Bad Homecoming

The dull throbbing in her head was what woke her. Vanessa sat up and, elbows on her knees, put her head in her hands. Even with the restorative of Cyrus's blood her entire body ached. Slowly she got to her feet and made her way, leaning against the wall with each uncertain step, to the bathroom. Splashing the cold water on her face made her feel marginally better but made her realize just how thirsty she was too. For a moment she worried she would have to crawl up the stairs as she plodded up them one stair at a time. She was sure it was mid afternoon, but exhaustion still hung over her.

Standing at the sink she drank the first glass, and then a second. She hesitated before setting the glass on the counter and making her way to sit in one of the leather chairs near the table. She sat there, one leg over the arm of the chair, head lolling back and stared at the ceiling. Slowly she began to feel better and was able to think past how miserable she felt. Unease replaced the hunger in her stomach as she realized she hadn't heard from Lilah yet. Jumping to her feet she went to run downstairs before a dizzy spell almost sent her careening into a bookcase. Hand to her head she stabilized herself and made her way downstairs carefully. Digging in her pack she pulled out her phone and called Lilah's number. As the connection was made she hoped to hear it ringing in another room.

"Please let her have come in and let me sleep," she whispered.

Ring followed ring, each one adding to her fear until the call switched to Lilah's voicemail. Hanging up, Vanessa gripped the phone tightly. She had been too late. With a growl she poured the contents of her pack out on the bed. Picking through what she had brought she selected a dark outfit that she could move freely in.

Dayflower

After she had changed she knelt beside the bed again and pulled her wooden chest free from the mess she had made. The lid felt heavy in her fingers as she opened it. She had bought these things long ago hoping she would never have to use them. Reaching in, she pulled out the pistol crossbow. Its black aluminum grip was cold in her hands as she gave it a test pull. When she had picked it out the man at the store had said that there was no way she would be able to cock it. She remembered her satisfaction at the astounded look on his face as she pulled the lever back and locked the string in place. That satisfaction was gone now as her arm trembled, unable to do more than bow the arms slightly. With a scream she braced her hand against her knee and pulled until her arm burned. Still falling short of cocking it she had to fight the impulse to throw it across the room.

Frustration gnawed at her as she sorted through the rest of her arsenal. Setting aside the keepsakes the box held she looked at her meager selection of weapons. She went ahead and belted the belt hook for the crossbow and the holder for its bolts to her waist. The two bottles of holy water she slipped in her pocket along with the rosewood rosary. She hesitated for a moment before adding the small belt knife to her collection. It was nothing special, but like the bolts for her crossbow, its sheath was saturated with anointing oil. For a moment she held the bottle of anointing oil and considered bringing it as well before tossing it back into the box.

She wasn't sure what she was planning to do, she just knew she had to do something. Considering how weak she was she figured her only hope lay in using the daylight to her advantage. As she started to climb the stairs she stopped. Turning around she crept down the hall. Grateful that she knew every inch of the house she checked the rooms she thought Meri might be in. At the end of the hall she found her lying on Cyrus's bed, her day planner on the nightstand beside her. Vanessa inched across the room to the table, careful not to make a sound. While most vampires wouldn't wake without something earth shattering happening at this time of day, she didn't know Meri and wasn't going to take chances. Cyrus, she knew, could wake at the faintest whisper.

The zipper sliding open sounded like a chainsaw to Vanessa. Slowly she eased it open and slid one of the vials free from its holder. Her hand on the cover she went to close the planner and stopped. There on the page in front of her was Cyrus's hotel information. All she had to do was call the number Meri had written there and she could talk to him. The temptation proved to be too much. She had even written what time sunset was in Belfast and the time difference. Looking at her watch Vanessa saw that it was only half an hour away. A deep sigh escaped her and she wilted in on herself.

"I'm sorry Lilah," she breathed.

Closing the book she crept out of the room, the vial of blood still in her hand. Upstairs she pulled out her phone and went out to sit on the steps in the warm afternoon sun. Her panic was passing and she began to think a bit more clearly. It dawned on her that she had no idea where Lilah may be. She leaned her head back against the aged stone of the house and let the sun warm her. Her thoughts drifted back to the vial she still held in her hand. Meri obviously didn't believe she was human, but sitting there in the sun she found it harder to doubt than she did some days. That made her wonder what drinking Cyrus's blood did to her. She knew about its healing properties but she also knew that vampires could make human familiars. Never having done it herself, she didn't know what it took to do it. How much blood would it take to make her Cyrus's familiar? Was that all there was to it?

There were so many things she had never managed to learn and somehow those gaps kept coming back to haunt her. She knew that a familiar had a portion of the vampire's power tempered by a touch of their weaknesses. The strength was highly variable too. Other than that she was at a loss. No matter how hard she tried she couldn't remember anything more. She had spent most of her life bonded to Cyrus and wondered if it was the same. Part of her realized that she was grasping at straws to avoid thinking about Lilah. At the same time she wondered how much of her curiosity was spurred by the helplessness she felt. Most of the time she didn't miss what she had sacrificed by becoming human again, but at the moment her helplessness made the loss cut like a knife.

As the time Meri had recorded for sunset approached she dialed. The phone rang for what seemed like an eternity. She whispered an apology to Lilah for what this was going to do to her phone bill while she listened to the droning ring. Her thumb hovered over the end button on the verge of giving up when she hear it picked up on the other end.

"Hello Little Flower," Cyrus answered.

"How did you know it was me?" Vanessa gasped.

"Do I really need to explain, Flower? Is all well?"

"No, Cyrus. On both counts. I'm at your house. I think they have Lilah." The line was silent for a long moment. When Cyrus answered Vanessa could feel the menace in his voice through the phone.

"Is Meri with you?"

"Yes."

"When she wakes tell her to remember what I told her. There is much I must do here before I return but I will deal with those responsible soon enough. Promise me you will not do anything foolish."

"But what about Lilah?" she screamed into the phone.

"I said I will deal with it. Promise me!" The command was so clear in his voice Vanessa almost jumped to obey except she refused to lie to Cyrus. She was glad they weren't face to face.

"How are familiars made?" she blurted out, the words coming out on their own.

"It requires intent. I did not leave you enough blood for that in any case. Please put whatever foolish notion you have in your head away. This is a matter for those of the Blood. We must take care of it." Vanessa wanted desperately to argue with him. That he would think that she could sit by while Lilah was in danger because of her was infuriating but it wasn't an argument she was going to win.

"How are things going there?" she asked in an attempt to change the subject.

"The Senate is in much worse shape than I imagined. I will correct the problem and return. You still have not promised to let us handle this." It was clear she wasn't going to evade him like she wanted.

"I love you Cyrus. I'll be careful," she answered and ended the call.

Her anger burned inside her, warring with the indecision that tore at her as well. She hated having hung up on Cyrus, but there was too much of a chance of him wearing her down and getting her to promise to stay put. Sitting there toying with her phone an idea struck her. Pulling it out she scanned the menu for what she wanted. Lilah had signed them up for some program that allowed them to see where each other were. She had made it so that Vanessa could see where she was too, but Vanessa was sure that it was mainly so Lilah could keep tabs on her. Apparently she and Cyrus were afraid that her tendency to disappear would continue.

The app showed Lilah being at home and Vanessa groaned. Wracking her brain she tried to figure out how she could get there with enough time before dark. Pacing up and down the walk the sports car Meri had brought them here in caught her eye. She only hoped that she wouldn't get stopped on the way. It was over four hours until dark. Hopefully she would have plenty of time.

Back inside she crept back down stairs and held her breath as she looked for the keys. Not finding them anywhere she could see she leaned over the bed and gently poked at the pockets of Meri's jacket. A cry of frustration tried to well up before she stifled it when she felt the keys in the inside pocket. Inch by agonizing inch she lifted the edge of the jacked and slipped the keys out. Meri stirred fitfully as she let the edge drop back down and darted out of the room.

She couldn't tell if it was weakness or nerves making her hands shake as she dropped behind the wheel of the car. After almost two years not being allowed to drive, Vanessa thrilled a little at being behind the wheel again. The car started with a throaty roar and pulled smoothly onto the street. She didn't think she would get home nearly as quickly as Meri had brought them here but she was sure she could get here faster than Lilah would have.

Panic welled up every time she drove by a patrol car but none of them seemed to notice her. The drive was agonizingly slow since she was too afraid to drive over the speed limit. As she sat there behind the wheel it struck her that this was the first time she had ever driven in daylight. Rolling past the businesses seeing people come and go suddenly seemed more novel than it had when she was just riding as a passenger. For a moment she allowed herself to smile. The feeling of freedom was a welcome joy in an otherwise miserable day.

Doubt began to worm its way into her thoughts though. For all she knew Lilah had come to Cyrus's and decided to go home during the safety of the day. She began to wonder if she was on a fool's errand as she went. Just as it always had, her mind continued to wander as she drove, alternating between worry that she was making a fool out of herself to what she was going to do if her initial instincts proved accurate. The thought of facing three vampires as weak as she was right now was sobering, even given the advantage daylight gave her. Her greatest fear was finding that she was too late to save Lilah. Visions of finding Lilah hurt or dead pushed everything else out of her mind.

By the time she pulled into her driveway she had began to imagine them having turned Lilah into one of them. Storming up the steps to the door she hesitated as a dizzy spell hit her. Her hand on the knob she noticed that the door was unlocked. Lilah's car wasn't there either. Neither discovery made her feel any better. With a deep breath she steeled herself and stepped into the living room. Bright sunlight streamed in to the room through the windows giving everything a bright glow. The first thing she noticed was the mess. Her backpack had been upended and her books scattered across the floor. Other things from the room were tossed around to litter the floor. It looked like things had been broken for the sheer sake of destruction. She was sure some of it was vented rage at her escape last night.

Stepping gingerly through the mess she tried to make as little noise as possible. Room by room she made her way through the house, finding mindless destruction at every turn. Her room was the worst. She was sure it was meant to intimidate her but it only served to increase her rage. At least her hope chest was intact. Black scorch marks showed where one of them had tried to move it before discovering she had treated it with holy oil. Deep gouges marred the surface where whomever it had been had tried to break it open and failed. In the rest of the room long slashes bled the foam from her mattress out onto the floor to mix with the shattered remains of her bookcase. With a grimace she went on down the hall.

Lailah's room made her blood run cold. It too had been ransacked, though not as badly. The bed had been stabbed several times but worst of all was the smear of blood on the bedspread. Touching it she knew it was Lilah's. She couldn't have said how she knew but there was no doubt in her mind. That was when she saw the phone. The display showed her missed call as well as a couple from her office. Lifting it she found a folded piece of paper covered with a thick handwriting.

"I hope you enjoy our gift to you. I wish I could say I was surprised at how things turned out last night but I warned them how dangerous you are. Now that you know that you can't use your nice little technological toys to try and find us before dark I want you to listen. I have the woman and she is relatively

unharmed. If you want her to remain that way you will go the theater by Donovan's an hour after sunset for more instructions. Do not try any of your little games or she will suffer for it.   Ivan"

A piercing scream ripped from her throat as she kicked the nightstand sending the lamp crashing to the floor with the rest of the debris. Shoving the wadded note in her pocked she walked back down the hall, a red rim of rage blurring her vision. At the dining room she stood there amidst the shattered remains of Lialh's china and clenched her fists. Falling back against the wall she slid down to sit on the floor and hung her head between her knees. Anger, frustration and fear boiled in her mind choking out all other thoughts. For several minutes she sat there envisioning what she would like to do to Ivan if she could. Finally the worst of her rage burned itself out and she calmed down. She was tired and felt sick. Dragging herself to her feet she stepped into the kitchen and decided to see if she could get some food.

While she didn't feel hungry she knew she was going to need her strength tonight. The refrigerator door had been left open and much of what was inside was ruined. Sifting through what there was she managed to put together something resembling a lunch. The food made her feel much better but the exhaustion still gripped her. Before she left she paused and threw some of the remaining food in a bag to take along. If she made it past tonight she would likely be at Cyrus's for a while and groceries weren't something he kept on hand.

She made the drive back in a daze. Seeing the way her house had been violated left her feeling numb. Her mind kept going back to the smear of blood on the bed and Ivan's words that Lilah was relatively unharmed. What he would likely consider relatively unharmed made her stomach sink. Somehow she managed to make it back to Cyrus's without incident and pulled into the drive. Her feet dragged the sidewalk as she made her way to the door. On the steps she stopped and dropped the bag of groceries, sliding down to lean against the wall. Head against the stone she stared blankly at the sky waiting for darkness to fall.

Chapter 12
Debate

The plastic earpiece of the hotel phone sighed with relief as Cyrus released it to the cradle. His anger burned low and solid. He had a moment of irritation at the way Vanessa had ended their call. He was certain that she was going to fly off into some poorly thought out scheme, but all he could do at the moment was hope that the girl's preternatural luck had stayed with her in her new life. Either that or that Meri could keep her safe. There was serious doubt that she would deliver his message to Meri before doing whatever she was contemplating. He looked at the clock and did the quick adjustment for the time in New York. She had several hours of daylight left there. He was as sure she would try to use it to aid Lilah as he had been of who it was calling him.

But she wasn't why he was angry. Long ago he had learned that if he was going to be angry with Vanessa's foolish ways he would have to either be angry all of the time or push her out of his life. In the end he had decided it was easier to simply accept her for the force of nature that she was; something akin to standing in the tides. The breath of life she had brought into his otherwise sterile life of artifacts and books was worth the inconvenience she occasionally brought to his door. This was the first time her presence in his life had caused him more than a few tense conversations. When he considered what he was discovering about the way the world had changed around him he was glad he had been rousted from his self imposed exile.

This business of Lilah having been taken fired his spirit in a way he hadn't been sure was still possible. Not since Gordon had kicked his door in near dawn had he felt like this. And then the perpetrator had been right there for him to deal with. Now someone he cared for, had placed under his protection at Court over a year ago, was in danger or dead despite all of the laws and customs his kind had adhered to for millennia. If they had taken Vanessa he would have still been upset but would have had to admit how hard it would be for anyone to grasp the fact that she was no longer a vampire. Taking Lilah, however, was a clear violation. If he had his way someone would Stand Before the Dawn for this.

It was still a few minutes before sunset and he stood at his window watching the last dying rays of the sun as it set. While his eyes took in the sight he didn't see any of it. He would have to return to the Senate tonight. He had yet to even begin to argue for Vanessa with the unexpected detour things had taken the night before. Hands clasped at his back so hard that the ancient joints creaked, he tried to put his feelings out of his mind. As badly as he wanted to go directly to dealing with the issue of Vanessa's Blood Price he felt an obligation to Alaric. Hopefully that would be a simple matter and they could move on, but he doubted it. For reasons he couldn't begin to fathom he was sure that Landina was stalling him. It would be easy to assume that it was because she was behind the hunt for Vanessa but he wasn't so sure. In her position that should be a very small matter for her. And as adept at making enemies as Vanessa seemed to be he couldn't think of any way she could have earned Landina's ire.

There was something more going on than he could guess. Once again in his short trip he chastised himself for becoming so far removed from his world. While he had grown weary of the bickering and backstabbing of the Senate he still firmly believed in the value of the laws they were sworn to uphold. His world and the world of the humans had to maintain a balance. As superior as most vampires thought they were to humans the sheer number of his kind that had fallen to hunters proved how much of an illusion that superiority was. If the humans knew of them and thought them a threat there wouldn't be a vampire alive within a decade he guessed. The church had done a fair job during the inquisitions and they didn't have near the technological advantages humans had today.

"Dear Gods, that can't be it can it?" he asked into the fading twilight.

One of the ideas Gordon had whispered where he thought only his men could hear had been the idea of a new hierarchy with vampires as the ruling class over the cattle of mankind. Cyrus had seen that idea come and go countless times over the centuries.

Dayflower

Usually someone got too bold and drew the watchful eye of the hunters and the problem took care of itself. That quickly showed how much the vaulted superiority of the blood was really worth.

Cyrus began pacing the room, his anger lost in the new insights he had stumbled upon. His mind began to race as he weighed its merit. Gordon was apparently Landina's spawn; that was clear now that he had seen her. If she had been working towards this for that long it was no wonder she had so much control in the Senate. That would explain why she would want Alaric deposed. He had been the most moderate Magistrate the Senate had until the Americas had truly begun to develop. The younger, more democratic attitudes of the new Blood from America tended to temper the aristocratic nature of the rest of the Senate. The more he thought on it the more plausible it seemed to him. Sheer horror at the magnitude of the folly of such a thing in this day and age shook him. He was just glad that he was here to bring an end to things.

While he abhorred violence, Cyrus was sure he could use force to bring the Senate to bear if that's what he had to do. As much as he sympathized with humans he didn't want to see a hunt of extermination on his own kind either. And that was what he was sure would result if Landina planned anything like the rumblings he had heard from Gordon. Again he found himself before the windows staring out into the deepening gloom. Slowly the city took on its twinkling mantle for the night. It was some time before he felt he was calm enough to proceed to the meeting. He was sure the others would chafe at his tardiness but it wasn't concerning to him. If anything the delay may unsettle them a bit.

It was a pleasant night and he enjoyed the walk. A thin cloud cover added to the darkness of the night and just a hint of mist gave the air a damp feel. After an eternity in the desert he found the damp delightfully novel. That was part of the reason he had taken to living in the new world after all. The sheer variety of weather he was able to experience was amazing. He took his time in getting to the meeting and was not disappointed in his expectations of Landina's mood.

"While you may be an elder the Senate is not here to wait idly just for you!" she chided him.

"I was detained by a call from home," he countered with a cold smile. She was far too shrewd to let her reaction show but Cyrus could feel her flare up at the news.

"I hope that all is well then?" she asked flatly.

"It is not. I will get to that in a moment; however there is one thing I would like to see resolved beforehand. According to you Alaric was deposed by harboring a fugitive which you named as myself. Since we have determined that judgment to have been in error then Alaric's deposition was likewise in error. Since I have not heard it reported that he was Stood Before the Dawn I assume he is still alive."

"Ah but again your logic is flawed," she replied.

Her satisfaction was thick in her voice. Cyrus had met several of his kind that he had not cared for in his time but this woman was beginning to kindle a true feeling of hatred within him. Instead of rising to her bait he remained silent, waiting for her to resume.

"While the warrant was ill placed it was still an instrument of Our authority. He refused that authority and has been punished for it. Since the matter is past now We will commute his sentence. His has been placed in the Embrace in Valence. Is that all?"

"But he will not be restored?" Cyrus had no real hope that Landina would go that far. He was somewhat surprised at how quickly she had acquiesced the matter at all.

"No," was her only reply.

Cyrus could feel an almost electric tension in the air. Landina herself was giving off sharp pulses of emotion in the moments her careful guard slipped. He was reminded of a predator on the hunt. The sensation made him uneasy which he decided was just as well. He was not among friends he reminded himself. How differently the law was being applied by Landina and her toadies would make the elders that had crafted it rise from the earth if they knew. A very old and tired part of him wished he hadn't seen this day come. He scanned the group around him and saw none worthy of the responsibility they wielded. Shaking his head he looked up into the mist to collect himself before continuing.

"Fine. As to the Blood Price on the head of Vanessa Miller."

Landina strode forward until they were almost touching. Drawing herself up to her full height she stood eye to eye with him and glared at him in a cold fury.

"You WILL NOT try to excuse her actions to this body! She has earned that sanction a dozen times over. She should have been burned the day she was turned!" she screamed. The sudden heat of her rage was startling enough Cyrus had to force himself to stand his ground.

"I come here not to argue the nature of her crimes."

"Good!" another member interjected.

"What I come to argue," Cyrus continued, "is the jurisdiction of our Courts over her."

"Every vampire on the face of this Earth is under Our jurisdiction," Landina spat.

"That is my very point. She is no longer one of the Blood."

The silence in the park was sudden and total. For the first time since his arrival Cyrus felt he may be in a position to take charge of things rather than being on the defensive. His short lived hope was shattered as Landina spoke again.

"I was told that you may try such a ridiculous ploy. To be honest I didn't think a sage as respected as you would come here telling us fairy tales."

"If it is a 'fairy tale' as you put it, then please explain to the assembly how she walks in the light, attends a school and eats food," Cyrus boomed. His anger had been stoked to the boiling point and he was through trying to be civil. If Landina was going to act as a spoiled girl playing princess then that is how he was going to treat her. The fact that the rest of the Senate seemed to treat her as though she really were such a princess only strengthened his desire to swat her down.

"When she cries her tears are as clear as water and holy relics do not harm her. By what measure then do you call her a vampire?" His voice had reached a low roar as he continued. Not waiting for her to respond he charged on, "You, a woman brought back from the dead by the demon dwelling inside of her to walk the world for what? Fourteen hundred years? You have the gall to talk to me of fairy tales! Will you walk into the halls of the Fay and speak to them so?"

As he finished he saw that the rest of the group had stepped away from him. Landina had not moved but she was visibly shaken, one hand to her throat in a protective gesture. Only then did he realize that in his ire he had allowed his fangs to drop. Abashed, he marshaled himself and fought for calm. It was not easy in claiming as angry as he had gotten.

"May I take the floor?" she asked, for the first time since he had arrived using the proper protocol. He nodded acquiescence.

Dayflower

"Entertaining the possibility then, I find it much more likely that she has just undergone transference. Since that seems to have been the fate of the man she turned after Anton it seems plausible to me that she would be likewise affected."

"That was nearly two years ago!" he gasped, "Tell me of a single case of a Therian surviving more than a few cycles of the moon, much less not transforming for over a year and a half and I might believe that."

"Then I guess we're at an impasse," Landina replied.

He realized that any argument he used to bolster his claim could be equally applied to hers. They stood there for several minutes attempting to stare one another down. Before long other members began to murmur and shift about. That none of them even attempted to speak without Landina's lead sickened him. Cyrus hated the uncertainty he felt. He wasn't about to concede the point but didn't expect the cutting opposition Landina offered. If it weren't for how unpleasant he found her personally he would be enjoying the mental exercise. As it was he felt as though he were swatting at an unusually persistent wasp.

"While our arguments may be balanced I will remind you that you said yourself that I am a sage. I have made the study of our kind and our very nature the work of my life," Cyrus continued at last. "Do you, a mere child at my knee presume to know more about this than I, who have studied the powers of the blood for over six-thousand years?"

He hated what she had forced him to do. The way some of their kind used age alternately as currency and a bludgeon seemed so childish and simple to him. His age didn't matter to him beyond having allowed him to see so much of the world. That he had been forced to resort to such measures was humbling.

"It seems to me that Cyrus's testimony would carry the greater weight, if we could be sure he spoke the truth," another Senator added. He was a small, bookish looking fellow, turned no more than five hundred years by Cyrus's estimation. Landina gleamed. She knew her word would be taken here among her prodigy.

"Will you submit to a reading then?" she asked him with saccharine sweetness.

"After your attack last time, I do not think so," he said flatly.

"Would you submit to the Truth Stones?"

Once again he felt like he was being led. The very course the conversation had taken screamed of being a trap to him. If it were simply his own life that was in question he would walk away. That act would undoubtedly earn a price on his head but he had no doubt that his exile would be fairly peaceful. No more than a handful would try to claim him before it was deemed too costly. But it wasn't his life. It was Vanessa's. Somehow he had come to care for her more than he had anything else in the world. And while he could protect her it would be a prison worse than death for the girl. So knowing that treachery was afoot he resolved to move forward anyhow.

"I will submit on these conditions. First, I want it sworn to that Alaric will be released without prejudice immediately. Secondly, I grow weary of the games you seem intent on playing. I want the matter of Ms. Miller to be dealt with expediently and for us to be done with this. Last, I demand that once you have seen that I speak the truth the Blood Price on her will be lifted, or I swear I will destroy you."

"That is acceptable to Us," she cooed.

He was not surprised when she produced the stone. They were ancient, having been made before Cyrus had been born by a type of blood magic that had long since been lost. It was a small simple thing, a marble bowl half the size of a hen's egg. He could feel the same radiance of power from it he did from the Sanctuary stones. Those, at least, a few knew how to make. The secrets of the other artifacts were lost to time. Whoever presided over the Senate usually had access to one, though Cyrus knew a few had been lost to the tribulations of time. When he had last involved himself the fates of only three or four were known.

Landina brought out a small silver knife and prepared the Stone for him.

"Before you is the Stone of Truth. Do you give freely your blood so that We may know your words to be true and to see the will of the Senate be done?" she asked in the ancient formula.

"My blood is freely given so the truth may be known, so long as justice is served," he replied. He had to choose his words carefully. The stone required him to give his blood freely and honestly or its power wouldn't hold, and all here would know it.

Holding his hand over the small cup, he let Landina make a small cut with the silver knife. Drops of blood dribbled into it barely covering the bottom before the cut healed, stopping the drips. It wasn't much, but it was enough. Anything more than a single drop would allow the stone to hold him in its sway. Already he felt its influence. Landina smiled and held the stone before her triumphantly. More than ever he knew he had been trapped, he had but to wait and see the jaws when they closed.

"Very well, Cyrus, to make sure that we appease your conditions I will ask straightaway about Ms. Miller. Do you still claim her to be human?"

"Having reclaimed her humanity is the only explanation I can see for the changes I have seen in her," he answered carefully.

"And how is this miracle supposed to have occurred?" Landina demanded.

"As you are aware she was turned too young," he paused as Landina nodded before continuing, "Because of that she was not like the rest of us. Her demon possessed her, but was not a part of her like it is in all of us here. The young man that she turned the night she destroyed Anton was likewise divided. When he turned he became a Therian and she became human."

"Well, at least it's clear you believe that," she conceded. "Very well Cyrus. Since the girl is inconsequential I hereby suspend the Blood Price for you. But you understand, as many enemies as she had made if she ever proves to be one of the Blood or becomes one again then it will be waiting for her."

"That is acceptable," Cyrus agreed, "but what do you mean by saying she is inconsequential?"

"You haven't figured that out yet?" she smirked. "This was all to get you before Us. Honestly it was a windfall when you called for the meeting. When you arrived I was sure you were just another intermediary. I was expecting to have to resort to her trial to drag you out of your hole. "

Cyrus was stunned. The fact that he was the target of her machinations left him unbalanced and grasping for a response. He realized that she still held the stone and he could still feel its pull.

"Why," he asked, afraid he already knew the answer.

"Because those damned American Magistrates will listen to you and it's time for a change. I can't believe how easy it was to get you to agree to the stone. It seemed impossible that you didn't realize what they can do!" Her voice was a shrill harpy's cry to his ears. Anger swept over him again and he began to stride across the clearing to crush her.

"Stop!" she commanded with calm surety. Cyrus was brought up short as though he had hit a stone wall. However hard he tried he couldn't force himself to move towards her.

"I will tear you apart and leave the pieces for the sun to find," he hissed.

"No. No you won't," she crowed, "I would just make you wait for the sun but Alaric finally let us know how futile that would be." As she spoke one of the others from the circle produced a roll of some variety of cling wrap. With exaggerated care they wrapped the stone, sealing Cyrus's blood inside. He could see another pair coming in from the side carrying a coffin.

"So we'll just stick you in a hole until I think of a more permanent solution."

Chapter 13
Dinner and News

Meri opened her eyes and was grateful for the utter darkness of the room. Cringing she rolled over and dropped her feet to the floor. For several minutes she sat there, head cradled in her hands as pain tore through her head. Before the last few days she had never used her ability this heavily and it was wearing on her. A tickle on her hand brought her head up. Looking down she could see, in that strange twilight way her kind had, a smear of blood on the side of her hand. Shocked, she brought her fingers to her face to find blood dripping from her nose.

"Christ!" she gasped and made her way to the bathroom.

Flicking the light on sent new waves of agony over her as the lights came to life. Holding onto the edge of the counter she tried to fight it back, her vision swimming red as her eyes watered. Slowly the pain eased until she could stand. She was going to have to feed tonight. Normally she would be able to get by with the blood Cyrus kept on hand but there was no way that was going to cut it tonight. Muttering to herself as she worked Meri set about cleaning herself up. When she was done she examined herself in the mirror. Everything still had a slightly red tint because her eyes wouldn't stop trying to water. They looked almost black as she studied her reflection. Her skin was normally very pale but tonight it had a distinctly gray color to it.

With a sigh she turned off the light and went back into the bedroom. Her planner was exactly where she had left it but she knew before she touched it that Vanessa had been into it. She didn't have to feel to know her car keys were gone as well. Two more critical crossroads had passed while she had slept. The absence of her keys told her that the first hadn't gone as she had hoped. It had been clear to her that Vanessa was going to look to go on the offensive by herself. Meri had made a point of putting

99

Cyrus's contact information where she would find it hoping he would be able to talk her down. Things would have gone much better if he had.

Now she was left wondering how the second tipping point had gone. Vanessa was destined to go home once she left here. Meri knew that much. The question was did she return. If she decided to continue her hunt and go after Ivan herself then all was lost. As it was things were sitting on a razors edge and Meri wasn't sure she was going to be able to continue her mad efforts to tip the balance. Another lance of pain as she began to trudge up the stairs reminded her of that. If the girl wasn't there when she got to the top of the stairs she wasn't sure what she would do. Despite her ability to see the future every path where Vanessa died ended swallowed in blackness she couldn't see past. That, if nothing else, made her whisper a prayer under her breath to a Goddess she wasn't sure was listening that the girl was safe.

The perpetual half light Cyrus maintained upstairs made her uneasy. She was sure that Vanessa would have turned on at least another light or two. A quick scan of the room told her she was alone. Panic tightened her chest as she checked the other rooms she might be in. Desperate she tried to catch some image that would tell her if Vanessa had come and gone again. Her effort was repaid but a crushing blast of pain that took her to her knees. Holding her eyes tightly shut she willed herself not to bleed again. Somehow she kept control and got back to her feet. Leaning heavily on the front door she became dimly aware of a feeling she had missed in her panic.

Vanessa was sitting outside. That strange aura she gave off was plain now that Meri was aware of it. It was a sign how clouded her thinking was that she had missed that before. She opened the door and looked out to find the girl asleep on the front porch. Stepping outside Meri knelt beside her. Meaning to carry her inside Meri found herself struggling to keep control. Her fangs dropped as she caught the scent of the girl. With her predator's senses she could feel the blood coursing through Vanessa's veins. For a moment her hunger made her want to succumb to the temptation. But that way lay a darkness she feared more than she desired blood.

Not trusting herself to get any closer until she had fed, Meri drew her thumb across the tip of one of her fangs, slicing it open. Repeating the binding Cyrus had taught her she ran a line down the center of Vanessa's forehead and placed a line on each of her cheeks. Her mark wouldn't offer the girl much protection but it was better than nothing. The new magistrate hadn't revoked the protection Alaric had given Cyrus's property. Only Ivan or his men would dare violate that. Hopefully this would keep any of his flunkies from harming the girl and Mari wasn't sure how much she could protect Vanessa if Ivan showed up anyhow.

Shaking herself she pushed the thought from her mind and set off down the sidewalk. Holding her head high she moved with a purpose. Her normal hunt would take her somewhere a lone woman would not go lightly. She particularly enjoyed the fear and anger she caused in the men that would have hurt her. She knew how the girl hunted a similar prey, but Meri's motivation wasn't out of any similar moral concerns. Her making came at the hands of someone who reveled in his power over her and left her taking her revenge on those she saw as like him. The rage would eventually give way to fear. Oh how sweet that was! A cold smile touched her lips allowing her still extended teeth to show.

Tonight was not the time for that, though. She would have to take whatever came her way this time. Passing by people as she walked it was difficult not to just grab someone and feed. But the last thing she needed now was a price on her head too. The Night Courts had no mercy on the perpetrators of messy kills. She was forced to range farther than she would have liked to get to thinner groups of people. Her strength was beginning to fade and the pounding headache was back. Stepping into an alley she tried to collect herself. Pain shot through her again and as she extended her hand to lean on the wall a drop of blood splattered on the back of her hand.

"Are you alright?" someone asked her.

For a second she was too dazed to respond. She stood there looking up at him as her blood continued to fall through her fingers. Her knees buckled dumping her to the ground. The man was beside her in an instant trying to hold her up. As he knelt there, his neck inches from her, her hunger overwhelmed her. She reached up and grabbed him, sinking her teeth into his neck. Life flowed into her just as it flowed out of him. His pulse was weak by the time she was sated and she forced herself to stop short of killing him. Standing there she hesitated before walking away. Reaching down she grabbed one of the broken bottles in the alley and used it to mar the bite she had left behind. With that done she searched the man's pockets until she found his cell phone. Using the tail of his shirt to hold it she dialed nine-one-one and waited for the dispatcher to answer.

"Nine-one-one operator. Where is your emergency?" answered a woman's voice.

Meri dropped the phone to the ground and screamed before walking away. As she made her way back towards Cyrus's house she couldn't say why she had done that. Perhaps it was because he had been trying to help her instead of hurt her. Walking slowly she began to look at her actions and realized she had changed since she had first come to Cyrus. A few years ago she wouldn't have cared if the man had lived or died. In fact she would have been more likely to have drained him than not.

She wondered what had prompted the change. Cyrus tried to reclaim his humanity. That much was clear to her. But he never forced his way upon her. For a brief moment she thought of the girl before casting the thought aside. It had been less than a day since she had found her. The only reason she was even protecting her was a request from Cyrus. Even her feelings of obligation to him seemed strange to her. He had helped her to control her abilities, true, but she had never felt like she had owed him anything. This train of thought made her uncomfortable so she moved on to other things.

Before long she was walking through the arch over Cyrus's walk glad to see Vanessa where she had left her. Picking up the bag of food that sat beside the girl she went on into the house and started putting things away. The worst of the deciding points were now behind her and Vanessa was still alive. That much was promising. She had no idea why the girl was so important, but it was clear to Meri that she was. There were a few finer points coming tonight but none that ended in blackness. Meri drew a deep sigh as she returned to the porch. Disaster was still in the cards if things went wrong. Once again she wondered how all of this had fallen in her lap. She didn't want to be responsible for such big decisions. Shaking her head she crouched down and tried to decide if she should wake the girl or let her sleep.

Lilah shifted against the ropes that bound her arms behind her back. She wasn't sure how long it had been since she could feel her hands. As she tried to turn her shoulder dug painfully into the rough cinder block wall she was leaning against. Dark rivulets of water trickled in through cracks in the rough concrete to run down her back. Gritting her teeth she pulled her legs up to her chest and pressed harder against the wall until she could turn some. Finally she managed to shift enough to force a tiny bit of slack in her bonds. Blood flowed into her hands making them come alive with a fire that brought tears to her eyes. The strain of holding herself up from the floor like this soon drew her breath out in short gasps while sweat ran down her face. Unable to hold herself up any longer she dropped back to the floor just glad to know her fingers still worked.

The single bare bulb hanging from its cord in the ceiling cast harsh shadows around the cellar she had been thrown into. One more time she looked around the room for anything she could use to try and escape and again saw nothing. She was more angry than she was afraid, at least that was what she tried to tell herself. It wasn't that she had any doubts about the fact that her life was in danger. That she knew for a fact. But she refused to give in to panic or fear. Not allowing herself those options all that was left to feed her growing resentment of her captors. She didn't know a tenth as much about vampire law as she did about American laws, but she had learned enough to know that what was happening to her went against every law or tradition they were ruled by. Somehow it was almost that disregard for the law that angered her the most. Snorting to herself she had to admit that maybe that was just what she was clinging to so she could keep from thinking about what else was going on here.

"Yeah. Got it. No problem, Mistress." The voice came to her through the door at the top of the short set of stairs on the opposite wall. She recognized it as belonging to the one she had figured out was Ivan. He came swaggering into the room with a leer on his face that made her stomach turn.

"So you're awake. Damn. I was looking forward to waking you up," he said with just the faintest trace of a Russian accent to his voice.

"What do you want?" she sighed, sounding a lot more tired than she would have liked.

"I just got off the phone with my boss," he sneered, "The old man is in a box. Do you know what that means?" Lilah just stared at him. "We don't need the Miller girl for bait anymore." Reaching down her grabbed Lilah's chin and pulled her up painfully. "Don't worry though sweetheart. I'm going to keep you around for a little bit yet. I'm saving you for the celebration after I take care of her." His tone left no doubt what he meant by that. "Besides, I don't know if she has you bonded or not so I can't kill you until we have her."

"She isn't one of you anymore," Lilah growled through clenched teeth.

"Yeah. I keep hearing that. Considering she beat the crap out of three of my guys forgive me if I doubt you. Not that it matters now. I really hope you're right. This will be so much easier then. And I will really enjoy sucking that little bitch dry."

With that he released her to fall back to the floor, her head bouncing painfully off the cement. He didn't look back as he left the room leaving Lilah to think about what he had said. She knew she had been taken as bait for Vanessa. The fact that Vanessa was just meant to be bait for Cyrus left her reeling. Tears burned her eyes as she recalled his words. *The old man is in a box.* If Vanessa was still a vampire she might be able to do something, but Lilah didn't see what she could do now. And with Cyrus taken she didn't see how much hope was left to her. Vanessa had said she was with someone Cyrus had sent. She had to hope that whoever it was had some tricks up his sleeve. Exhaustion began to take its toll and she drifted off to an uneasy sleep wondering if she should dare hold out any hope.

Chapter 14
The Theater

Vanessa opened her eyes and was startled to see that it was full dark. She knew she had nodded off, but couldn't believe she had been out for so long. Looking to the side, she saw that the bag of food was gone. She hoped that Meri had taken it in. As she stood she had another bout of dizziness that threatened to send her down the stairs. Grasping the rail, she put a hand to her head and felt the dried blood there. Once the dizziness had passed she scrubbed what remained of the blood from her face. At least she knew that it had been Meri now.

With a sigh she went inside. The sounds of Meri putting things away in the kitchen drifted to her through the house. She was less than happy with how much sleep she had apparently needed. It was one more way her frailness was making itself abundantly clear to her.

Content to let the other woman put things away without her, Vanessa dropped into one of Cyrus's leather chairs. Staring at the ceiling she tried to think of some way out of the situation she found herself in. Checking her phone, she saw she didn't have much time before she was supposed to be at the theater. She should have felt more urgency about the situation, but she was just too numb for it. Wearily she pushed herself from the chair and made her way to the kitchen. She tried to brace herself for the confrontation with Meri.

"Finally up?" Meri greeted her as she walked in.

"Yeah," Vanessa sighed, "Ivan has Lilah. He wants me to meet him at the old theater by Donavan's soon."

A look crossed Meri's face that Vanessa couldn't pin down. It was obvious something had touched a nerve with her though.

"You know it's a trap, right?" she finally asked.

"Yeah."

Dayflower

"Well, I guess we should get going then," Meri said with a shrug as she tossed the empty grocery bag on the counter.

Vanessa was flabbergasted. She had been certain that there would be some argument about going. In fact she was sure Meri would insist on staying here to wait for Cyrus's return. She wasn't sure what to make of the woman's cavalier acceptance. Her train of thought was interrupted by Meri coming to a sharp stop in front of her and turning to face her.

"Do you have your phone?" she demanded suddenly.

"Yeah," Vanessa replied as she pulled it from her pocket.

"Turn it off and put it downstairs."

"Why should I?" she argued.

"You've been out of school, Lilah will have missed work. Someone is sure to have looked into it by now. Someone could track you through that thing and somehow I doubt that would help Lilah very much."

While Vanessa wasn't normally attached to her phone like her classmates were, she was still loathe to part with it right now. Too many things could go wrong and even if she didn't know exactly who she would call she still liked having the option. She prepared to say as much when Meri fixed her with a withering stare that made her rethink her argument. Intimidation aside she couldn't really argue with the woman's reasoning. After she had done as she was told she returned upstairs to find Meri waiting by the door with her arms crossed, one hand held out towards her.

Vanessa handed Meri the keys to the car earning her an annoyed look, and the two walked outside wordlessly. There was something more to Meri than Vanessa knew. She was sure of that. The things she chose to argue over didn't add up based on anything Vanessa had ever seen. Watching Meri drive, Vanessa tried to figure out exactly what was going on with her. Before long she shook her head in resignation. Figuring out how to save Lilah was more important than unraveling the eccentricities of some vampire she had just met. Vanessa reminded herself that she needed to keep that in the front of her mind. While she had faith in Cyrus's judgment on Meri's trustworthiness, the woman was still a vampire.

While they were driving Vanessa remembered her conversation with Cyrus and his command to remind Meri of what he had told her. Reluctant to break the peace she wasn't sure she wanted to say anything. It would be a lot simpler if Meri was willing to help. Minutes ticked by and the thought continued to bother her. Guilt pricked at her until she began fidgeting with the zipper on her jacket distractedly.

"I already know so you might as well say something," Meri said suddenly.

"Know what?" Vanessa shot back, using her best innocent voice.

"That you talked to Cyrus," she replied, "I have a pretty good idea of what he said to you too."

"Oh. You talked to him?"

"No. I knew you were going to call him before I went to sleep. Why do you think I left his number where you would find it?" Meri answered with a slight air of superiority.

"You're a reader!" Vanessa gasped.

Meri shot her a puzzled look, but didn't respond right away. The silence stretched uncomfortably long as neither said anything. Vanessa watched Meri with a new wariness; all of the pieces she couldn't put together fell in place. It was going to be a lot harder for her to deal with Meri now than she had originally thought.

"Okay, what the hell is a reader," Meri demanded harshly, cutting Vanessa's train of thought off.

"It's something I read in some books a guy I used to know had," she answered.

Thinking about Jason washed guilt over her again. She absently ran her hand over the sleeve of her jacket and wondered if everyone who took her in would die because of her.

"That doesn't answer my question," Meri said flatly.

"They're people that can see things. Kinda like an oracle, I guess," Vanessa answered halfheartedly.

"Close enough," Meri shrugged. "What did Cyrus say?" she asked, obviously trying to change the subject.

"He said to remind you what he had told you," Vanessa admitted reluctantly. "What did he say?"

"I'm supposed to take you and go to ground. Hide somewhere until he gets back." Meri sighed and gave Vanessa a weary look. "But I think we both know that wouldn't work. You'd run."

"Yeah," Vanessa mumbled.

She wasn't surprised at Cyrus's instructions, but she couldn't say the same about the fact that Meri didn't plan on following them. She wanted to be relieved that Meri was still going to help her. Somehow that wasn't the feeling that came to the forefront. Her trust in Meri was pinned to Cyrus's faith in the woman. If she didn't do as he said then what else could she not be counted on for? In spite of feeling like she shouldn't trust Meri she didn't have much choice. Her instincts were telling her something about the woman, but it wasn't that she shouldn't trust her. With a mental shrug Vanessa decided that if her instincts didn't throw up any red flags about Meri then there wasn't any reason not to trust her.

"So do you know what's going to happen tonight?" Vanessa wondered out loud.

"No," Meri admitted, "I know a few ways things could turn out; a few things that I can't let happen, but I don't just see the future."

"Will we save Lilah?" Vanessa's voice was pitched low, almost a whisper as the words left her mouth.

"She's not even there," Meri replied, "But if we don't go she would die. Ivan doesn't bluff."

Vanessa paused for a moment thinking. She had been certain that the meeting was going to be a trap, but she hadn't thought of the possibility of Lilah not even being there. Now that she knew it didn't surprise her. Ivan wasn't forthright on the best of days, much less when he was out to get someone. Letting her thoughts wander she was struck by something.

"How do you know Ivan?"

"Great Goddess you ask a lot of questions," Meri sighed in exasperation.

"Well?" Vanessa insisted, clearly not planning to let it drop as Meri had hoped.

"He created me," she growled, her voice as cold as iron.

"What!" Vanessa gasped. "What the hell was Cyrus thinking?"

The last words came out before she even realized it. Disbelief rocked her as she realized she was going to face Ivan aided only by his own progeny. Even without compulsion like Cyrus, or until recently herself, possessed a creator could compel their offspring. Suddenly her hope that everything would work out began to fade.

"I ask myself that a lot as well," Meri spat, fixing Vanessa with a heated glare that left no doubt as to what subject she doubted Cyrus's judgment on.

Dayflower

"What the hell is that supposed to mean?"

"You know damn good and well what I mean. For whatever reason he has a blind spot where you're concerned and it has caused no end of trouble."

"You don't know what you're talking about," Vanessa hissed.

She instantly felt defensive and angry, but she knew exactly what Meri was talking about. A lump formed in her throat as she thought about Lilah and the trouble she was in. Before she had the chance to follow her train of thought any farther she was jarred by the car slamming to a stop. Meri had swerved to the side of the road so violently that they had clipped the curb before shuddering to a stop. Vanessa looked over at her as she knocked the gearshift out of gear with a rough slap. The woman loomed over her adding a hint of fear to Vanessa's indignation.

"Don't tell me what I do or don't know you little twit," she growled in a low cold voice, "Cyrus is in serious trouble right now because of you. And your Lilah. Not to mention that I don't see too happy of an ending for myself in all of this." She paused for a moment obviously trying to calm herself before continuing, "I have had to walk a fine line ever since that bastard made me because I broke rules I didn't even know about. Everywhere I turn I find your tracks all over the place, usually with disaster having been left in your wake while you just went on your merry way."

She was going to continue, her ire gaining heat as old angers bubbled up, until she saw the tears running down Vanessa's face. The girl was mad Meri knew, but at herself. She didn't need her gift to read the look on Vanessa's face, the defeated slump of her shoulders. The girl was aware of the trouble she had caused and obviously felt bad about it. It reminded Meri of the pain she had seen in the girl's past earlier deflating Meri's self righteousness in the process.

"Goddamn it," she muttered as she threw the car back into gear and pulled back onto the road. "Don't worry about Ivan. For whatever reason he can't compel me," she explained once she had calmed down.

Vanessa nodded, but remained silent. Meri struggled not to sigh as Vanessa continued to sulk. While she had no desire to make an ass out of herself she certainly didn't feel any need to apologize for the exchange. It seemed to her that someone bringing the girl to task was long overdue. *A lot of this shit could have been avoided if everyone had been as harsh with her as they had been with me,* she thought to herself.

On the other side of the car Vanessa tried, and failed miserably, to keep from crying outright. Hot angry tears flowed despite her attempts to stop them. She was furious at Meri. Not because she was wrong, but because she was right and Vanessa knew it. It wasn't just Meri, though; she was mad at herself as well, and at fate, or whatever it was that kept putting her into these situations. Not to mention Ivan. The man had been a constant source of grief to her from the first time they had met. Letting her thoughts drift to him she found that hatred much more satisfying than feeling sorry for herself. The tears stopped, replaced by a dark hardening of her eyes as she began trying to figure out a way to take him down.

Several minutes later Meri pulled the car to a stop less than half a block from the theater and killed the engine.

"I don't want to park where they can see the car," she explained when Vanessa gave her a questioning look.

"Do we have a plan?" Vanessa asked hopefully.

Meri cringed inside at the expectant look the girl gave her. She could tell that the girl was putting more faith in her abilities that she felt herself. Turning to face her Meri reached out and grabbed Vanessa's arm, braced to block out the torrent of images she knew would be there.

"I don't know what's going to happen; it doesn't work like that. It's like if you drop a ball on the sidewalk. You can have a good idea of where it will bounce, but a million things can send it wild."

"I know," Vanessa replied.

She made a sour face and searched for the right words. Meri held her peace despite the increasing urgency they both felt.

"But you know *something* or we wouldn't be here."

"Yeah, I do," Meri agreed, "And I can't tell you a word of it or everything will go to hell in a hurry. What we're going to do is step into the trap, spring it, and hopefully walk out the other side."

She paused for a moment struggling with her own thoughts. Her arm dropped as she ushered Vanessa back into motion.

"I will tell you this," she continued, "Whatever happens to me, you have to get clear of this. Go back to Cyrus's, hide, something. Okay?"

"Okay," Vanessa said at a whisper.

Meri wasn't doing anything to make her feel more confident about the situation, but she wasn't going to back down now. *I've made it out of some real nightmares, I'll make it through this too,* she thought with a grim determination.

They continued walking in silence. Meri wasn't eager to return to the nursery that had spawned her, but refused to let the past control her. The dark facade of the theater was just in sight when Meri pulled Vanessa into an entryway. She gave one last furtive look down the street before she pulled out her day planner.

"Since I don't know if I'll be able to give this to you if you need it I'm going to give it to you now."

As she opened the case she saw that one of the vials was already missing. She fixed Vanessa with a withering glare as she handed over the remaining vial without comment. The look rolled off of the girl without effect as she took the vial. Vanessa watched Meri with a blank face, waiting for the woman to indicate their next move.

"Come on," she sighed as she resumed walking, expecting Vanessa to follow.

It only took moments to cross the remaining distance to the front of the theater. As they approached Meri motioned for silence and paused, pressing her hand to the plywood core of the door. Vanessa was struck by the similarity between Meri's appearance and her own when she would extend her senses. She looked briefly at the rest of the abandoned theater's facade. Not a single pane of glass was left intact, every opening having been filled with plywood. It had been over eighty years since the theater had closed. Then the vampires had taken it over. Using the opportunity before they entered Vanessa pulled the cork on the vial, examining it with a mixture of anticipation and fear.

"What are you doing?" Meri hissed in her ear.

"It doesn't have to be afterward to work," she whispered back.

Meri looked dubious but nodded once, letting the matter drop. She motioned that she was ready to go and waited for Vanessa to drink the contents of the vial. The power ran through her with an overwhelming force. The previous time she had thought that the sensation was intense. Now she knew that her weakness and wounds at the time had drastically diminished the potency. Every nerve in her body came alive in a way she could barely understand. Once the initial onslaught was past she knew things were different. She had been able to feel Meri before, knew that the woman was a vampire, but now she could feel her in the way she had before her change as well as the presence of more inside the entrance. All of her senses were amplified and more. It was a familiar feeling, one that had defined most of her existence.

Without a word she pulled out her crossbow and cocked it. She couldn't help smiling as she did so, reveling in the return of her old strength. Meri could feel the change as well. The look she gave Vanessa was a mixture of confusion and relief.

"When I kick open the door go left and drop," Meri whispered as she pulled a handgun from a holster on her ankle.

Vanessa nodded and braced herself for the fight. She had been in hundreds of fights before. Every time she had been terrified and desperate to survive. For the first time she was almost anxious to step into the fray. Now that her former strength was returned she was forced to admit that she had missed it more than she thought. The vampires on the other side of that door were Ivan's men; some of the same that hunted her and had taken Lilah. Within a heartbeat she decided that there was no "almost" to it; she was ready for a fight.

A single kick from Meri sent the plywood sheet spinning out of the frame into the lobby of the theater. It was still standing upright when Meri entered the room with Vanessa half a step behind. As it fell Meri fired two rapid shots into the hip of the man on the right. He fell with a strangled scream that was silenced when a third round caught him in the neck. The second man darted forward to attack Meri faster than she could react.

The bolt from Vanessa's crossbow hit him in the chest just wide of the heart. He spun and dove for Vanessa. Sidestepping his grab, she dropped into her fighting stance. With a casual motion he pulled the bolt from his chest and walked towards her, a dark smirk on his face. She waited for him to come, ready to counter his attack when the loud report from Meri's pistol made her jump. He toppled over backwards, a large hole above his left eye.

"I said to drop," Meri barked as Vanessa turned to face her.

Vanessa didn't have a chance to say anything before another man stepped out from the recess on the other side of the door and drove a stake into Meri's back. She went stiff and fell into his arms, her eyes turning black with rage. Instantly Vanessa was aware of two more coming up behind her from the wings of the lobby. She turned trying to load her crossbow before they got to her. A moment's hesitation when she realized that they were two of the men that had grabbed her in the van gave them the opening they needed. The blond man stepped to the front and fired a pistol at her legs. Using every ounce of speed she had at her disposal she lunged to the side making the shot go wide.

A second shot followed the first still lagging behind her as she moved. The second man cut her off and tried to grab her making her pause to evade his grasp. She heard the click of the action and threw herself back hoping to beat this shot as well. A sharp pain in her upper thigh told her she hadn't been fast enough, but the wound wasn't bad enough to slow her down. Her lunge, however, threw her enough off balance that the second man was able to catch her with a blow to the side of the head, taking her to the ground.

He stepped in delivering a kick to her ribs that knocked the wind out of her. Anger welled up in her as he went to kick her again. As he pulled back to deliver the kick she slid around and locked her wrists behind the ankle of his planted leg and drove her shoulder into his shin just below the knee. The move toppled him over backwards as she pulled his leg out from under him.

She scrambled to get to her feet, but another slug tore through her leg dumping her back to the floor. Gritting her teeth against the pain, she pushed herself up to her hands and knees. The wound was closed by the time he grabbed her from behind, but healing it had taken all but traces of the strength Cyrus's blood had given her. He locked his arm across her throat and began pulling her up. She drove her elbow back into his crotch as hard as she could on the way up. Before he could even respond she pushed off with her legs and threw her head back smashing him in the mouth.

His grip loosened enough for her to go limp and drop, sliding out of his hold. Out of the corner of her eye she saw the other man rising and had to push down a rush of fear. The moment she was free she turned, her momentum from dropping taking her to her knees. In a panic she grabbed one of the bolts from its quiver on the side of the crossbow she still gripped and drove it upward in between his legs with all of her strength. Smoke from the anointing oil meeting his flesh rolled out from between her fingers as she let go of the bolt and turned.

Dayflower

The second man caught her with a hard slap across the face knocking her to the ground. She rolled away from him and found herself laying on the gun dropped by the first man as he collapsed. With trembling hands she pulled it out and started firing at the attacker standing over her. Her finger kept squeezing the trigger until the slide locked back and the gun ceased to fire. Three of her shots had found their target in his chest, the others knocking plumes of plaster from the crumbing ceiling and walls of the lobby.

Her attacker stood stunned for a moment by his injuries. Vanessa was grateful he was young enough to still react like a human to his wounds. An older vampire would have barely acknowledged being shot. His shock gave her the time she needed to retrieve her crossbow from where his blow had made her drop it. Luckily it had stayed cocked through the tussle and all she had to do was slide a bolt in place. Her assailant had recovered by the time she brought her weapon up to fire. He closed the distance with a burst of speed she could barely follow now that Cyrus's blood had left her system.

She pulled the trigger just as he reached her, the bolt not even clearing the end of the crossbow as it drove into his chest paralyzing him. His momentum carried him forward to land on top of her. Vanessa grunted as she heaved his frozen form to the side and pulled her legs the rest of the way out from under him. Quickly scanning the room she saw the four downed men but not the fifth or Meri.

With a growled curse she retrieved her crossbow and reloaded it. Warily she made a quick check of the rest of the doorways off of the lobby. Only the short hallway that led to the backstage area seemed to be used, thick dust and cobwebs coating the floor elsewhere. She strained to hear any signs of movement as she crept through the gloom to the open doorway. A quick peek revealed an empty room, but what she saw chilled her to the core. On a rough, battered table in the center of the space sat a silver thermos alongside a few other familiar tools.

At a run she entered the room and grabbed the cursed thing. The point of her crossbow swept the room as she scanned for anything or anyone else important. Satisfied that there was nothing else significant she hurried back to the lobby. It was clear at a glance that the two Meri had shot were still out of commission, but that wouldn't last for long; their wounds nearly

114

closed. The two she had fought were still down as well, the first still screaming as he tried to claw the bolt free.

"Shut up," she commanded coldly as she stood over him, crossbow aimed at his heart.

"Fuck you, bitch," he panted.

"Where does Ivan have Lilah?" she demanded.

"I'm not telling you shit you little whore," he spat, reaching to grab her.

Lowering her aim to where his other hand still gripped his groin she fired. The bolt drove through the back of his hand burying itself in what lied beneath. A fresh howl of agony tore from him as she stepped back slightly.

"I have three more bolts ready," she informed him as she reloaded, "Where is Lilah?"

"The basement of B-block," he grunted, trailing off into a guttural growl as he pulled the latest bolt free.

Vanessa turned and headed for the door at a jog without reply. In the doorway she paused. Laying on the concrete was Meri's pistol. Picking it up, she gave it a quick look. It was a compact gun with a sloped front and rounded back end. She couldn't find the safety, but figured out one lever let her ease the hammer down. Hoping that was good enough she stuffed it in her pocket and hurried away from the theater.

She knew the place the blond vampire had meant. It was a low income housing block several vampires controlled. Trading cash and drugs for blood they treated it like their personal buffet. The practice sickened her, but since it kept their feeding from drawing attention it was ignored. She had pressed Alaric about it once. He simply shrugged, informing her that it was a practice that had existed as long as man had built cities. No one wished to change a system that worked.

With a curse she went to check her phone for the time before realizing it had been left behind. Sirens cried in the distance, getting closer as she ran. *All the gunfire got somebody's attention,* she thought to herself. Coming to a stop beside the car she hesitated. She was sure Meri had stolen the car at least a couple of days before. With police coming this way she was afraid it would be noticed.

Grimacing, she took off walking. Her thigh still ached where she had been shot. Apparently there hadn't been enough power left from the blood to heal it completely. Grateful that the dark would hide the blood on her clothes she began the long walk to Cyrus's.

Chapter 15
Choices and Messages

What had been a quick drive to the theater was a decidedly longer walk back. Every time she thought she wouldn't draw too much attention she dropped into a distance eating run, grateful for the months of track training behind her. Any sight of a squad car would send her ducking out of sight. Her nerves were strung tighter than a bowstring as she moved through neighborhoods nearly unchanged since she had lived here.

It was nearly midnight by the time she reached Cyrus's house. Using her key to let herself in felt strange. Cyrus being gone left her feeling adrift. Even in the decades she had lived here he had never been gone more than briefly. Walking to the center of the twilight lit room she set the thermos on the table with a metallic clink.

She sat down resting her chin on her laced fingers staring at the stainless steel vessel in front of her. That such a simple, mundane thing could hold so much menace struck her as strange. It was dented and scuffed; its life had obviously been rough in the two years since Anton's men had used it to catch the blood they drained from her. Out of morbid curiosity she sat up and slowly removed the cup, setting it aside. Her finger traced the outline of black plastic stopper in the mouth of the thermos. Hesitantly she removed it and gingerly set it inside the cup. In the dim light she could still clearly see the crimson liquid inside.

It was as fresh and bright as the moment it had left her arm, just as she knew it would be. Staring at it she could almost feel it pulling at something within her. She swiped at the edge and looked at the red droplet on her fingertip. There *was* some sort of power to it; it was almost as if she could hear it crying out to her. Everything started to feel distant, darkness swimming at the edges of her vision.

117

Dayflower

The thermos felt heavy in her hand and she forced herself to set it back on the table. Moving it away from her was difficult, as if her muscles were resisting her command. Quickly she forced the stopper back in place and staggered away from the table. She ran into the kitchen and washed the blood from her fingers. As she watched the thin red trail swirl down the drain she pulled in deep, ragged breaths. Everything slowly started to feel normal again and she turned the faucet off.

Stepping back to the doorway she glared at the thermos on the table like it was a venomous snake. What was in that simple container had the potential to undo everything for her. But at the same time it could give her back the things she had lost. She remembered the strength and the speed, and the helplessness when Ivan's men had caught her. If she used it she would be able to save Lilah, she was certain of that. She would also lose Lilah as a mother, as well as the entire life she had built. With Lilah and Meri taken and Cyrus gone she didn't know what to do; who to turn to.

Suddenly she was exhausted. The weight of the last few days came crashing down on her making her weary to the core. With dragging feet she made her way downstairs and into the bathroom. Moving mechanically, she stripped and washed the blood from herself.

"God is it always going to be like this?" she moaned trying to remember how many times she had done this same thing.

After she dressed she collapsed on her bed. She felt guilty going to sleep in her own bed while others suffered for her, but there was nothing she could do tonight. Her only chance was in the daylight. With that thought she drifted into an uneasy sleep.

"Please tell me you are kidding me!" Ivan screamed at the men in front of him. "Christ what the hell is wrong with you!"

He kicked a table across the room in his rage sending papers and glasses flying against the far wall of the cellar. His men watched him pace back and forth in silence. Enough were his progeny, and as such his to destroy at will, that the whole group was nervous. As far beyond the law as he had already gone the others weren't sure he wouldn't kill them anyway.

"At least you brought me this bitch," he sighed at last, his anger apparently spent.

Dayflower

Meri laid against the wall in front of Liah, the point of the stake still protruding from her chest and rage seething in her eyes. Ivan walked over to her and knelt down. Seeing the hate in her eyes he smiled and ran the back of his hand across her cheek almost tenderly.

"I can't wait to teach you some manners, girl," he said in a near whisper.

He shoved himself to his feet and turned back to face the still silent group behind him.

"So she got away again. I guess at least this time she had some help," he said, giving Meri a kick. "So if I send all of you after her do you think you can catch her? Or is one little girl too much for the five of you?"

"She got the blood, Ivan," the blond man interjected hesitantly.

"The blood doesn't fucking matter," he spat, "That was only for if she really was human like the old man said. It sure as fuck doesn't sound like that's a problem now does it?"

The group shuffled uncomfortably refusing to meet his icy glare.

"Here's what we're going to do. She's probably at the old man's house. Kick the goddamn door in and get her. If she's not there, leave her a message."

"But what about the boundary?" a dark skinned man objected.

Ivan crossed the distance to the man in a single stride. He gave the man a shove that bounced him off the wall to land on the floor alongside the ruins of the table. Before he could rise Ivan shoved him back down with a boot on his throat.

"The old man is in the fucking ground. To hell with his neutral ground bullshit!" he screamed at the man. "I said go get her!"

"What about the magistrate? She's still enforcing it," the blond offered meekly.

Ivan stepped away from the fallen man and let out a heavy sigh. Shaking his head he ran his hand through his hair and chuckled softly to himself.

"It really hasn't sunk in yet has it?" he asked the group. "The old order is falling. These old rules are going to go away. There are what seven more magistrates on this side of the world?"

He waited for a murmured agreement from the other men before continuing.

"As soon as the majority here are ours like back home everything will change."

He spoke with the manic fervor of a zealot; an irrational glow to his eyes. All of the men had heard his revolutionary rhetoric before. Most of them agreed with it or they wouldn't be here, but there was still a fear of retribution in their eyes. To a man they had heard stories about Cyrus, and most had seen even Ivan show the man deference. Despite being told that he had been dealt with they were reluctant to cross him. Ivan saw none of this, however. His confidence blinded him to the uncertainty in his followers so he forged ahead.

"Now to send the little whore a message if she did think to find another hole to hide in."

He walked over to Lilah and knelt beside her. Untying the knot binding her hands he smiled at the sigh of relief that escaped her as the tension on her shoulders eased. Roughly he grabbed the hand closest to him, her left, and pulled it to him.

"I wouldn't get too happy just yet," he told her before biting her pinkie finger off.

Lilah shrieked as she felt his teeth sever her flesh and bone. In a small way she was grateful that her hands were still mostly numb from being bound. As bad as the pain was she realized that it could have been worse. She felt sick as he nicked his finger and rubbed his blood over the wound, closing the damaged flesh.

"I wouldn't want to waste anything," he said with a sickening calm. "Nail this to the door if she isn't there," he commanded the men as he tossed the finger to one of them.

"You're going to lose, you know that don't you," Lilah told Ivan with more confidence than she really felt. "She'll find a way."

A rich throaty laugh filled the room as he sat back slightly. He looked truly joyful as he stared her down. Lilah tried not to react to the unsettling coldness in his eyes. For a moment they just sat there and stared at each other as his men shuffled up the stairs and back into the night.

"I hope she tries," he replied, "I've been waiting for that for a very long time."

Lilah was scared, but she didn't want to let him see that. She considered saying something more, but she didn't have a chance as

Dayflower

Ivan shoved her back down and retied her bonds. Gritting her teeth she tried not to whimper as he cinched the ropes tight wrenching her aching shoulders again. Despite her best efforts a small moan escaped her as he finished the job and left her lie.

Hearing that Vanessa had eluded the trap gave her a bit more hope. She thought back to some of the things Cyrus had told her the girl had been through and survived. Vanessa was reluctant to tell Lilah much about her violent past herself, but she had heard enough to know that her daughter was not to be taken lightly. Looking at the paralyzed woman in front of her Lilah assumed that this was the help Cyrus had sent. She knew she had been told the woman's name, but she was too exhausted to remember it. With a ragged sigh she pushed down her fear and tried to figure out if there was any way she could free either of them.

Ivan climbed the stairs out of the crumbling basement to the back service entrance of the apartment complex. He was frustrated at the ineptitude of his men. They were all young for one thing. Even he was young for his kind as far as that went, but he had a hard time believing that was the sole source of the problem. The Miller girl had been an irritant to him from the day he set foot in this territory. He would have gladly returned to his homeland if he were allowed to. His Mistress commanded him to remain, so remain he would. As much as he hated following her orders he had learned it was foolish to do otherwise.

Since he was stuck here he would make the most of it. Right now that meant taking care of the girl. Seeing her dead would be a satisfaction long in the coming. He would never forget the first time he had met her. And while the incident wasn't reason enough on its own for his ire, it had certainly showed him what the future would hold.

~~~

It was his first appearance at Court here in the new world. The entire place seemed so packed and busy he could hardly imagine what it was like in the daytime. That business and the steady flow of immigrants like himself had its definite advantages. As small as the new world was, the population of his kind was unusually large. With so many people moving through the city at any given time it was an opportunity like none he had ever seen. For the first time in his new life he could feed almost at will with no fear of reprisal.

121

Dayflower

The magistrate here was strict and closely followed the old ways, but that was bound to change. Such a change was what he was here to put into motion. Back into motion he corrected himself. He had never met Gordon, the progeny whose place he was taking, but he couldn't make himself feel any respect for the memory of the man. In such a wild place of change and plenty how could he have failed to gain support for the new order?

At heart he had always been a revolutionary. He had always had a way of defying death as well. As a soldier for the Russian Empire he lived when scores of others died. Then the Decemberist revolution had come and he eagerly joined with his brethren to bring in a new regime. Unfortunately his revolution had been easily crushed and he was sentenced to hang. When the noose had been placed around his neck he was sure that his luck had run out. That was proved wrong when the rope had unraveled dumping him to the frozen Russian ground still very much alive.

Many of his unit were not as lucky. Oh plenty of ropes failed that day, but going against tradition they were ordered to be rehanged. He, however, escaped a second noose for exile to Siberia. Instead of a fast death at the end of a rope it would be a slow death from cold and starvation in a mine. That was what he expected anyhow.

Instead Landina had taken him one night. She said she had been watching him; that she could use a man with his dedication. Once she explained the bargain to him there was no option other than to accept. He assumed he had never really had a choice in the matter and that she was just being diplomatic about it. Nothing he had seen since made him think otherwise. Now he was to stand before the magistrate here and argue for division of the territory.

"This is a separate land from the old order and the home of the Senate. Just as this new country stands apart from the nations that made it we too should stand apart as our own conclave," he had said using the arguments she had given him.

"You do realize that what you suggest is akin to treason?" Alaric had asked cautiously.

This was the argument Gordon had been sent here to make years before, but had failed to get the support he needed to be effective. But Ivan knew how to make men follow him. It wasn't through excitement about ideas or personable camaraderie. It was about respect and fear. That was the Russian way. Even though he was younger than the men that followed him he had their respect because he had their fear.

"A traitor is a man that fails to change his country. The man that succeeds is a patriot," he announced with conviction, "I don't propose overthrowing the Senate, I propose standing apart from it."

Unknown to anyone here besides himself overthrow was the plan, though. The number of his kind here was so much higher than in the old world Landina wanted it separated. If they could control this place openly it would make wresting control from the elders much easier. If that plan failed her family would still have a haven to retreat to. One that was ruled the way she saw fit.

"That's idiotic," cried a female voice from the back of court.

It was clear she hadn't intended to be heard, but the room had fallen so silent that her voice rang out like a bell in that space. Ivan looked and saw *her*. He had heard about her. A child turned. She was a violation not only of Senate law, but of Ivan's personal sensibilities. The ancient one living here officially in exile, Cyrus, kept her like a pet. He was the danger to their plans. Even though he had renounced the Senate the magistrates here relied on him for advice and guidance. While he never came to court his little spy did.

"Listen child, you should keep your silence and let your betters conduct our business," he told her mockingly.

He was not about to be called down by a girl, much less one that was obviously still a child. It was clear that she had taken offense to his words. Drawing a few gasps, she marched across the floor to stand before him. At her full height she barely reached his chest and he smiled down on her in amusement.

"Go sit down before I put you over my knee, girl," he commanded in a tone much colder than his smile conveyed.

"I think you need a lesson on respecting your betters, *boy*," she hissed.

"Go sit down," he growled at her.

It was more than a command. He put the full weight of his compulsion behind it. His ability had always been abnormally strong. Even freshly made he had been able to compel those much older than himself. Landina warned him that it was a violation, but in his home territories the point was never raised.

Instead of scurrying away as he expected she gave him a wide eyed glare.

Dayflower

"How DARE you," she yelled, "You sit, you cur."

The compulsion wasn't strong enough that he was forced to obey, but it had enough power that his knees nearly buckled making him step back to steady himself. It was a greater affront than he had ever been dealt other than by his maker. Even then she had the decency to deal with him in private, not in the center of Court when he had the floor.

"That is enough."

Alaric's command wasn't shouted. It was a low cold voice that left no doubt that it would be obeyed. Looking abashed, the girl returned to her seat now at nothing more than a word from him. Ivan was left feeling even more the fool for the intervention.

"I don't know how things are managed where you are from, Ivan," Alaric continued, "but you won't try to compel another of the blood in these lands without consequence."

"Yes sir," Ivan answered through clenched teeth.

After that he had been dismissed and his argument had never even been discussed. After court had closed he had found the girl on her way home. He shoved her into an alley and freed his belt intending to teach her respect his own way. Before the first lash had fallen his arm had been stopped by a grip like iron. He had turned to find a solidly built middle eastern man not much taller than the girl.

"This is a warning," he said as if he were commenting on the weather. "If I hear so much as a rumor that you have touched my Little Flower I will break you. Only then will we go before the magistrate. Tell me that you understand."

There was no threat to the words. Ivan was a man that knew threats and this was no threat. The man, presumably Cyrus, was stating a fact. Judging from the strength in his grip when Ivan struggled against it he would be able to deliver too. He simply stared passively at Ivan as he tried to pull his arm free. Only after Ivan had nodded in agreement was he released.

Things had only gotten worse from there. Now that the girl didn't have Cyrus to protect her, she would see how things really worked. He was looking forward to it.

Chapter 16
Reflection

Cyrus had no idea how long he had been in the coffin. He had never been as acutely aware of the hour as others of his kind seemed to be so he wasn't even sure if it was day or night. After his initial anger had burned itself out he had decided to sleep. He had rested very little in the preceding days and the resulting fatigue had apparently taken its toll on his judgment. Perhaps he would be better able to do something about his situation well rested.

A glance around the satin lined confines of his prison made him glad that Landina had at least had the decency to bury him in a nice casket. A rough wooden box was the norm for punishments ordered by the courts. Pushing a finger through the lining he pressed experimentally against the lid of the coffin. It was made from a heavy steel. He was sure that he had been placed in a concrete vault as well. There were no illusions on his part that his relatively comfortable prison was a move of kindness on his captors part. No, it was a practical decision. He had to wonder if the average vampire would even be able to break open this heavy model. The concrete sarcophagus he was sure surrounded him would certainly contain almost any of his kind hampered as they would be by the coffin.

Out of curiosity he pushed at the lid. Hands pressed to the cushioned interior he found himself unable to exert any pressure on the lid. Landina's compulsion of him with the Truth Stone prevented him from trying to leave the coffin. Instead of being irritated or angry at this turn of events he merely examined the problem. At the moment he was more concerned with learning about his prison that escaping it. This clarified purpose fixed in his mind he sought to extend his arms again.

The seal on the coffin snapped easily under his hands, but the lid didn't move more than a finger's width before hitting something

125

Dayflower

solid. Craning his neck Cyrus could see that his assumption about the vault had been correct. He exerted a bit more force distorting the lid of the coffin even farther. The moment he went to shift the lid of the sarcophagus his strength failed him dropping the lid of the coffin back into place. His thoughts had strayed too close to the idea of escape and the compulsion had taken hold preventing further action.

Being stopped again by Landina's command to stay in the coffin finally began to irritate him. Considering that she had also accosted him using the power of a reading he realized he shouldn't have been surprised by her reprehensible misuse of the Truth Stone. One thought was a balm on his ego. However else she may have manipulated the law to her ends she had overstepped here. Her life was forfeit by violating the stone just as surely as if she had committed an act of violence in a Sanctuary.

He had always had his suspicions that the stones were capable of more than forcing the truth from a subject. Now he had his confirmation. Cyrus wanted to know where Landina had learned lore that he hadn't managed to unearth almost as badly as he wanted to destroy her.

It was time to examine the bond that held him here, he decided. Reaching inward with his senses it was easy to find the compulsion wedged in his mind like a sliver. Pushing against it with thoughts of escape he gauged its strength much as he had judged the resilience of Meri's ability to resist him. Slowly he pushed ever harder against the compulsion. As he committed more and more of his will to the task he felt the demon stir to life within him. He could feel the power bowing under his onslaught, but his hunger and anger rose as he pushed. His own animal growl brought him back to himself. It took longer than he would have liked for him to regain his sense of calm.

A cold truth was now clear to him. Even after thousands of years of domestication there was still a demon beneath the surface. All it needed was an opening to reassert itself. He now knew that he had the power to defeat the compulsion. It had been on the verge of collapse when he had relented, but so had his self control. Was his freedom worth his hard won humanity? Not yet, he decided. He still had other hopes before he went down that path. Though he knew time was not on his side. Lilah was in grave danger and he was uncertain if he could trust Landina to be true to her word to call off the hunt for Vanessa. He didn't want to leave

126

their fates to chance, but he would do them little good if he was freed bereft of his humanity.

His attention turned from his personal predicament to the plight of those he cared for. It was possible that Meri already knew of his situation. He hoped that she did. That might mean that help would arrive of its own accord. If she did know, he couldn't fault her for not warning him. They had experimented and he knew how fragile her visions were. One piece of information too much and everything she saw would crumble away. If she had seen something and not told him about it he knew that there was a good reason for it.

Not content to leave everything to the hope that Meri had managed to foresee this turn of events he tried to come up with another option. He had not bonded Meri as he had Vanessa so he couldn't reach out to her. At this distance it was doubtful he could even reach her if he had. He had never made any progeny and Vanessa was the only soul he had even bonded. He was proud of that choice even if it proved very inconvenient at the moment. With Vanessa no longer being of the blood he didn't see any hope there.

The only hope he had would be if he was wrong about Vanessa's humanity. It wasn't a thought that he relished. All she had ever wanted was to be human again so she could grow up. Since that was her desire it was his as well. Her new life was a bittersweet joy to him. Seeing her so vibrant, so alive was a deeper joy than he had known since he had last seen his own daughters so long ago. It was also painful to have her so absent from his life. He still carried regret for his misjudgment in wrongly throwing her out over Anton. Of all the damage that Anton had done Cyrus felt the theft of those decades from his time with her more keenly than any of the lives he had taken.

Now that he was forced to face it Cyrus had to admit that he may have been seeing what he wanted to see. Landina's arguments that Vanessa could be a therian certainly had merit. He wasn't prepared to abandon his own counter arguments just yet, though. No therian he had ever read about or encountered had gone more than one lunar cycle without changing, much less two years. For a moment he marveled at how therian lore had been distorted over the years. He never understood how the therian's full transference to a demon became confused with the legends of lycanthropy; even if therians had a somewhat wolf-like appearance. Not to mention the juxtaposition of the new moon and the full moon in the lore.

Shaking his head he pushed those thoughts aside. Now was not the time for academic musing. If Vanessa was a therian she was like no other that had existed. By any measure he could think of she was human. Though her presence was still clear in his mind just as it had been since he had bonded her. If she truly was human would that still be so?

There was also the possibility of a familiar. He was well versed in the technical aspects, but had never preformed that act either. Vanessa being a familiar to him had its own unique set of complications. That would explain every oddity Meri insisted on pointing out to him without negating her humanity. Unfortunately it would also place her back in the jurisdiction of the Senate.

He wasn't going to unravel this riddle trapped within this box either, he admitted to himself. There was only one option left to him so he might as well attempt it. Reaching out to Vanessa was all he could do besides wait.

At such a great distance he wasn't sure if he would have been able to reach her before she had changed. Now he was even less certain so he fixed a singular impression in his mind. All he could do was hope it would be enough if he got through. Clasping his hands together on his chest he stilled his mind. With an ease born of centuries of practice he cleared away every thought except the one he focused on. Seizing on his awareness of Vanessa he concentrated on that bond.

It was easy for him to work with the bond. Even in her decades of exile he was always aware of her through it. Now he pushed with it, pouring every ounce of energy he dared through it hoping to reach her. After several minutes he stopped, more exhausted than he could remember feeling in ages. He could only hope that she had felt him. There was no way she would be able to respond even if she had. With a mental shrug Cyrus decided since there was nothing to be done other than wait, he might as well sleep.

Chapter 17
Going to Church

Vanessa woke with a start. She had been having another dream about the past; something that had been very rare until recently. Suddenly she had an image push its way through her dream. It was hazy and indistinct, not clear enough that she could pick out specific details from what she had seen. As hazy as it was it still left a clear impression of what it was. She was as certain that it was a cemetery in Ireland as she was that the vision had come from Cyrus. The feeling of his presence in her mind was all too familiar for her to mistake.

Rolling out of bed she once again reached for her phone to check the time only to curse its absence. There was no clock in her room here since time had been relatively meaningless when she had lived here. Still, she was sure that it was before dawn. Exhaustion weighed too heavy on her for it to be too far into the morning.

The worst thing was that she knew Cyrus didn't have clocks around the house. The man had always kept his own hours and expected others to conform to them. She padded upstairs hoping that by chance one of the appliances in the kitchen would be set correctly. As she walked she had a growing sense of dread. Any reason to doubt her instinct had long been burned out of her so she retreated to her room and loaded her crossbow.

Silently she crept up the stairs and peeked around the corner. The library looked the same as it had when she had gone to bed, but her fear was not assuaged. Step by agonizing step she moved through the chest high stacks looking for any sign that someone had been in the house. Finally convinced that the library was clear, she moved to the kitchen. The clock on the stove told her that it was still over half an hour before sunrise. Counting on Cyrus's methodical ways she assumed that it was correct.

Dayflower

Vanessa was sure that no one but Ivan himself would dare violate the restrictions on Cyrus's home. Unfortunately she wasn't entirely sure that Ivan wouldn't be a problem so she spent the next half an hour sitting in front of the door with her crossbow aimed at it. Only when the first rays of morning light seeped through the crack under the door did she dare open it and look outside.

Throughout the time she sat there staring at the unmoving door her sense of dread never lessened so she wasn't surprised to find a package on the front steps when she opened the door. What did surprise her was the contents of the package. Inside she found a finger she knew had to be Lilah's and a note that read simply "B."

A multitude of emotions ran through her as she stood there in the morning sun holding the severed finger of her adoptive mother. The one that stayed was pure undiluted rage. She stormed back into the house and slammed the door behind her. As she had sat her vigil at the door she had thought about the thermos on the table, about the power it could restore to her. And about the cost of using it.

With an angry swing she knocked it from the table and sent it flying across the room. It slammed against the wall by the kitchen doorway leaving a deep gouge in the plaster before falling to the floor with a dull thud. She marched over to it, intending to do more violence upon it, but paused. It took her several minutes to gather herself enough to set it back on the table without slamming it down as hard as she could.

Suddenly it was clear to her. This *thing* contained her past. All of the pain and loneliness of the last three and a half centuries sat before her in a stainless steel container. Right now, in this moment, Ivan was forcing her to choose between that time and the life she lived now. Feeling the euphoric rush of power last night she had her moment of doubt, but it was past now.

With a sickening lurch in her stomach she knew that Lilah had been wrong Sunday; Cyrus wasn't going to be able to save her this time. Meri was gone as well, so it was up to her.

She looked at the thermos with hatred burning in her eyes. This was the price that Ivan wanted her to pay for Lilah's life and she would be damned if she would pay it. Not that she intended to let Lilah go without a fight. The front door was still standing open letting the morning sunlight pour into the room. Slowly she walked over and stood in the bright light, reveling in it. Somehow, she had no idea how, she would kill Ivan for what he had done just as she was.

For a moment she considered calling the police. They would be able to get Lilah if she told them where to go. At least she hoped they would. The fact that it was a haven for vampires left the possibility of several dead cops on her hands. That was if she were lucky and no one involved was under the influence of the magistrate. Even if they did manage to rescue Lilah there would be a price. Getting the police involved would violate a multitude of vampire laws, most likely revoking Cyrus's claim of Familiar Blood.

The more she thought about it the worse an idea it seemed. In the best case scenario she would likely end up with a price on her head. At worst Lilah and several policemen could end up dead, and she would still have a price on her head. The only way she could see her way through this would be on her own. Fortunately she had more than her fair share of experience with vampire hunters. Admittedly that experience was from the side of the prey and not the hunter, but she still knew what types of weapons and techniques hunters used against vampires. She also knew that those methods proved far more effective against most vampires than they ever had against her.

She once again stepped into the bright morning light. Here was her best weapon; the one thing that would undo any advantage they had in the darkness. All she had to do was capitalize on that. Holy water would be another requirement. Only a small handful of hunters had ever failed to use that powerful tool against her. The ones that didn't were without exception former military types with more conventional ways to damage someone.

A small, but very specific list formed in her mind. Some of the things she already had at least a small supply of. There was no way that her small stash would be enough for a full assault on B-block though. Just as she had taken up self defense she had taken other measures to keep from being helpless. For centuries she had lived in this house with its ever growing collection of rare, often unique, tomes and scrolls. Never before had she truly realized how much information resided inside these walls beyond what Cyrus himself knew.

Once she had regained her humanity everything had changed. She knew she couldn't continue to be as ignorant of the world around her as she had been while immortal. As little as she had

cared for the details of vampire society and history while she had
been a vampire herself, she now felt the need to know everything.
If there was a law she could use against them she wanted to know
it by heart. Her first visits to Cyrus's after Lilah had taken her in
were spent in heavy research. Cyrus was surprised, but very
approving of her new dedication to knowledge. Often he would
guess where her research was taking her and suggest new books to
read.

One piece of that information was vital to her right now.
Vanessa had gathered that a lot of people had heard of Pope
Innocent VIII's papal bull *Summis desiderantes affectibus* that had
opened the door to the witch hunts in 1484. The History Channel
had even had a show on it she had watched. She wondered how
many knew of the other edict he had issued that day. The one that
declared all "cursed dead that walk God's earth in defiance of His
will are a scourge that all men of God are bound to destroy." It
also directed the church to give any aid possible to "God's
servants" working to destroy them. She knew where she could get
her supplies if the church between here and B-block had anyone
who knew their history.

Time was of the essence. It would take her about two hours
to get to B-block without a car. And that was if she didn't run into
any trouble on the way. There was a nagging fear in the back of
her mind that the police would find her and take her into custody.
Hopefully things went well at the church. If they wouldn't, or
couldn't help her she didn't know how she would get what she
needed. Urgency suddenly pressing in on her she dashed
downstairs and gathered what little she had, tossing in her pack
before running out the door. It was all Vanessa could do to keep
from breaking into a full run as she jogged down the sidewalk. No
one would notice a girl jogging with a backpack at this time of the
morning; there were a lot of kids out making their way to school,
but a full run might draw more attention than she wanted.

Vanessa anxiously watched the sun move higher in the sky as
she ran. It was at least something of a relief when she finally
reached the church just over half an hour later. Finding the
massive front door open was also promising. The inside of the
massive building was dim and cool. The smell of candles and old
paper were strong in her nose as she moved farther into the
sanctuary. She was somewhat surprised to find the place
apparently empty, for some reason she had expected there to be at

least a few people inside. Not that she had much experience in churches. The last time she had set foot in a church had been the last service she had attended with her parents. It was a bittersweet memory she hadn't thought of in a long time.

Her nerves began to get the best of her as she milled around trying to decide how to find someone. She was just about to go through a doorway at random when a voice from the entrance caught her attention.

"Can I help you?" the young priest called out to her.

"I certainly hope so," she sighed with relief.

She walked towards him not wanting to shout the length of the aisle.

"Do you know about the papal edict of 1484?" she asked bluntly.

"The condemnation of witchcraft in Germany? A little, why?"

"The other one," she replied flatly.

He gave her a confused look and shook his head.

"I'm sorry. I don't know what you're talking about," he said with a touch of remorse. "Is this for a class project or something? Perhaps the library..."

"No it's not for a class project," Vanessa interrupted, "This is a matter of life and death. I need to talk to someone who knows about church history. Detailed stuff."

"Father McKay is here somewhere. He might know something," the priest offered looking a touch uneasy at her comment.

"Great. Let's go talk to him."

"Well, I don't think..." he stuttered obviously unsure of what to do.

"Listen, I'm in a hurry and this is very important," Vanessa said through clenched teeth. At the moment she was seriously missing the ability to compel people. Things like this went so much smoother when she had been able to force people to do what she wanted. "Right now I'm trying to be calm, but I'm sure I can be loud enough for the good father to hear me wherever he is, if I need to."

The priest was obviously uncomfortable. Vanessa felt a little bad trying to bully him like she was since it was obvious he really didn't know what to do. The silence stretched uncomfortable between them as he tried to decide whether to take her to his superior unannounced or risk a scene, although it wouldn't be much of one given the empty sanctuary.

"Is there a problem Jonathan?" an older man asked from behind Vanessa making her jump.

"Father Mckay, this young lady had a question for you," he gushed with obvious relief.

"What can I do for you miss?" he asked as Vanessa turned to face him.

He was shorter and overweight. His eyes looked too large, magnified by his round rimmed glasses. Seeing him made Vanessa feel a bit embarrassed that he had come up behind her without her noticing. But he did give her the feel of someone who would know history.

"Please tell me you know about the Papal Edict of 1484," she pleaded.

"The *Summis desiderantes*? Of course."

"No!" she sighed heavily, "The other one. The secret order Innocent issued that day."

The older priest's face went from friendly to serious in a heartbeat. He looked nervously at his fellow and wiped his face with a handkerchief. Vanessa could see that he knew something so she held her peace, waiting to see if he would admit to it or try and stonewall her. Finally he laid a hand gently on her shoulder and leaned in closer to her.

"I'm quite surprised that you do. Can we discuss this in my office?"

Vanessa nodded and let the older man usher her though the building to a shabby little office in one corner. Well worn rough bookshelves lined the walls and stacks of both papers and books filled most of the space. One small window let in a weak shade of the bright morning light outside. As they entered father McKay gestured for Vanessa to have a seat in one of the well worn leather office chairs in front of his desk. She took an uneasy seat on the edge of the chair and waited impatiently for him to shuffle his way around the desk to take his seat on the other side. Finally he had settled into his chair and steepled his fingers before him before addressing her.

"I must admit that I'm curious as to how a teenage girl knows about a secret church order from the fifteenth century," he said once he had settled in.

Vanessa paused for a moment. Impatience burned within her, but she was afraid that if she pushed too hard that things would take even longer than if she played whatever game the priest was working.

"A dear friend of mine has a copy," she admitted.

The priest's eyebrow shot up at her comment and he sat back in his chair.

"A facsimile?" he probed gently.

Her patience wouldn't last if the old priest insisted on questioning her on every detail.

"One of the handwritten edicts," she said, her words heavy with frustration. "Not to be rude, but there are lives on the line here. If you can help me great, but if not say so now so I can go elsewhere."

He looked at her as though he were weighing her. Again silence stretched as he thought about what she had said.

"Fine, since your need is so urgent tell me why we should help you." he said at last.

"If invoking the order isn't enough," she replied, her voice flat and cold. She stared him down as she continued, "I know that the monsters are real. The stories that you use to scare your congregation are real. And if you gave a damn you'd help me fight them."

"No one has tried to invoke that edict for quite some time," he mused, unfazed by her glare.

"Since the mid fifties, right?" she asked, remembering a fight from her past.

He gave her quizzical look, obviously surprised.

"How long have you been with this church?" she demanded, "How many hunters have you dealt with?"

Finally she had made an impact. He was still calm, but her talk of hunters had certainly touched on something with the old priest.

"I *promise* you that I have dealt with more vampires and more hunters than you have ever seen." she declared.

There was no boasting to her statement, no teenage drama. It was a cold declaration of fact and that was apparent to the old priest. For just a second he looked into her eyes and saw something there that convinced him of what she was trying to tell him. With relief she watched the change sweep over him.

"What do you need?" he asked, suddenly sounding very tired.

Dayflower

Half an hour later she left the church feeling much more prepared than she had when she had entered. For the most part they had gladly provided the things she had asked for, but they had balked at her taking the black wool prayer rope she had seen. In the end she had managed to get her way and left with everything she had hoped for. The sun was much farther overhead than she would have liked, however, forcing her to hurry to get to the complex in time.

Chapter 18
Going Back

The trip across town went much smoother than Vanessa had feared. In fact her trip went so well that she was getting paranoid. Experience had taught her that if things were going extraordinarily well it meant something was terribly wrong. Not a soul seemed to so much as look at her as she rode the bus to the stop closest to her destination. As she walked the final blocks towards the project that held B-block the street seemed strangely empty. Unease crept up on her making her doubt what she was doing. She knew from the beginning that it was a bad idea, but the eeriness of her journey drove that point home firmly.

Rounding the last corner the project came into view. It looked the same, but different all at once. The decrepit collection of buildings that made up the housing project were scarred and filthy; refuse dotting the courtyards between the building. None of that was different from the last time she had been here, but the neglect was more pronounced. Out of the corner of her eye she could see curtains close as she passed. The residents here had learned to keep their heads down and avoid anything having to do with the vampires that controlled the area. Word must be out that something was happening. She wondered if the older residents recognized her. That would explain the abandoned feel to the place.

The moment the "B" building came into view Vanessa's stomach churned. For a moment the fight in the theater came back to her. A wave of nausea swept over her making her lean against a nearby streetlight. She pressed her forehead against the chipped and ragged surface of the pole grateful for the feel of the cool metal on her head. The spell didn't last long, but she hesitated before continuing. It wasn't the violence of the fight that bothered her; most of her existence had been defined by violence, but before

137

it had always been in self defense or because of the demon that had been within her. For the first time in her life she had initiated the fight and she didn't like the way that felt. She felt no remorse for what she had done; Ivan's abduction of Lilah had forced her hand, but it bothered her.

Forcing herself to keep walking she thought about everything that had happened. The whole situation was something new to her. For centuries she had survived by either running or letting Cyrus protect her. Now she couldn't do either. The impulse to run and hide was as strong as it was familiar, but she refused to give into it. Too many people she cared about had been stolen from her or died protecting her. There was no way she was going to add Lilah to that list without a fight.

Fear tried to creep up on her as she entered the vestibule of the building. A quick tug told her that the inner door was locked. She had expected as much, but thought it was worth a try. Turning her attention to the tattered collection of buttons beside the door she looked for the right name. The person answering the call might changed, but the name was always the same. Finding what she was looking for she pressed the button. An obnoxious buzz emanated from the panel in reply.

"What?" a tired voice demanded.

"Blood is thicker than water," she replied.

Another buzz clawed its way from the panel before the clack of the door latch releasing. Vanessa smiled as she slipped inside. It had been decades since she had been here, but vampires were creatures of habit. Change, including passwords, was hard for them. That was a fact that she was counting on today. Turning down the first hallway she stopped at the first apartment she came to. With a prayer to whatever deity that might be listening she punched the code she remembered into the pad on the door. Sighing heavily with relief she pushed the door open and slipped inside.

The apartment was dark and thick with dust. Turning the lights on she could see that it had been a while since anyone had been here. That was a good sign. The last thing she needed was someone coming in while she got ready. A thick cloud of dust kicked up as she dropped onto the couch. The brown and orange plaid pattern belied how filthy the thing really was. She shook her head as she looked at the rest of the furnishings in the room. The newest item had to be the monstrous console television in front of her, and it had to be at least thirty years old. Maybe thirty-five she decided.

Forgetting the furniture she began emptying her pockets onto the coffee table. A selection of bottles and tools lined up beside the pieces of the crossbow before her. The weapon was too bulky to carry assembled on public transport without drawing attention so she had taken it apart. As she opened her small tool kit and went about putting the pieces together her mind drifted to the past. Looking down at the worn leather of the jacket tears burned her eyes as she thought about the first human that had died trying to protect her even though he knew what she was.

~ ~ ~ ~

She had just managed to escape from the hunter. He was a sinewy southwestern type in a cowboy hat and boots, a heavy wad of tobacco in his cheek. She had seen his type before; not driven by a religious zeal, but by a personal hatred of her kind. The religious types wanted to destroy her kind, the ones like him wanted to hurt her. He was certainly of the latter type. Someone close to him had been taken by a vampire, she was certain. A spouse or a child, that was the only thing that ever gave them the cold malice she had seen in his eyes.

He had been armed with a shotgun and a bowie knife, not the usual hunter gear. Of course it wasn't a normal shotgun either. He had loaded the shells with a mixture of silver and wooden shot. She wasn't sure where the silver myth had gotten its start, but it had saved her more times than she could count. She held her arm across her body not against the chill, but from the pain of the shrapnel still working its way out. The wooden shot went to splinters as soon as it hit which was painful. She didn't know what would have happened if he had caught her in the chest with it, but she wasn't eager to find out.

What she wanted more than anything was to go home. The pain of Cyrus's exile was still fresh. Fighting back the tears that threatened to fall she kept walking. She needed a ride desperately and bloody tears wouldn't help her any more than the shredded clothes she was wearing. She had been forced to leave her coat behind as she ran from him. There might be another shirt in the bottom of her pack, but the blood splattered jeans she was wearing were the only pair she had left.

Dayflower

The few years she had been on her own since Cyrus had thrown her out had been hard. She still didn't know what she had done to earn his ire, but knowing his convictions she was too scared to go back. Since that night it seemed as though she had been constantly on the run, constantly hunted. Alaric had warned her how dangerous it was to live outside the tight rules of the territories, but she had never imagined it would be like this. As it was she had no choice but to do the best she could. For the moment simple survival seemed to be pushing the limits.

The roar of the motorcycle interrupted her morose train of thought. She turned to see the ratty old Triumph pull to a stop beside her.

"You need a lift?" the young man asked with a smile.

She couldn't imagine how he could stand to ride the bike in the cold. As immune as she was to the elements, even she was aware of how cold the wind was.

"Yeah," she replied uncertainly.

Looking down at her bare arms she was sure he was thinking of the weather. In reality she still didn't trust herself to be able to hold on. She rubbed herself to sooth the crawling pain she felt as bits of wood and silver worked out of her skin under her hand.

"Here," he offered, stepping off of the bike.

He pulled off his leather jacket and wrapped it around her. It was quite a bit too big for her, but it was warm. She picked up his scent from the lining and couldn't help but pulling in a deeper breath. He had a deep earthy smell that made her feel at home. While she was preoccupied he had pulled open a bundle on the back of the bike and began to pull on a few extra layers.

"I know it's not exactly a Cadillac, but she's a decent ride," he smiled as he climbed back onto the Triumph.

She smiled and stepped on behind him. As she wrapped her arms around him the smell she had picked up from the jacket hit her even stronger. The demon within her surged in hunger, her earlier wounds driving it. Gritting her teeth she forced it down. The last thing she wanted to do was hurt the first person to show her any kindness in quite a while.

"Name's Kevin," he called to her as he pulled back onto the road.

"Vanessa," she shouted back.

"Where ya heading?"

"Somewhere warm!" she yelled.

Dayflower

She could feel his laugh as she gripped him tight. The road slipped by beneath her feet faster than she had ever imagined. For most of her life she had never traveled anywhere her own feet hadn't carried her. Recently she had ridden in a handful of cars, which seemed a marvel to her, but never had she been moving at this speed in the open before. A terror unlike any she had felt facing hunters or anything else gripped her. Closing her eyes she pressed her head against his back and held on for everything she was worth. Before long the wind was biting in until her hands were numb from the cold. She was astounded that he could stand the bitter cold as they moved through the night.

It was near dawn when he stopped to fuel the bike. She stepped off from behind him and slowly pulled off the jacket he had given her. For some reason she was loathe to part with it, but there was no way she could stay with him through the day.

"Thanks for the ride," she said holding the jacket out to him, "I need to crash so I'll hop off here."

"I was going to call it a night too," he replied. He smiled a warm smile that made her stomach flutter and ran his hand through his sandy blond hair. "You're welcome to crash with me if you want."

Her instincts told her that it was a bad idea, but there was something about him that made her feel giddy in a way she hadn't ever felt before. She had to fight down the urge to giggle and he wrapped the jacket back around her and led her into the gas station to pay. Soon they had found a small motel and he got a room with double beds for them. Feelings she had never had before were at war with her pragmatic survival instincts, but the last few years since Cyrus had thrown her into the night had been so bleak she was just glad to let someone take care of her again.

Somehow she found herself traveling with Kevin far longer than she had meant to. He would stop in a town for a few days, perhaps a week or two, and work odd jobs to get enough money to get back on the road again. The time was euphoric for her. All at once she had someone that she cared for and that seemed to care for her in return, but still had the freedom of the open road. Whenever they stopped he would say she was his sister. It made her angry every time he did, but she couldn't say why.

More than anything else she enjoyed the fact that he never seemed to question her peculiar habits. Whenever he would ask if she wanted to eat he would simply nod when she declined. Not once did he question her insistence to stop before dawn or the fact that she slept until dark. He usually took evening shift work so he was gone for a while when she awoke, but would spend the night talking with her or doing any of a hundred little things to pass the time. On the rare occasion that she needed to hunt she would slip away before he got off of work and when she returned he never questioned where she had been. Usually he would decide to get back on the road on those nights so she rarely had to worry about getting caught.

They were stopped in Nevada when it all came to an end. She went to the restaurant where he was washing dishes to wait for him to get off work. They were walking back to the motel when she caught the smell of tobacco from behind them. She spun around to see the hunter she had fled months before. Without a word he pulled up his shotgun and fired. Kevin shoved her to the side putting himself in the path of the blast. Before he had even hit the ground Vanessa was on the hunter.

She pulled the gun from his hands with a twisting jerk and drove the side of the action against the side of his head. He staggered back from the blow, but didn't fall. In a fluid motion he pulled his bowie knife and launched it at her. She was surprised by the motion and caught the knife in the throat. Often she had seen young vampires react to such wounds as if they were still human. Vanessa had long since had those reflexes burned out of her and simply pulled the knife free and threw it back at him. The hunter was not nearly as able to shrug off the wound as she had been and fell clutching at the blade.

Vanessa took a chance and turned to check on Kevin. The shotgun blast had torn an ugly hole in his chest. He was breathing, but barely. Blood coated his lips as he struggled for air.

"You idiot," Vanessa sobbed, "It wouldn't have killed me."

"I..." he began, a coughing fit interrupting him, "wasn't sure."

Vanessa stroked his face as red tears streamed down her cheeks.

"I can save you," she offered. The wound was too great for her to simply heal, but she could still turn him; the demon could restore him then.

"No. Not like that," he protested, grabbing the wrist she was bringing to her mouth.

"But you'll die."

142

Dayflower

Kevin shrugged, put his hand on her cheek and smiled. She could feel her heart breaking as she watched his eyes grow dim.

"When did you know?" she asked as she pulled him close.

"First night," he murmured, "Your breath didn't steam. Didn't shiver."

"Why?"

Again he didn't respond, just shrugged. For the next few minutes Vanessa held him is silence, her tears falling on his chest to blend with his blood that was already there. She had no idea how much time had passed, but she knew he was gone. Glancing over at the hunter she saw that he was dead as well. Gently she slid out from under Kevin and closed his eyes. Scrubbing at her cheeks with her palms she walked back towards the motel to get her things. She almost left his jacket behind, but she couldn't bring herself to do it. The memory of him insisting she keep it that first night bright in her mind. As she walked into the night she felt more alone than she ever had before.

~ ~ ~ ~

Her hands had long since finished putting her weapons together while her mind was otherwise occupied. The memory was a painful one that she rarely let herself dwell on. Wiping the fresh tears from her face she started for a moment to see them clear on her fingertips. Shaking her head she stood from the ratty old couch and took a deep breath.

"That was then," she reminded herself, "It'll be a different fight today."

Walking into the bathroom she was glad to see that there was a mirror over the sink and that it would come off of the wall fairly easily. There was a narrow window of time for her to do what she meant to and it was coming fast. She gripped the mirror tight and made her way back into the hallway. It was a short trip down to the service door. Carefully she leaned the mirror against the wall and broke out her tool kit. A large red handle sat in the center of the door. Pushing it would open the door to the emergency exit and basement entrance beyond, but would also sound several alarms.

As Vanessa pulled screws from the cover of the latch mechanism she was grateful for some of the more questionable skills she had learned in her years on her own. It didn't take her

143

long to bypass the alarms and get the door open. Dragging the mirror behind her she tried to be silent as she slipped into the short hallway. Illuminated by nothing but the red glow of the exit light over the steel door on her right, the space was a murky blur. Trusting her memory and once again relying on the vampiric resistance to change she released the mirror and made her way slowly towards the basement door. Right where she was expecting, she found one of Ivan's men in an office chair propped against the door.

She took a deep breath and hoped she was strong enough to do what she planned or it would be a short fight. Pulling out the thick wool cord of the prayer rope she made a loop in her hands and dropped it over his head. Twisting it so that the knots of the rope locked together she quickly pulled back towards the emergency exit behind her. As soon as the rope made contact with the vampire's skin it began to sizzle and smoke. The rope had no more than pulled tight and he began to flail, the pain pulling him awake despite the hour.

Vanessa didn't hesitate as he began to fight and kicked the door open as his struggles flipped over the chair. The sudden shift threatened to pull the rope from her grip, but she gritted her teeth and put everything she had into pulling him back towards the door. Bright afternoon sunlight streamed through the door blinding her for a few seconds and redoubling the fury of his struggle. Grabbing at the rope he tried to shake her free, slamming her against the door frame painfully. Even weakened by the sunlight he was several times stronger than her. If this continued for much longer she was going to lose this fight.

Desperate, she stepped forward and kicked him in the side of the head as hard as she could. The impact sent a lance of pain through her foot, but it did slow his struggle enough for her to get through the doorway. Planting her foot on the frame she pulled on the rope until her shoulders and back screamed at the strain. Somehow she managed to get him most of the way through the door into the sun. With some satisfaction she realized that he was the blond man from the van. The rope wound tight around his throat kept him from screaming as he began to blacken and burn in the sun.

Sweat drenched her as she held tight while the sun did its brutal work. She was exhausted by the time his struggles had stopped and she could release the rope. Nausea threatened to overwhelm her as she watched the decades since he had been turned catch up to his body in seconds. She had never seen what happened to a slain vampire before now. In fact it had never occurred to her to even wonder what happened. It was sobering to watch the body crumble to ash and dust before her; to realize how close she had come to that fate herself.

Shaking the thought off she stepped over the remains and set about putting the rest of her plan in motion. After the struggle she had just gone through she had some serious doubts about her ability to pull it off, but it was too late to back out on Lilah now.

Chapter 19
B Block

Vanessa slipped through the small crack she had opened the door using her body to block most of the light from the mirror. Carefully she let the door ease shut wincing at the click of the latch. Bright spots swam before her as her eyes adjusted from the bright afternoon sun to the pitch black of the utility room. Her stomach lurched again as she scrubbed her hands against her jeans. Digging through the charred ashes outside the door to find the key had almost been more than she could handle. She wished she had thought of that detail earlier. Clenching her jaw she tried not to think about it.

Slowly she pulled the crossbow from her belt and carefully cocked it. She still couldn't see, but she could feel the presence of vampires in the room before her. Struggling to pull up a mental image of the space she wished she had paid more attention the times she had come through here. It wasn't a large room and she knew that the door to the basement was straight ahead. Unfortunately she could tell that someone was between her and the door. In the back of her mind she had hoped that there would be a chance that she could get Lilah out of here through stealth instead of needing to fight her way through. That didn't seem likely right now. She might be able to slip past them, but then they would be between her and the exit which wasn't a thought she relished.

Her heart was pounding in her chest as she stood like a statue against the door. Slowly the spots faded from her vision and she could make out shapes in the dim red glow from the exit sign over her head. A chill ran through her as she saw that one step forward and she would have tripped over the driver from the van that had caught her. Finally adjusted to the dark she peered into the gloom and made out three other figures scattered around the room. All of the vampires from the theater she guessed. Ivan was still at large, which made her almost as uneasy as the four figures before her.

Easing herself to her knees she carefully aimed the crossbow at the driver's chest. It seemed strange to her that her hands weren't shaking. Inside it felt as though she were coming apart with fear. The twang of the string was loud in her ears as she launched the bolt at its target. He jerked as it hit sending Vanessa's heart into her throat, but it was a single movement before he was paralyzed. In the dim light she could see his black eyes boring into her, almost glowing in his rage. Not leaving things to chance she rose and stepped out of his reach. The last thing she intended to do was fall for a ruse she had used so many times. It wasn't until she had the crossbow reloaded and an open bottle of holy water in hand that she got close again. She almost felt bad as she poured the holy water in his mouth, but remembering what he had tried to do to her on top of taking Lilah quashed that sympathy.

Confident that he was in the very least out of the fight she moved on to the next figure. Once again she took careful aim and pulled the trigger. Instead of the solid thud she expected it hit with a sharp crack as it hit something solid. The bolt shattered sending splinters flying. He sat up with a roar clawing at the fragments that had penetrated.

"Oh hell," Vanessa hissed as the other two stirred.

Scrambling to reload the crossbow she was glad to see that her shot had at least had some effect. He lurched to his feet with unsteady, jerky movements. Drawing back the string Vanessa realized that she wasn't going to have time for a second shot. Dropping the crossbow she knocked his lunging grab aside easily with one of the blocks Miles's had taught her and stepped into him. With a sharp pull she slid the end of the prayer rope from where she had it coiled on her arm and wrapped it around his neck. Smoke rolled from where it dug into his skin and he frantically tried to pull it free.

Groaning, Vanessa saw that the other two were on their feet now. Desperate she pulled the rope away from the door. Out of reflex he resisted, slamming himself into the wall next to the door when she released the rope. As soon as she let go he pulled the rope free and took a step forward. In one motion she shattered a bottle of holy water against the wall beside him and opened the door. Recoiling from the scorching spray of the water brought him into the bright afternoon sun reflected through the doorway. Not giving him a chance to recover Vanessa kicked him as hard as she could into the doorway and slammed the door into him knocking him the rest of the way through. For a moment he pounded and clawed at the door before she heard the sound of shattering glass.

With a sinking feeling she realized that he had probably managed to get the outside door closed before the sun had finished him off. Her vision was ruined by the sudden flash of light too. She only hoped that the remaining two were as blind as she was. Reaching down she managed to find the crossbow, grateful to find it still cocked. Sliding a bolt in place by feel she strained to listen for any sign of movement. She berated herself for being in this situation. Even groggy and weakened by the day they were both going to be stronger than her and better suited to the dark. Hopefully she would still have speed on her side.

A slight crunch on the cement floor was all the warning she had before a blow fell. Out of reflex she pulled her elbow up to shield her head and sidestepped. The swing still made contact, but her dodge took the power out of it. As it was she still stumbled over the body of the vampire she had staked and tumbled into the basement door. Reaching above her head she sought out a handhold to pull herself upright. On her feet once more she realized that her hand was on a light switch. With a swipe of her hand she threw the switch bringing the overhead lights flickering to life.

The sudden light blinded the two she had left to deal with; which she realized with horror, were right on top of her. Before they could recover she fired at the closest one, realizing when he didn't fall that she had missed his heart. Growling, he advanced on her. Her sharp kick to his knee did nothing but send pain shooting through her shin. Too late she realized he was much older than the others.

Scrambling to get out of his reach she fought to pull Meri's pistol from her pocket. He stepped in and pulled her jacket down over her arms pinning them to her sides. She thrashed wildly trying to free herself, but he held her tight. The other man was on her in an instant forcing her head back and to the side. Desperate, she angled the gun still caught in her pocket at the one holding her and pulled the trigger. The report was deafening in the small room. Through the ringing in her ears Vanessa could just make out his scream as the slug tore through his hip. His leg buckled dumping him to the floor. While he didn't release his hold on her jacket, his grip opened enough for her to slide her arms out as he dragged it down.

Grateful that the jacket was so big on her, Vanessa managed to keep her hold on the pistol as the jacket slid free. The vampire holding her head hesitated for a heartbeat at the sound of the shot, but her reprieve was short lived. As his partner hit the floor the one still holding her kicked her feet out from under her. All of her weight was held painfully by his grip on her hair as he pulled her into him. Despite the pain she let herself go slack making him support her. He moved over her coming in to bite her neck. Making an upward swing with all the strength she could put behind it she drove the pistol into his face. The action of the gun caught him in the mouth shattering his front teeth. He dropped her suddenly, his hands going to his tattered mouth.

"Dammit!" she spat as she hit the floor between his feet.

Her heart sank as she heard the basement door open. She didn't need to look to know that it was Ivan. For a split second she debated trying to shoot him, but she didn't trust her aim with the pistol. Instead she settled on a closer target and raised her arms and fired a round into the groin of the vampire standing over her. Pain ran through her leg as she tried to roll away from his collapse. The one she had shot in the hip had a vice like grip on her leg, pulling her towards him. She sat up and fired with the gun just inches from his head dropping him nervelessly on her legs. Without hesitating she raised the gun and aimed at Ivan, pulled the trigger once more. Horror settled on her when nothing happened and she saw the action was locked back.

"So much for that little toy," Ivan smirked as he slapped the gun out of her hand.

Vanessa rabbit kicked her way free from the body on her legs and tried to roll away from Ivan. He responded with a kick to the ribs that bounced her off of the wall leaving her in a breathless heap. Stars swam in her vision as she looked desperately for a weapon. An iron grip yanked her upright by the hair and Ivan leaned in with a sneer.

"I can't tell you how long I've looked forward to this."

"Fuck you," she hissed.

His slap rang like a shot. She could taste blood before she even really felt the sting. Dazed she wondered at how little Ivan was weakened by the day. Normally a vampire as inhuman as him could barely move while the sun was in the sky. It convinced her that his cruelty was his own and not the influence of the demon.

"Do you hear me?" he roared.

She realized he had said something while she had been dazed, but she had no idea what.

"You never did listen," he stated coldly before slapping her again.

This time she expected the blow and turned to take the worst of the force out of it. As he drew back to hit her again she yanked a bolt from the clip on her belt and drove it into the wrist of the arm holding her.

"You bitch," he growled and swung again.

Pulling her elbow up she blocked the blow, wincing at the bruising impact on her arm. He tried to maintain his hold, but the burn of the anointing oil forced him to let go. She pushed off from the wall and dove for her jacket as he pulled the bolt free. Frantically she dug for a pocket. Ivan grabbed her legs, sticking the bolt in her calf before pulling her back dragging a choked yell from her. Dropping to his knees over her he pinned her to the floor and pulled her head back. Vanessa twisted violently and brought her extended arm back to smash a bottle of holy water on his face heedless of the cuts to her hand.

The water boiled on his skin leaving deep furrows in his face. With an inhuman growl he wiped at his face spreading the damage to his hands. Not wasting the opening Vanessa crawled free and retrieved the prayer rope, winding it around her hand as she lurched unsteadily to her feet. A sharp pain reminded her of the bolt in her calf. Pulling it free she braced to face Ivan again. She ran her hand down her face bringing it away wet with her blood. Dizzy from his blows she couldn't bring herself to approach him again. Hoping she could free Meri she staggered to the basement door praying that this had been all of Ivan's men. She had barely opened the door and turned on the lights when her world exploded.

Chapter 20
Exodus

Lilah didn't know how long it had been since anyone had come to check on her. She knew she had been down here at least a day when Ivan had taken her finger, but time had become mostly meaningless to her since then. Now her thirst was almost more unbearable than the pain in her arms. Her head was pounding and she kept having dizzy spells. Though she tried to fight it she was drifting in and out of consciousness. She had given up on trying to free her new companion some time ago; no matter how she squirmed she couldn't move enough to do any good. On top of it all her bladder had felt like it was going to burst for what seemed like an eternity.

"Hey!" she cried hoarsely, finally giving in to the urge, "Is anyone there?"

"What?" one of the men demanded tersely as he opened the door a crack.

"I need to go to the bathroom."

"Well nobody's stoppin' ya." He grunted and slammed the door.

Lilah burned with indignation. Unfortunately she knew that was the end of the matter. These creatures, she couldn't see them as human anymore, honestly didn't care about her welfare. Even so she needed at least some water.

"Hello," she croaked, even hoarser than the first time.

He didn't come at first and Lilah was forced to yell three more times before he finally burst back into the basement.

"I don't give a shit what you want," he told her, "If you don't shut up, I'll shut you up."

"I need a drink," she pleaded.

He gave her a flat look before shrugging and turning back to the stairs.

Dayflower

"People die from dehydration," she pointed out to him.

He paused, looking at her. She was hoping Ivan had told them not to let anything happen to her. Apparently he decided that it was in his interest to keep her alive since he turned and came back down the stairs and walked over to a mop sink in the corner. Turning on the water he aimed the short section of hose attached to the faucet at her. The water splattered all over her face soaking her almost to the waist. Feeling the water was too much and her bladder released, adding to the pool she was now laying in. She wanted to be furious at being forced to endure this, but she was too relieved to be taking in large swallows of the stale rusty water to care. The sudden rush of water sent pains shooting through her stomach making her wince and choke. Only when she was coughing and gagging from the continued spray did he turn the water off and walk away.

After that she felt somewhat better. With her two largest concerns dealt with, however crudely, it was easier for her to drift off. It wasn't exactly sleep since it was nowhere near as restful as sleep should be, but she did manage some actual rest. In between spells of unconsciousness she kept working to keep some blood flow to her limbs. Each time she could hold herself up a little less, and it took a little longer for feeling to return. She began to worry that if something didn't happen soon the finger Ivan bit off wouldn't be the only one she lost.

Idly she began to wonder if anyone was looking for her. She knew that her office would have missed her by now. Surely Vanessa's school would be trying to find out why she hadn't been at school either. Lilah knew that in theory someone should be trying to find her by now, but the police finding her seemed like a fantasy trapped where she was.

No one entered the basement for a long time after that. For a while she heard muffled conversation from the room at the top of the stairs, but then that went silent. At some point Ivan had come in and set up a lounge chair that looked like it had been stolen from a pool somewhere. He settled into the seat and laced his hands behind his head. He never looked at her, but eventually he smiled and started talking to her.

"The boys say that they couldn't find your girl. I bet they're afraid of the old man. What do you think?"

Lilah didn't respond. Ivan seemed almost jovial which made her nervous.

Dayflower

"They left her a present though," he said, giving her a meaningful look. "If I know her she'll be along shortly. Of course we have a welcome ready for her upstairs. She never was much for thinking before she sticks her nose into things. Have you noticed that, *Mom*?"

She knew what he was talking about. Learning to temper her tendency to just blurt things out had been hard for Vanessa when she had started school. There wasn't a doubt in Lilah's mind that Ivan was right. She just hoped that Vanessa wasn't alone when she did come.

Lilah wasn't sure how long it had been since Ivan had fallen asleep. Laying here in the dark she had nothing but the hum from the emergency lights and her own breath for company. It was eerie knowing that Ivan and the woman were inches away, but not hearing them breathe. Even though she was exhausted she couldn't find any rest. The thought that Vanessa might show up kept her mind racing.

She was almost convinced that she was hearing things when she heard sounds of movement up stairs. Her heart leapt into her throat at the thought that perhaps a maintenance man for the building could have stumbled upon them. Straining she tried to catch any sound she could. For several minutes there was nothing but silence before she heard the sound again.

This time she was certain someone was in the room at the top of the stairs. Before long there was a muffled yell and the sounds of a struggle. Anxiety gnawed at Lilah as she tried to decide if she should yell or not. If it wasn't Vanessa up there she needed to let them know she was here, otherwise she didn't want to wake Ivan and add him to the fray.

The choice was taken from her when she heard the loud report of a gun from the other side of the door. Ivan was up in an instant moving towards the door. As he went through the doorway Lilah heard two more shots and another vicious struggle. Her stomach clenched at a yell she recognized as Vanessa's. Seconds later the door began to creep open and the light came on. She watched with horror as it suddenly slammed open against the stop and Vanessa was launched through hitting the rail and pin wheeling over to land in a heap on the floor below.

Blood covered the side of her face from a cut at her eyebrow and trickled from the corner of her mouth. Her hands left bloody prints on the staircase as she pulled herself unsteadily to her feet. As she limped back from the door Lilah could see more blood coming from her leg and huge bruises already taking color on her arms. Tears welled in her eyes watching her daughter turn to face Ivan as he charged through the door after her. Lilah didn't know how the girl could stand, much less fight looking like she did.

Ivan vaulted over the rail to land on the floor directly in front of Vanessa. His face was a ruined mess. Deep furrows were etched through his skin, bone showing in places. Half of his nose and lips were gone leaving his teeth exposed on one side. A thin seeping of blood from the wounds gave his entire face a ghoulish look. As he raised his hands Lilah could see that they too were raw and bleeding.

Without even waiting until he had his balance Ivan swung in a huge hay-maker that Vanessa easily ducked under. She countered with a backhand blow with a hand wrapped with a black rope. Lilah guessed it was some holy item when smoke rolled from the point of contact on Ivan's face. With an animal roar he charged her like a bull catching her in the ribs with his shoulder. The hit was savage, making Lilah wince just seeing it. Though Vanessa cried out as he hit she didn't shirk away from the fight. As he carried her to the wall she wrapped the rope around his neck and pulled on it, growling with the effort of the move.

Dropping her Ivan clawed at the rope as it scorched into his throat. As soon as she hit the floor the girl staggered forward and delivered a front kick to Ivan's groin. The man grunted, but that was all. He had the last wrap of the rope free as she pulled a crossbow bolt from her belt clip and drove it into his chest, crying out as her ruined hand drove the bolt in. He responded with a backhand that knocked her to the floor. Tears streamed down Lilah's face as she watched her daughter struggle to her feet once more to face the monster before her.

"Sit down!" Ivan bellowed.

Vanessa's legs buckled nearly dropping her to the floor. She managed to stay on her feet, but just barely. Ivan caught her with a solid grip on her throat and held her against the wall with one arm, using the other to hold her face towards himself.

"Maybe you're human after all," he panted, "I can actually feel a pulse in there. Not that that's going to last long."

"Go to hell," Vanessa croaked, spitting blood on Ivan's face.

"Oh I've been looking forward to this," he sneered.

Dayflower

Vanessa pulled a knife from her belt and drove it into his chest as he gloated over her. Smoke rolled from Ivan's chest as the blade bit into his flesh. He doubled over slightly and growled, but didn't release her. Knocking her hand away from the knife he yanked it from his chest.

"Nice try," he told her, "Blades don't hold the oil like wood though."

He hefted the blade before him and then scrubbed at the smoking wound in his chest. He grimaced as the oil spread to his hand and burned into it.

"Let's see how you like it," he said as he drove the knife into her chest.

"NO!" Lilah screamed.

Vanessa's eyes went wide and she gasped slightly as the blade pushed through her flesh. Ivan held her for a second as she went limp in his grip. With a shrug he dropped her to the floor and walked over to Lilah. Crouching down he held his face inches from her own. Wracking sobs tore through her as she stared at Vanessa's still form. Reaching out Ivan grabbed her face and forced it to face his own.

"I was going to drain the little bitch, but I just couldn't help myself," he told her.

His words were slurred and indistinct from the damage to his face. Up close it was even more ghastly than it had seemed from across the room. Lilah hoped he would be scarred forever from the wounds.

"I'm sure you know how it is," he said casually, "Of course now I really need to regain my strength."

He forced Lilah's head back painfully and leaned in. She closed her eyes and braced for the worst. She expected to feel him tear out her throat, but instead she heard him make a choking sound and he released her. Opening her eyes she saw Vanessa standing over him, the knife in her hand as she drove it again into the base of his skull.

"Over my dead body," she whispered as she pushed him over, knife still embedded in his head.

A mixture of emotions rolled through Lilah as she stared up at Vanessa. It was an unbelievable relief to see her standing, but Lilah was transfixed by her eyes. They were as black as pitch as she stepped away from Ivan and pulled the stake from the woman's chest. Turning the point down she drove the point into Ivan's body, making sure she got the heart.

"Vee," Lilah croaked as Vanessa turned towards her.

Fear tightened her throat seeing Vanessa like this. The girl never had a chance to respond. Before she could take another step here eyes cleared and she collapsed in front of Lilah.

"VEE!" she screamed.

Vanessa didn't respond, but she saw the woman Vanessa had freed stand. Slowly she pulled herself to her feet and made her way to Vanessa's side. Holding her fingers to Vanessa's throat she began to mutter to herself. Casting about the room it was obvious she was looking for something.

"Goddammit," she muttered as she made her way to the stairs and worked her way unsteadily up them.

"Wait!" Lilah wailed as she went through the door.

That was the last straw for her. Sobs tore from her as the door closed. The woman was a vampire and after how Ivan and his men treated her it only made sense to Lilah that the woman would just leave her here. All hope left her as she stared at Vanessa's body.

"Great Goddess don't start that," the woman barked as she came back into the basement.

Her reappearance stunned Lilah to silence. She was carrying Vanessa's jacket, riffling through the pockets as she went.

"She even brought my Sig," she muttered more to herself than to Lilah.

Reaching in the inside pocket she pulled out a small vial of dark liquid with a relived look on her face. Dropping the jacket she knelt next to Vanessa and pulled the girl's head into her lap. Opening the vial she poured some of its contents in Vanessa's mouth. For several moments she watched her with anxiety clear on her face. Finally she nodded to herself and eased Vanessa back to the floor. Casually she pulled the knife out of Ivan's head and sliced through Lilah's bonds with it before sticking it back in.

The sudden release from her bonds sent fire coursing through her hands and feet. She had to bite her lip to keep from screaming from the pain. For a moment she thought she might pass out as she struggled to sit up. Falling forward she was caught and pulled upright.

"Drink this," the woman commanded.

Dayflower

Lilah did as she was told. It felt as though she had been struck by lightning as the thick liquid entered her system. Though she still felt weak she felt much better than she had. Most of the agony from her captivity was erased by the time she handed the vial back.

"Thank you," she said, stumbling over not having a name to use.

"Meri," she supplied, "I work with Cyrus."

Lilah was half aware of Meri changing clips in a handgun she had produced from somewhere as she crawled over to Vanessa. Sitting by her head Lilah stroked Vanessa's face tenderly. She could feel her breathing which was a relief. Looking at her chest the stab wound was obvious.

"How did that not kill you Vee," Lilah whispered.

"Funny huh," Meri observed dryly, "Almost like she isn't a normal girl."

"What do you mean?"

"You saw her eyes. Your girl isn't human."

"But Cyrus..." Lilah protested.

"Cyrus refuses to see it," Meri muttered, heat clear in her voice.

"See what?"

"I thought she was a therian," she replied, "Now I'm not sure what she is. Listen, we don't have time for this."

Reaching down she grabbed the jacket and staggered. "Damn," she groaned, dropping it, "put that on her. We need to get going. Those guys aren't going to stay down for long."

"What about him?" Lilah asked as she pulled Vanessa upright.

"I'd love to drag his ass out to bake in the sun, but I don't think any of us are in any shape to do that. We just need to be gone."

With that she grabbed one of Vanessa's arms, wincing as she did so, and gestured for Lilah to do the same. Neither woman was steady on their feet as they struggled to get up the stairs. The scene in the next room took Lilah's breath away. A ruined corpse was lying just inside the door. Two other bodies were farther away, both with grievous wounds. Sprays of blood from the gunshots peppered the walls and smeared blotches and hand prints showed her where more of the fight had ranged.

Dayflower

Meri led her through with an impassive face until they reached the opposite door. Opening it a crack sent bright beams of sunlight into the room making her recoil away and slam the door shut. Leaning against the wall behind the door she wrapped her arms around Vanessa and sighed.

"Go out there and close the outside door," she ordered, "I can't go out like that."

Lilah nodded and slipped outside. A set of charred remains spilled across the threshold of the door outside amidst the ruins of a shattered mirror. She could see another outside the door. It was a struggle to force herself to kick what she needed to out the door so she could close it. While the carnage made her queasy, she didn't feel the slightest sympathy for them after what they had done. By the time the trio reached the drab lobby of the apartment building it was a welcome relief in its normalcy.

"What do we do now," Lilah asked, feeling completely overwhelmed.

"You get someone, anyone, to call nine-one-one and go to the cops. You two are in the system so people will be looking for you. I'm going after Cyrus."

"What do we tell them?"

"Tell them the truth," Meri replied, "Leave me and vampires out of it. Tell them some guys took you two and there was a fight and someone cut you loose. Let them try to sort it out." She took on a pinched look as though she had a bad taste in her mouth. "The magistrate will make the worst of it go away. If the cops don't hide you, you need to go to ground. Ivan will be out for blood."

Lilah nodded. She was too tired and shell shocked to do any more.

Meri left her and Vanessa before they got within reach of the hazy light coming in through the glass of the front doors. Step by step she fought to stay on her feet as she dragged Vanessa out and to the street. She considered trying to get help in the building, but right now she felt more safety in the daylight. At least she knew none of Ivan or his men would follow her here.

Everything was a blur after that. She didn't even really remember stopping the car and getting help. All she could think of in the ambulance was how much she wished that the nightmare was over, and how certain she was that it wasn't over at all.

Chapter 21
Consequences

Her hunger was maddening. It had been all Meri could do to keep herself under control until she bolted from Lilah and Vanessa. She knew that the two probably needed more help than she had given them, but the risk was too high. Her recent feeding had barely made up for the energy she had been spending the last few days. Being staked on top of that had taken every reserve she may have had.

Slamming the door behind her she turned, pressed her hands to the door, and ground her forehead against the cracked veneer. She could still feel Lilah's blood singing to her. Once she had been free there had been a moment that she had almost lost control. Then she had gone to pick up the girl's jacket. As weak as she was she couldn't even try to control her visions so she had been hit especially hard. Images of the way things would be if she fed on Lilah had nearly made her black out. She shivered just remembering what she had seen. The memory of the carnage from the fight today left Meri without a doubt that her vision was accurate; what the girl would have turned into promised disaster for her kind.

For the time being Meri had her hands full trying to figure out how to make it through the rest of the day. Ivan's goons, the two that were left anyhow, would be able to move soon. If the cops didn't show up first she knew they would come straight here. Looking around the ratty apartment she considered her options. She could gamble that the police would arrive before they could get Ivan and come here. Weighing how her luck had run since she became entangled with Vanessa she didn't feel inclined to take that much on chance. Hiding within the apartment wasn't much better. The girl's smell was still thick in the place so there was a chance that she would be missed, but again that was taking a huge chance.

159

Even staying awake against the pull of the hour was becoming more of a struggle. There was no way she could make it to any other cover like this.

"Goddammit," she muttered and strode back through the door.

As she staggered back to the basement she could hear sirens in the distance. Rolling her eyes she hoped she had enough time. When she reached the door she had to bite back a torrent of curses. The door had locked as soon as it closed and she didn't have a key. Stepping back she fired three quick shots into the lock and used what strength she had to pry the door open.

The two were still where she remembered them, but they were starting to move. Before they could get up she stepped up to each of them and fired. There would be hell to pay for what she had just done, but it was the only option she could see. She ran back to the apartment in a staggering gait, hand dragging on the wall to hold herself up as she went. As she opened the door to the apartment she could hear the sirens pulling into the complex. It was a relief to lock the door and slide the chain into place before the police entered the building. Meri looked at the distance to the bedroom and decided to just collapse on the couch. As she fell into sleep she could still smell Vanessa's presence and wondered if the bedroom wouldn't have been worth the extra steps after all.

A piercing pain running through her head woke Meri. She knew it was after dark, but had no idea how long. Pushing herself to her feet was a herculean effort that made her head swim. As she shuffled to the door she was glad she didn't have a pulse; she was sure that would have made her head throb as well which might have been more than she could handle.

Dragging her hand down her face she tried to decide if she would be better off dead. *And not this walking around with a blinding headache dead, but real oblivion dead,* she amended to herself. The only time she could think of that she had felt this bad had been on that first night she was turned.

As she exited the apartment she could hear the chatter of radios from the main hallway. Apparently the police were still cleaning up the mess from earlier. If Lilah had done as she had been told then she and Vanessa should be safe for a little while at least. Meri hoped that they had been as vague as possible. The magistrate would have her hands full making this debacle disappear and any wiggle room would help. Not even Meri liked the idea of a big exposure. Having seen what Vanessa had dealt with when hunters were around made her understand Alaric's hard line a little better.

She moved away from the sounds towards the fire exit at the end of the hall. Unlike the one to the basement exit, she knew the alarm was disabled on this door. All she had to do was get through and she could hopefully avoid any complications.

Sodium lights overhead cast murky shadows everywhere and sent new shots of pain through her head as she opened the door. With her eyes on the ground trying to shut out the harsh light she stepped away from the door. It wasn't until she had actually run into him that she saw the cop leaning against the wall smoking a cigarette. Both of them jumped, Meri stammering an apology as she stepped back.

"What are you doing?" he asked as he dropped the cigarette, grinding it out with the toe of his shoe.

"It seemed like there was an awful lot going on in there and I didn't want to get in the way."

"Do you live here?" he pressed.

"No, I was just visiting a friend," she answered uneasily.

Meri could feel the conversation going south for her. Almost as though thinking about the situation getting worse made is happen she saw the cops eyes go wide. Following his gaze she saw the hole in her shirt and the blood soaked patch around it.

"Aw fuck," she breathed as she saw him drop his hand to the taser on his belt.

Before he could pull the device from its holster she was on him. Blood-lust drowned everything else out for her as she shoved him to the ground. He didn't even have a chance to yell before she had her teeth in his throat. His blood flowed into her with the sweetness of life itself. Greedily she drank until he was dry before dropping him. As she rose she looked around, glad that no one had witnessed her attack. With a grimace she pulled the cop's own gun and shot him in the neck to obscure her bite marks. By the time she had wiped her prints from the gun and dropped it his radio crackled to life with calls from the rest of the police presence in the complex trying to find out what had happened.

Meri sprinted away from the project with every ounce of speed she could muster. As she ran she started a tally of the crimes against vampire law she had committed in the last twenty-four hours. By the time she was finished she knew she would be lucky if all they did was sentence her to stand before the dawn. What was more likely was a blood price on her head. While she knew that the outcome was sure to be the same the path there would be a lot rougher with the blood price.

The night streaked past her in a blur as she ran. Without even thinking she had began to go to Cyrus's house. Muttering an oath, she brought herself to a stop and tried to see where she was. Irritation pricked at her at the thought of her destination. The last thing she wanted to be was another pet project of the old man like the girl was. She might have her problems, but she was able to take care of herself. Leaning against the wall of the storefront she had stopped in front of she thought about what she needed to do next.

She had expected at least something resembling the current state of affairs. While she hadn't figured the police or having been staked into things, she knew that it was likely that she would be on the run once the girl and Lilah were free. Cyrus was sure to have been buried by now, that much she knew. The irritating part was that she wasn't sure exactly where. Vanessa was the key to that piece of information. She had made sure that the girl had her phone number tucked into the pocket of her jacket. At this point all she could do was hope that Vanessa would be able to find it and call before Meri was forced to put the next step of the plan into action.

There was a little time before she could do that though. Even with having fed on the cop she was desperately hungry. Turning away from her original destination, Meri began to make her way to her usual hunting grounds. The way things had been going she was sure she would need to be more careful than usual.

It didn't take her long to make her way to the neighborhood she wanted. The housing project that contained B-block wasn't in a good part of town to begin with so she didn't have far to go. Meri wished she could afford the time a true hunt would take. After having been taken by Ivan's goons she would love nothing more than to turn the tables on some guy looking to take advantage of her. Instead she would be lucky if she found an opportunity for a clean kill that wouldn't dig the hole she was making for herself any deeper.

After nearly an hour of hunting without any good prospects she began to worry. Every person she saw was either part of a group or too close to a high traffic area for her to approach. The piercing headache and weakness were gone, but she still felt a vicious gnawing hunger. It was getting very tempting to just make a messy kill and deal with one more charge on her list.

"Meri Watts you are hereby called before Magistrate Graves. Please come peacefully," a stern voice called out from behind her.

Meri turned to see a tall angular young man with skin the color of espresso. She had dealt with him on Cyrus's behalf quite a bit in the time around Alaric's deposition.

"Derek, I absolutely don't have time for this."

"I'm sorry Meri," he said apologetically, "There have been some ugly charges made against you. Graves is pissed."

"Fuck her," Meri spat, "Ivan and his dogs can burn for all I care. He's been violating every custom there is and now all of a sudden he's worried about 'the law'!"

"So it's true?" Derek asked with shock.

"What? That I shot his guys and left them for the cops? Yeah." Meri crossed her arms defiantly, her patience with the exchange wearing thin.

"What were you thinking?" he demanded.

Meri's temper flared. She was still furious over having been staked foremost, not to mention the rest of the situation.

"Are you stupid or something?" she countered, "You were friends with Alaric. Doesn't this whole thing seem strange to you? He shouldn't have been deposed; much less Cyrus being called before the Senate."

"But Anton…" he began before Meri plowed on over his interruption.

"To hell with Anton! His crimes were his own and Vanessa should have burned for creating him, but that has nothing to do with Cyrus or Alaric! There's a coup going on here and you're helping it along!" Meri's voice had risen as she went until it was almost a yell. She strode towards Derek while she talked; her last words delivered with a finger jabbed into his chest.

Derek looked at her thoughtfully. From the look on his face Meri was sure that he had been harboring doubts of his own about how the deposition had come about. Shaking his head he let out a long sigh.

"Even if I agree with what you're saying, and I'm not saying I do, there are still three of the blood dead and three more that went to the morgue. That's a hell of a mess you left to clean up."

"The mess I left!" Meri shrieked, "They're trying to dump ALL of that on me?"

She spun and stomped away from him, a growl like an angry cat in her throat. Turning back to Derek she had to fight to keep from completely unloading on Derek.

"That was all everybody's little pet, Vanessa. Ivan took Lilah, violating Familiar Blood I might add, and then had me staked and brought to him like a piece of meat," she told him in a cold fury. Derek tried to interject something, but Meri plowed on over him forcing him to silence.

"I shot the two once before going to ground so that Ivan couldn't come after me," she barreled on, "I was laying there with a fucking stake in my heart until the very end."

"You mean to tell me that Vanessa did all that on her own?" he said skeptically.

Meri nearly reached out and punched him. Having resisted that urge, she was left staring at him dumbstruck. Derek saw the shock on her face and understood. He deflated as he put the stories he had heard together with what he knew and realized Meri was telling the truth.

"So what am I supposed to do?" he asked quietly, "If I just let you walk away it'll be my head."

Reaching down Meri pulled her Sig from the holster on her ankle.

"What…" Derek got out before she shot him in the knee, dumping him to the ground.

"Problem solved," Meri said before walking away.

"Dammit Meri," he shouted at her back as he pulled the injured leg out straight to heal.

Now she knew that there were bailiffs out looking for her. That gave her hunt a new urgency she hadn't expected. Moving quickly she made her way through the crumbling neighborhood. At every intersection she scanned the side streets for someone alone. She didn't have either the time to be picky, or the reserves to put off feeding. Her chance finally came as she rounded the corner of a shaky looking apartment building and ran headlong into a young man.

"Watch it," he said as he tried to brush past her.

Meri reached out and grabbed his arm in an authoritative grip, spinning him back to face her. Not giving him a chance to react she lunged. His startled yell was cut off as she clamped her hand over his mouth and forced his head back. Hurried, but not desperate as before, she fed. Her hunger was quickly sated and she still felt a strong pulse as she pulled away. The temptation was strong to finish the man off and give herself a bit more time before she would have to worry about this again. In the end she decided against it. Slicing the tip of her finger on a fang she closed his wound. He was unconscious, but his pulse and breathing were strong so she was sure he'd live.

Now she just had to do was make it back to Cyrus's to retrieve the package she had stored there without running into Derek or another bailiff. After that it was just a matter of getting to the warehouse she had the casket staged in and leave a message for the courier she had hired. Normally the thought of a few days locked in a box would horrify her, but after the last few days she was almost looking forward to the chance to rest.

Chapter 22
Questions

Consciousness crept up on Vanessa slowly. At first she was only aware of the all encompassing ache she felt. *At least I know I'm not dead,* she thought. Bit by bit she began to make out sounds. A crackle of an intercom, several different beeps, and the dull roar of an air conditioner that was far too loud to allow any peace. *Great. I'm in the hospital again,* she thought bitterly. Old habit took over and she remained still, listening for trouble.

"Ms. Malone, are you sure there isn't more you can tell us?" a deep baritone voice asked sharply from near her feet.

"I'm sorry," Lilah replied, "Vanessa called me and said not to go home; that someone was after her. I went to turn around and was going to go back to the office and was blocked in by a van full of men who drug me to that basement. I don't know what more I can tell you."

"What about this Ivan. You said he seemed to be the leader?"

"From what I could see. He would yell and the others cowered from him."

"What did he yell about?" he asked.

"Lots of things. I don't remember it all. Something about a new order and 'Showing that little bitch what was coming to her.'"

"Referring to Vanessa?"

"I assume so," Lilah answered, nodding.

Vanessa could tell that the officer had been pressing Lilah hard for information. The woman sounded exhausted and Vanessa's heart went out to her. That all of this had fallen on Lilah because of her threatened to crush the air from Vanessa's chest. She had a strong impulse to keep still and stay out of the conversation, but she couldn't do it. There wasn't a doubt in her mind that she would be better able to deflect the questions they couldn't answer.

"It's Nivikov," she croaked, just above a whisper.

"Vee, you're awake!" Lilah gushed.

Leaning forward, she gently swept Vanessa's hair from her face with her right hand. Her bandaged left glaringly still in her lap. The sight made Vanessa's eyes sting with guilty tears. Anger and regret welled up in her until her throat was tight. She knew better than to hope that Ivan was gone. Blurred memories from after he had stabbed her swam in her head, but nothing was clear. Since she couldn't remember seeing him crumble to ashes she had to assume he was still out there. That was something she meant to remedy.

"Vanessa, welcome back," the officer said, his tone much softer than he had been using with Lilah. He was a solidly built man with graying hair and a complexion like scorched oak. His broad, heavy features made him look overly tired to her.

"Do you feel up to answering a few questions?" he continued.

Lilah fixed him with a withering stare which he ignored. Vanessa nodded slowly before reaching for the water pitcher. With a shooing motion Lilah forced her back down and poured her a glass of water that she swallowed almost in a single gulp. The detective, Vanessa judged by the look of him, waited with a look of forced patience as Lilah mothered her.

"Thanks, Mom," said earnestly, squeezing Lilah's hand.

Lilah returned the squeeze and the two shared a look conveying more than the detective knew. With a nod Lilah sat back and drew a pensive breath. It was clear that her maternal instincts were operating in full force, but she knew to let Vanessa take the lead. The look she was getting told Vanessa that there would be a long talk in her near future. After the last couple of days the thought of a lecture from Lilah almost left her feeling elated. With a half hidden smile she nodded for the detective to go ahead.

"I'm Detective Banks," he began, "There are a few holes we are trying to fill. Anything you can tell us would be helpful."

"I was walking home from my self-defense class when these guys in an old utility van grabbed me."

"When did you call Ms. Malone?" detective banks interrupted.

"Later," Vanessa replied, irritation chilling her voice. "There were two in the back trying to tie me up. A third was driving."

The detective tried to ask another question, but Vanessa drove on over him.

"They stopped so the driver could help and I managed to get away from them."

"The driver came back to help the other two contain you and you got away," Banks repeated with a tone of skepticism, scribbling furiously in his notebook. "What happened then?"

"I happened to run into a friend who gave me a ride home."

"What is this friend's name?"

"I'm not going to drag her into this," Vanessa replied flatly.

The detective locked eyes with Vanessa for a moment. Seeing that she wasn't going to budge he turned to Lilah. Drawing a deep breath it was obvious that he was trying to find the right tone. Suddenly a cold feeling swept over Vanessa. She was aware of the woman before she had even entered the room. The familiar wrongness of her presence made Vanessa blanche, gripping the covers in fear. Sensing the change in Vanessa, Lilah leaned forward, concern written on her face.

"Vee, what's wrong?" she asked worriedly.

Before Vanessa could respond the woman walked into the room. Her appearance was striking. She was tall and lean with a finely angled face framed by dark brown hair. Her coldly severe expression was enhanced by the charcoal skirt and jacket she wore. All eyes turned to her as she walked in.

"That will be all, officer," she said with authority.

"Listen, lady, I…" he began, rising to face her.

"That will be all," she repeated coldly.

As the woman glared at the detective Vanessa could feel the power of her compulsion radiating from her. Involuntarily she pushed back against the bed, gripping Lilah's hand as the woman spoke.

"They have answered all of your questions quite satisfactorily," she continued, pulling his notepad from his nerveless fingers, "you will go back to the station and be most distraught that you lost your notes, but with what you already know you will remember enough to make sense of things in your report."

Banks nodded absently and shuffled out of the room with her a step behind. Vanessa and Lilah shared a concerned look as they heard her speaking with the policeman standing just outside. A moment later she stepped back in with them and closed the door. Vanessa steeled herself to act even though fear coursed through her with each hammered beat of her heart. This woman wasn't some youngling like Ivan's men, she was a true elder.

"You are a scrapper aren't you?" she asked Vanessa almost pleasantly, "Don't worry; I'm not here to kill you."

Vanessa realized she had drawn her legs beneath her and had a death grip on her covers. Forcing herself to relax she held her silence. Lilah's hand on hers was tightened into an almost painful grip. She wasn't sure if Lilah was trying to restrain her or sharing in her fear. A sidelong glance at her face revealed nothing though.

The silence drew out longer and more uncomfortable with each tick of the clock. The woman moved to the seat Banks had vacated and sat down, making a show of straightening her skirt and jacket while Vanessa and Lilah looked on. Finally she broke the peace leaning forward to peer intently at Vanessa.

"So you are *the* Vanessa," she said. There was a long pause before she continued, "Such a little thing for so much trouble. Do you even have any idea how much trouble you've caused?"

Vanessa felt her stomach sink. Shaking her head she whispered, "No Magistrate."

"So you know who I am. Good." Nodding to herself the magistrate sat back in the chair and folded her hands in her lap. "Just so that we're clear I would gladly drag you out of here for execution if that were an option. You do understand that don't you?"

She waited for Vanessa to nod before moving to continue, but Lilah cut her off before she could.

"What do you mean 'if that were an option'?"

The magistrate gave her a startled look. Rising, she took the television remote from the bedside table.

"You honestly don't know?" she asked, gesturing with the remote.

Vanessa and Lilah both gave her puzzled stares, making her grimace. Pointing with the remote as if she could impale the set with it she turned it on. A soap opera filled the screen drawing a sour look from the magistrate as she changed the channel. An anchorman and a woman filled the screen other than the ticker at the bottom.

169

Dayflower

"...can't know for sure if the abduction is tied to the incident in Missouri, it certainly seems likely that the two would be connected."

"Of course they are," the woman filling the other half of the screen interjected, *" You have the same girl turn up nearly dead in a semi trailer in Kentucky only to disappear until she's found months later in a ruined hotel four hundred and fifty miles away. Now not two years later the same girl and her adoptive mother are abducted? Things like that aren't coincidence!"*

The magistrate switched the set off and tossed the remote onto the table roughly. Turning, she saw Lilah with a hand over her mouth and Vanessa with a blank, unreadable expression.

"So this is what you've given me to deal with," she said sharply, "The police have had to set up a perimeter to keep the press at bay."

"Oh my god," Lilah gasped.

Vanessa rose sharply only to be pulled up short by the central line tube in her shoulder.

"ME!" she growled, "Ivan brought this on you. Even if there was a price on my head Lilah had nothing to do with it. She was declared Familiar Blood. Me getting her away from him was only righting his wrong!"

"Ivan is being dealt with," the magistrate hissed, "And while I don't think you could have made a bigger mess of things if you had tried, I agree with your reasoning. That's the only reason you aren't 'dying from your injuries' right now."

She returned to her seat and regained her composure. Letting the implications of her last statement sink in she waited patiently. Once it was clear that her audience was ready she continued.

"I'm sworn to uphold the laws of the Senate foremost," she stated soberly, "And for now that means keeping our existence hidden. Since you have this lovely media circus around you right now I'm going to walk away, but I want you to know that despite everything Cyrus has said you *are* in my jurisdiction. Sitting here I don't even need the evidence of what you're capable of to know that."

"What does that mean?" Lilah demanded.

"It means I can feel her just as clearly as she can feel me," she replied, "Isn't that right Vanessa?"

Vanessa dropped her gaze to her hands. She did know, and her silence was answer enough. The magistrate left without another word leaving her and Lilah alone. Looking up at her new mother she saw questions in her eyes that Vanessa didn't have answers for.

"So how long have you known?" Lilah demanded.

Vanessa cringed. She tried to sink further into her bed, not that the thin padding of the hospital bed allowed her to go very far.

"I never really knew," she answered hesitantly.

"Fine," Lilah sighed, "When did you suspect? I'm a lawyer; don't try to mince words with me."

Vanessa's gaze dropped to where her fingers worried at the edge of her blanket. She took her time answering. Much to her credit, Lilah waited patiently for her to put her thoughts in order.

"I've always been afraid on some level, you know?"

Lilah nodded in understanding.

"Sometimes the sun would seem to burn just a little too much, or I'd slip and do something from when I was still a..." she trailed off.

"I understand," Lilah said, reaching out and squeezing Vanessa's hand.

Looking up Vanessa saw that her expression was still stern and expectant. Drawing a breath she braced herself to continue, afraid of what Lilah would say.

"A little while ago there was a vampire at the pizza place we went to after track. I could feel him."

She paused and risked a glance at Lilah. She didn't like what she saw. She would be allowed to finish her account, but there was sure to be a harsh follow-up.

"When we left he followed us. I went back and confronted him."

Vanessa paused. Lilah had gone stiff at her words. Another quick glance showed her that Lilah had paled slightly. She could almost hear Lilah asking her what she thought she was doing. Vanessa swallowed and ducked her head at the imagined onslaught.

"It turned out okay," she offered weakly, "He left."

"That was foolish, Vee," Lilah said coldly.

"I can handle myself," Vanessa replied defensively.

"There was no way you could have known then..." Lilah began before stopping herself short. "Let's not argue about that."

She paused and the silence grew until it filled the room. She had a lot more that she wanted to say, that much was clear, but she didn't. For several long minutes neither said a word. Vanessa was caught between being indignant and embarrassed. She knew Lilah was right, but felt vindicated in her reasoning at the same time. She didn't know what Lilah was thinking so she was afraid to speak first.

"So you could feel him?" Lilah prompted at last.

"Yeah," Vanessa began hesitantly, "I even had a good idea of how old he was. It wasn't the same as it was before, but it was close. You know?"

Lilah nodded and waited for her to continue.

"That was the first time it was something I couldn't write off as being paranoid," she continued, "Until then I didn't think you or Cyrus would take me seriously."

"Why didn't you say something then?"

"I didn't want you to worry or lecture me for going back," Vanessa admitted in a whisper.

"I get where you're coming from," Lilah said, her voice thick with frustration. "You do realize that Cyrus is in trouble and all of this happening might have been avoided if you had said something?"

Vanessa nodded. She still couldn't meet Lilah's gaze. Ivan would have still done what he could have, but Vanessa knew things might well have gone differently if she had been forthright with Lilah. Perhaps Cyrus wouldn't have been lured into a trap on her behalf. In all of her life she had never felt as many 'what ifs' as she had in the last few days. She had always felt as though things were happening beyond her control and she simply reacted however she could. Now things had happened because of actions, or inaction, on her part and she didn't know how to fix it.

"Don't beat yourself up Vee," Lilah said softly as she took Vanessa's hand in hers. "I'm sure Cyrus will be okay and, while I may not be quite as fast a typist from now on, I'll be fine."

Reaching out with her free hand Vanessa touched Lilah's bandaged hand lightly.

"I'm sorry," she breathed, her throat tight.

"I don't blame you," Lilah reassured her, "But I want to know everything. No more surprises."

Vanessa nodded and tried to think of where to begin.

Chapter 23
News

A growing chatter in the hallway told Vanessa that the morning shift was beginning. She gave a pained glance at Lilah's crumpled form in the vinyl recliner beside her bed. The two of them had talked well into the night, her sharing more of her history with Ivan and what she had been going through than she ever had before. It made her ache inside to think of the trouble she had brought on this woman. Gritting her teeth she resolved to make sure that this was the end of it. Even if it killed her she was determined to see Ivan ended for what he had done to Lilah.

Even after they had finished their talk and Lilah was asleep Vanessa had been unable to find any rest. Her first instinct was to run. If she were gone Lilah wouldn't be a target anymore. Just shifting in her bed proved that wouldn't be an option for a while though. Instead she was left with nothing but her thoughts as the hours crawled by, interrupted periodically by the nurses coming in to check on her.

"Welcome back!" a doctor said warmly as he entered the room, making her jump.

He was an older man moving with a forced briskness Vanessa recognized as the gait of someone in pain, but determined to hide it.

"I really didn't expect to see you up this morning," he continued, "You had us hopping when you came in yesterday."

He flipped through her chart as Lilah stirred, sitting up with a confused look on her face.

"God morning Ms. Monroe," he said as she tried to focus on him, "You've got quite a trooper here. Has anyone explained Vanessa's injuries to you?"

"They kept me updated yesterday evening until she was stable," Lilah replied.

"Good," he nodded pulling a penlight from his pocket. "Can you follow this for me?" he asked Vanessa as he shined the light in one eye then the other before moving it. "So what's your favorite subject in school?"

"Music."

"Oh, what do you play?" he continued as he made some notes.

"Violin."

"Nice. I play piano myself. Do you have any headache, dizziness, blurred vision, or nausea?"

"No," Vanessa said with a sigh.

"I like Franck's 'Sonata in A-minor.' How about you?"

"Franck's was in A-major," she corrected him, "Schumann was in A-minor."

"Very good!" he smiled, "Miss Monroe I came in this morning worried about the small bleed we saw on the CT scan in addition to all of her other injuries. As it is now if I hadn't seen her myself yesterday I wouldn't believe she had a concussion at all. Even her bruising is much better than I expected. We'll need to keep an eye on her for a while longer to make sure that bleed really is under control and to monitor the chest wound. It doesn't look like we have any signs of pneumothorax or hemothorax so she's very fortunate considering the location. Did you have any questions?"

"No. Thank you so much, doctor," Lilah answered.

"You're welcome," he replied, "Now how are you doing?"

"There's nothing wrong with me that a queen sized pillow-top and a hot shower wouldn't fix," she said.

"Great. I'll let you get some rest," he said as he stepped towards the door.

Only the sounds of the hospital broke the silence for several minutes after he left.

"It wasn't luck was it," Lilah said finally breaking the silence.

"I don't think so," Vanessa agreed, "Though what Meri did probably helped a lot."

Lilah nodded and pulled herself to her feet stiffly. She moved to the restroom with a pained shuffle that made her look much older than she was. Guilt rose up again as Vanessa watched her. Once the door was closed she was left alone in the room for the first time since she had awoken. Taking a big breath she stopped short with a gasp. She had experienced broken ribs enough to recognize the feeling. Her fingers ran lightly over the dressing on her chest. The move had made it pull painfully as well. Tubes ran into and out of her in more places than she really wanted to think about as well. No matter how badly she wanted to, she didn't think running was an option this time.

Being helpless grated on her as she sat there unable to even reach the television remote. The worst part was that this was uncharted waters for her. Ever since she had began her new life she had never been really hurt. Now she had no idea how long getting back on her feet was going to take. Even though it was obvious she was healing faster than normal it was still going to take time.

A roar resembling an explosion made her whip her head towards the door. A moment later Lilah emerged from the restroom with a grimace on her face.

"You'd think someplace people are supposed to be resting that they could find toilets that don't sound like a seven-forty-seven," she said with a scowl. "I'm going to go find some coffee before someone gets hurt." She paused fixing Vanessa with a meaningful stare. "Don't get any bright ideas while I'm gone."

"What?" Vanessa said defensively.

"I know you," Lilah shot back dryly, "Just stay put."

Lilah stood there staring at Vanessa until she finally nodded. Alone again she was left trying to decide if she was insulted by Lilah's assumption, or touched that the woman knew her that well. By the time Lilah returned Vanessa had ended up just pouting.

A barrage of tests interspersed with long waits in various departments ate up the rest of the day. Too many people were around for them to talk about anything other than the situation at hand. Late in the afternoon Vanessa was wheeled into her room at last free from the majority of her tubes and lines. Even with her new found freedom the sleepless night combined with the constant tension of the tests left her exhausted and irritable. The sight of Detective Banks sitting beside Lilah when she came through the door made her clench her jaw in frustration.

"Vanessa, good to see you're doing better," he greeted her as they wheeled her next to the bed and helped her get back into place. "I was hoping you could help me out with a few details."

"Not today, officer," her doctor interrupted as he swept into the room. "She's recovering from a serious head trauma and needs her rest, which we've been keeping her from enough as it is."

"Doctor, I just need to ask her a few quick questions and I'll be on my way," Banks argued.

"Yes you will, but without the questions."

The two men stared at each other for a few heartbeats before Banks looked down at his pad and flipped it closed.

"Miss Monroe, you have my card. If you come up with anything please don't hesitate to give me a call," he said, thinly veiled frustration in his voice. "And we can have someone take you to the house if you want."

"Certainly. Thank you." As soon as he had left Lilah turned her attention to the doctor, "How's Vee doing?"

"I wish I had half her fortitude," he said with a smile, "Yesterday I would have expected her to be here for a couple of weeks in a best case scenario. If she continues to improve like she has today I'd say she can go in another day or two."

"Thank God," Lilah sighed.

"I heard she was up most of the night," he continued, "If she has trouble sleeping again I have an order in for some medication to help her sleep. Insomnia isn't uncommon after an injury like hers. Also, we can have someone come up and talk to her, or you if you need it as well."

"Thanks doctor. We'll keep that in mind. Vee, will you be okay if I leave for a while?" Lilah asked, looking tired. "They said they can take me by the house to get a few things."

"I'll be fine Mom."

Lilah leaned in and gave Vanessa a light hug and whispered into her ear. "They found a paper in your jacket that said 'Where is he?' signed 'M'." Pulling back she patted Vanessa's hands and smiled. "I got your phone back, by the way. One of the nurses charged it for me," Lilah said pointing to the bedside table.

"Thanks!" Vanessa said with somewhat exaggerated enthusiasm.

She reached for the phone trying to figure out how she was going to reach Meri since she didn't have the woman's number. Picking up the phone she was surprised to see dozens of texts waiting for her from teammates and other kids at school asking about both her ordeal and her condition. To a certain extent she knew that a lot of them were out of morbid curiosity rather than any real concern for her, but a few from the track team showed genuine worry. Her irritation melted as she sent out simple replies to many of the messages. It was an alien sensation to her knowing so many people cared about her.

The elation was short lived as she ran across a text from a number she didn't recognize, *"After shamrocks, let me know."*

At least she had Meri's number now. The woman's cryptic message could have been to keep Ivan's people in the dark or the police. Vanessa wasn't sure how paranoid she should be, but decided that it would be safer to assume that anything she sent might come back to haunt her. Her eyes closed as she focused on what she could remember of her dream.

"I hit a brick wall. There was Moore by a pond," she replied. There was every chance in the world that Meri wouldn't understand the message, but she didn't want to spell things out too much if she could avoid it.

Looking around her Vanessa was forced to accept that there wasn't much she could do about things at the moment. She picked at the edge of her gown, chewing on her bottom lip, as she weighed the turns her existence had taken. Now she was especially glad that she hadn't succumbed to the temptation held by the thermos at Cyrus's. Her phone chirped as another text came in. A smile touched her lips as she read it and replied, joking with Cari from track. Having traded super human abilities to end her solitude seemed like a better bargain now than it had then.

"Wow, I didn't know you could smile," Derek called from the doorway startling her slightly.

"How did you get in here?" she asked.

"You wear a tie and carry a clipboard you'd be amazed at where you can go," he laughed as he came and sat by the bed. "How are you?"

"I guess I'm doing ok. At least I can move around now. I'm kinda surprised to see you though."

"Yeah, well these are surprising times," he said, suddenly serious, "I talked to Meri the other day."

"Oh," she said with frown.

"Is what she was saying about a coup true?" he whispered, leaning in close.

"A long time ago there was this guy named Gordon that was pushing for the same line of crap the Ivan has been. I don't know if they are connected or not, but Lilah said Ivan was going on these rants about how 'after things change the old rules won't matter' and stuff."

Derek nodded and rubbed his chin thoughtfully.

"Why?" she asked.

He glanced nervously at the door. Vanessa could feel the tension radiating from him.

"Not everyone is happy with what happened to Alaric," he answered stopping himself short with a shake of his head, "I better not go into it."

Vanessa nodded and sighed. She was used to being left on the outskirts of the greater machinations of court. Not that she wanted any more involvement than she already had.

"So you look a hell of a lot better than I was expecting with what they were saying on the news," he continued, his easy smile back in place.

"Yeah, well..." she shrugged, fidgeting at his knowing look. "So this really is a big media thing?"

"All over CNN," he replied, "It's a mess. Graves is pissed."

Vanessa couldn't help but notice how much he seemed to enjoy that fact.

"Yeah, she already came by to see me. This is just great."

"Hey, enjoy your celebrity status while it lasts. It's keeping her off your back for now." He stood, reaching in his pocket as he did so. "Here's my number. Drop me a line if you hear anything about Alaric," he said as he handed her a card, "Or if you need anything."

She took the card with trembling fingers. Their eyes met, the look he gave her deep and intense. While he didn't say it, she understood that she had just gained another ally. Once he was gone she added the number to her phone and sat there with the card gripped tight in her fist. Tightness grew in her chest and her eyes burned. Every person that offered to stand with her increased the fear she felt. The end of her own existence was a possibility she had come to terms with a long time ago, but now others stood to be hurt; even if it wasn't necessarily in a physical sense.

Unwilling to fall back into her earlier melancholy, she set the phone and card aside and decided to see what they were saying about her in the news for herself. By the time Lilah returned around dinner time she was staring slack-jawed in disbelief at the screen.

Chapter 24
Holy Ground

Meri chaffed at the close confines of the coffin she was in. More than chaffed. Even though she had bought the largest coffin that the vendor offered she was still less than half a breath from sheer terror. Flashbacks to the month she had spent enduring The Embrace kept trying to force their way into her mind. Ruthlessly she forced them down and tried to focus on what she did have. As oversized for her frame as this model was she could roll onto her side and curl up. It seemed counter intuitive to her that curling into a ball would help with her claustrophobia, but she reasoned that doing so left more space around her.

The soft blue glow of her LED light helped a little bit. Compulsively she reached to make sure she had the extra batteries for the fourth time. Even being able to see in complete darkness the light gave her some small feeling of control. She knew that this was only going to be for one day. The flight was going to be fourteen hours. Then there was the wait for nightfall in Belfast. She wished she could have cut things closer with the courier she had hired, but they wouldn't guarantee delivery on time if she had tried. So now she waited for the flight to take off already having been trapped far longer than she could truly stand. Every time she went to take a breath she caught herself beginning to hyperventilate. Only not breathing at all kept her from it.

A small giggle with a hysterical edge to it escaped her as she thought about it; the notion of holding her breath the entire time.

As she let the breath out, feeling ridiculous as she did, she felt dampness on her cheeks. A swipe of her fingers came away red from the tears leaking from the corners of her eyes.

"God damn it!" she hissed, "I'll be damned if I'm going to lay here and cry." Scrubbing her face with a handkerchief, she seethed at her fear.

Dayflower

"It's just a few hours. If you survived a month, you can survive this," she said, her voice loud in her ears.

She chastised herself for not having scheduled the flight closer to dawn. Then she could have slept more of the trip. Not that this was her first time down this train of thought since the coffin had been sealed. She knew that waiting another day would have been disaster, but right now laying sealed in this box she was beginning to find a certain amount of disaster acceptable.

To keep herself distracted she began trying to piece together the flurry of images she had picked up as she gathered a few things at Cyrus's house. She knew she would get something from Vanessa. That boded well even if she wasn't sure what that something would be. What bothered her was that she knew there were a couple of major tipping points for the girl in the near future and there was nothing she could do about it. She knew for certain that staying stateside would be disastrous, but that was cold comfort knowing things could still go to hell on her while she was an ocean away.

Eventually she felt the plane lift off. Somehow that fact wasn't nearly as comforting as she had hoped it would be. While it meant that she was at least moving ahead, it also meant that she was trapped in a box thousands of feet above the ocean. Realizing where this train of thought was heading she went back to worrying about what would happen until she could make herself sleep.

By the time she had been unloaded and found an opportunity to escape her prison Meri was seething with impatience. Grinding her teeth in frustration as the taxi made its way to Cyrus's hotel she tried to remind herself that it wasn't the driver's fault she was so angry. The act of trying to control her anger only seemed to stoke it. In an attempt to spare the driver she let her mind go back to the most immediate source of her frustration. It had been almost two days since she had left Vanessa, and Meri had yet to hear anything from the girl. She knew that she would receive some message so it wasn't a matter of her note not finding its way into Vanessa's hands. While there were a multitude of possible explanations Meri wasn't interested them at the moment.

The fact that she had spent the last day in a box wasn't helping her mood, but the truth was that she wasn't going to feel better until she saw Cyrus again. There was nothing she could do about whatever it was Vanessa was going through so she didn't let herself dwell on that. At this point Meri had grudgingly decided that the girl probably didn't need her help as much as she had originally thought. None of that mattered if she couldn't find Cyrus soon, though. Even if things were destined to turn out badly should the girl die, it was nothing compared to where they would end up if she didn't find Cyrus soon; preferably tonight.

"That will be forty-three pounds, Miss," the driver said breaking her out of her thoughts.

She pulled a card from her pocket and swiped it through the hand-piece he gave her, making sure to add a decent tip. It was embarrassing that she hadn't even noticed the cab pull up to the hotel. Grabbing her one bag, she made sure she had everything before closing the door and stepping onto the curb. As she walked up to the hotel she braced herself for a flood of foreign images. Every area had a unique feel to it and until she adjusted to that it was much harder for her to filter things out. Fortunately for her the airport here was much like the one she had departed, and she had discovered that taxis all had the same awful blend of humanity to them.

The worn brass handle of the lobby door seemed to glare at her in the glow of the bright lights lining the walk. With a ragged breath she grasped it and felt the familiar falling sensation as random fragments of stranger's lives poured into her. Small snippets caught her attention as they passed, but the flow was too great for her to cling to them. She saw Cyrus as he arrived and again accompanied by a young vampire. The breath she had taken was ripped from her as she saw that same young vampire entering the hotel alone very recently.

Yanking the door open she rushed into the lobby, shoving the rest of the sensations back to a static roar in the back of her mind. A sharp pain ran through her head in protest, but she ignored that as well. As she hurried through the lobby she tried to decide if she should bother to stop and get a key to the room or not. The torrent she was still fighting made it hard to focus on the images she had seen, but she felt a crushing sense of urgency.

It was a small blessing that the desk clerk barely looked at her as she passed. Civil conversation would have been unbearable to her at the moment. Red tinged her vision as the pain in her head grew. Stepping into the elevator and pressing the button for Cyrus's floor brought another wave that dropped her to her knees. It took everything she had not to retch from the pain. She couldn't even remember making her way from the elevator to the door to his room.

The moment she laid her hand on the door everything changed. Time seemed to slow as the shift in sensation pulled her along. Cyrus had been in this room for two days. That was a short time for most people; barely a flicker in the tide of images she saw, but Cyrus's presence was so powerful that it pushed all others aside. For a moment she stood there, still as a statue, allowing the familiar presence to act as a balm to her tattered senses. It had barely dawned on her that the door was already ajar when it began to move away from her fingers.

Meri had never formally learned to fight, but she had been the only girl in a house full of older brothers. She had learned early on that her options were to be forever dominated or to learn to give better than she got. Those instincts rose rapidly to the surface as the vampire in the room grabbed her arm and attempted to pull her inside.

She hesitated just long enough for his grip to be secure before she planted her foot on the door frame and hauled backwards, dragging him along. As she moved she pulled the door along as well, slamming his wrist between it and the frame with a satisfying snap. He let out a yelp and recoiled immediately. Letting him go she kicked the door as hard as she could, slamming it into his face. He staggered back into the room grasping his ruined nose with his good hand.

Not giving him a chance to recover she lunged forward and planted a foot behind his and brought her knee upwards into the back of his. He collapsed just as she had planned, but managed to kick her in the face before she could move in closer. Stars swam in her vision as she felt him grasp her calf in an iron grip. With a swift twist he yanked her leg out from under her dumping her to the floor beside him. In an instant he had straddled her, resting his weight on her hips. As violently as she struggled, his arms were longer and he managed to get his hand on her throat and squeeze.

Panic threatened to overtake her until her rage began to build. Once she realized he couldn't make her pass out from choking her, she began to think more clearly. She couldn't reach his head or neck, but his broken arm was within reach. With a sudden snap forward she grabbed the wrist and twisted cruelly. Instantly he released her and pulled back. That was the opening she needed to kick her way free.

Dayflower

Scrambling to her feet she saw that she was in the alcove between the entrance and the bathroom. Directly in front of her a clothes iron sat perched in its wire holder. Pulling it free, she slammed it downward into her opponent's head as he struggled to sit up. A second and then a third blow landed before he stopped struggling and collapsed to the floor. Meri reached over and swung the door closed, hoping that no one had heard the struggle. She knelt down and pressed the point of the iron to his temple.

"Are you awake, or do I have to plug this thing in?" she demanded in a low voice.

"'M awake," he muttered thickly.

"Good," she said, pulling the cord out slowly. "Here's how this is going to work. You answer my questions and you get to leave with everything you came here with. Understand?"

He swallowed nervously and shifted his good hand slightly. The movement was rewarded with a savage blow from the iron that smashed that hand as well.

"Understand?" she asked again with a smile.

"Yes!" he agreed, beginning to nod until he saw her begin to raise the iron.

Less than an hour later Meri was walking purposefully through the night. A feeling of satisfaction had replaced her earlier irritation since she had been given an outlet to vent her frustration. The youngster she had caught at the hotel, Liam she had learned, had been just reluctant enough to talk that she had cause to use some persuasion. Gripping the handle of the shovel she had liberated from a landscaping truck she hoped that he had been telling her the truth. A buzz from her phone brought her to a halt as she fished it from her pocket.

"You're a little late," she sighed seeing that it was a text from Vanessa. After reading the message she shoved her phone back into her pocket. "Ok, so that was useful," she admitted to herself as she continued on her way. Seeing the wall in front of Roselawn she at least knew that Liam had told her the truth.

As she approached the wall she took a few running steps and leaped on top of the wall, a feral smile on her face. It was moments like this that she reveled in her new world. The cemetery stretched out before her with the marker stones in ruler straight lines. Small lanes and gravel paths wound around the graveyard following the natural contours of the landscape. Meri's jaw dropped at the sheer immensity of the place.

"Fuck," she hissed as she dropped down on the inside of the wall.

A wave of images crashed in upon her as she stepped onto the sanctified ground. Unprepared for the ferocity of the onslaught she felt herself begin to fall as her mind shut down from the overload. A strong grip caught her before she hit the ground accompanied by a presence that gave her an island of clarity to focus on.

"Are you okay?" Alaric asked as he shifted his grip, careful to keep her from touching the ground.

It took her several minutes to recover enough to answer. She pushed away from him to stand on her own even though she kept her grip on his arm to steady herself.

"No, not really. I haven't been in a cemetery since the one you stuck me in. It was a little more than I was expecting," she lied.

She wasn't sure if Cyrus had shared her ability with Alaric or not, but she wasn't about to be the one to tell him. Even if he wasn't at the top of her list of favorite people, she was glad Alaric was there. Besides saving her from what would have been a very ugly experience landing face first on hallowed ground, his presence was a familiar one. It gave her the anchor that let her shut out the tidal wave of emotion that saturated the place. She hadn't been lying about never having been in a cemetery since her Embrace so she hadn't known what to expect. With a sour grimace she realized that she should have expected as much since strong emotions left a stronger imprint.

Really looking at Alaric for the first time she saw he looked much as he always did in his trademark slacks and Oxford shirt. Unlike normal, however, were the smudges of dirt and burns on his hands and forearms. A pair of leather work gloves stuffed in his pocked caught her eye as well.

"Honestly I expected to find you a little farther down," she commented.

"Well apparently Cyrus made my release part of his terms before accepting the use of a Truth Stone or I would be," he said soberly, "Although they at least had the decency to bury me in France."

"Then why are you here?"

"Same reason as you I assume," he answered, pointing to a second shovel on the ground beside hers. "But I have no idea how we're going to find him. This place is huge."

Meri pulled her phone out and began tapping on the screen. Alaric stood by impassively. Several times she growled and almost swatted at the screen trying to undo mistakes. Only once she was frustrated enough to smash the device did she stuff it back in her pocket and kick the handle of her shovel up to grab it. Reclaiming his as well, Alaric fell in beside her as she stalked off into the cemetery.

"I'm going to guess that something fruitful came out of that?" he asked with a smirk.

"Yes," she growled.

Deciding that it was wiser to leave her be, Alaric gave up on conversation. With an uneasy glance around he hoped that they were adequately prepared to retrieve Cyrus. His own recent internment was still fresh in his mind as they walked.

Chapter 25
Freedom

It was far closer to morning than the pair would have liked when they finally hit the cap to the vault holding Cyrus's coffin. Both of them had dozens of burns from contact with the soil as they dug. An errant fan of dirt from a shovel was akin to a cloud of embers to them. This drove them to work with caution after the first few accidents occurred.

"Jesus, how are we going to get this thing off," Meri mused with disgust as she eyed the massive cement cover of the vault. "How did they even get the thing on there?"

"I think there were a lot more of them than there are of us," Alaric observed, "Let's see what we can do."

They hammered and pried at the joint where the lid met the body of the vault but were unable to get enough purchase with the shovels to do anything more than chip the cement and ruin the ends of their tools. Alaric wiped at his brow with the back of his hand then transferring the red tinged smear with disdain on his already ruined pants.

"Maybe if we..." he began.

"No!" Meri barked, "This is fucking ridiculous. I'm going to get a tractor or something!"

Just then there was a muffled boom and the ground shook beneath their feet. The cover suddenly lifted several inches and Alaric immediately shoved the haft of his shovel underneath it before it fell back in place. The pair exchanged looks before stepping to the corners of the vault and heaving on the lid.

It was all they could do to lift the lid, but they with the new handholds they managed to force it upright to lean against the side of the pit they had dug. Inside the vault they saw the ruined remains of a heavy stainless steel coffin. Alaric dropped into the vault and tossed the lid aside. Beneath the tatters of the destroyed interior of the coffin lay Cyrus, his face and hands drenched blood red from the sweat of his exertion.

"You are going to have to pull me out of this thing," he said through clenched teeth.

Meri was alarmed to see that his eyes were inky black and his canines pushed against his lips. In the time she had known him she had never seen Cyrus show any of the outward signs of their kind. Alaric reached down and took a firm grip on Cyrus's arm and hauled him violently free of the coffin. A look similar to someone plunged into ice water swept over his face as he cleared the confines of his prison. Teetering at the edge of the vault Cyrus put a hand to his face, the other reaching out to steady himself. The instant his hand touched the soil wall of the pit flames erupted from his skin making him recoil.

"I am afraid that this ordeal has cost me much more than I had anticipated," he sighed, leaning heavily against Alaric.

"I'm surprised that held you," Meri commented as she scrambled out of the pit.

"Were it not for the geis Landina placed upon me it would not have," he answered with a tremor in his voice.

Alaric hoisted Cyrus up to Meri who easily pulled him back above ground. Without touching them she shook the gloves from her hands and moved to check over Cyrus. He forestalled her with an upraised hand as he took his handkerchief from his breast pocket and tidied his hands and face. With a sour look he folded the ruined linen and stuffed it back into his pocket.

"Are you alright?" Meri asked with concern.

"I have certainly been better. Had I known at the outset that her prohibition would serve as a continual burden upon my will I would have broken it before they had brought forth the casket. As it is by the time I realized what was happening I was too far spent to break the compulsion."

"What exactly did she do to you?" Alaric asked, placing his hand on the older man's arm.

"She set the stage and snared me into agreeing to the use of a Truth Stone," he replied, "I can only assume she has found one of the lost codices since she knows how to accomplish things I had thought lost."

"But Truth Stones can only compel truthful speech," Alaric protested.

"My situation would indicate otherwise," Cyrus said bitterly, "Apparently the limit of their use as such is only customary."

"You haven't answered me," Meri interjected peevishly, "Are you alright?"

Cyrus took a deep breath and gave her shoulder a reassuring squeeze.

"I am well enough I suppose, though it is humbling to think that all this time I was one misstep from losing my so called control." A pained look swept over his face as he looked at his companions. "I am in your debt for the price you two have paid in freeing me," he continued, pointing out their burns.

"Can we get out of here?" Meri pleaded.

"Yeah, I've had my fill of the landscape too," Alaric added.

Cyrus nodded and fell in with them as they made their way out of the cemetery. Dark thoughts filled his mind as they walked. He had grown so accustomed to people deferring to him as a great wise man that he realized he had begun to believe his own legends. That hubris had led him to this point; once again in the thrall of the demon he had supposedly conquered. He reached down and experimentally touched the ground. While his fingertips didn't flame as they had when Alaric pulled him from his prison, the contact was still scorching leaving his fingertips blackened. Meri noticed the motion, but said nothing. He could feel her weighing the change in him. There was anger there, that much was clear to him even if he wasn't sure of its target.

Silence reined until they reached the hotel. Excusing himself from his companions, Cyrus showered. In some small way he hoped that returning to civil surrounding and attire would restore something of his sense of control. As he stood before the mirror once more restored to his normal countenance he certainly didn't feel any more in control than he did. Alaric's act of removing him from the coffin had broken that particular compulsion, but he could still feel the weight of his connection to the Truth Stone on his mind. Until he was free of that he wouldn't be able to fully focus on regaining his former mastery.

"We must return to New York," he stated as he rejoined Alaric and Meri.

"What about Landina?" Meri demanded.

"As long as she holds my blood sealed within the Truth Stone I cannot face her," he said solemnly, "My presence would be nothing other than a potential danger to you two."

"I don't think that we have to worry about that right now," Alaric added, "From what I overheard as they exhumed me she'll be in America soon enough."

"Why?" Meri asked.

"It would seem that she is comfortable in her control on this side of the world," Cyrus answered, "Now that she had a foothold with Alaric's former seat I imagine that she plans to complete her designs."

"So what do we do?"

"We go home and try to undermine her there," Alaric interjected.

"Exactly," Cyrus agreed. "Do either of you know of Vanessa's fate?" he added suddenly looking very old to his companions.

Alaric gave Meri a blank look. It was obvious that he hadn't heard anything since his release. Looking down at her feet Meri tried to think of how to explain the situation to Cyrus.

"When I left she was in bad shape, but I think she'll be fine," she said at last.

"You *think* she'll be fine?"

"Ivan had managed to take both Lilah and then me," she explained, "Vanessa managed to get us out, but she was in rough shape by then. It was daytime so I had to go to ground while they got out. She sent me a text tonight so she must be doing okay."

Cyrus nodded. It was clear that he had more questions, but he understood that no one here would be able to answer them. He walked to the window and stood there watching the pre-dawn glow grow on the horizon.

"I fear that my original travel plans will no longer be possible," he said turning back to his companions. "Can you arrange something Meri?"

"Sure. It's going to be a bit more complicated trying to get two more of us through in a hurry."

"Let me make a couple of calls," Alaric added, "I know a couple of charter outfits that may be able to do this. It won't be cheap though."

Cyrus waved his hand dismissively. "I am not concerned with that."

Returning to the window he was only dimly aware of Meri's departure and Alaric's conversations on the phone behind him. He felt the fool to have allowed things to have grown so out of control under his nose. Alaric had tried several times to warn him that there were ugly shifts happening in court. Even Vanessa had tried to warn him long ago of how dangerous Ivan was. At the time he had dismissed it as her personal dislike for the man, but he saw now that she had been right.

The pre-dawn light warmed him in a way he hadn't felt in millennia. A deep, hot rage built in him as he thought about all Landina had done. The anger fueled the demon and its demand to feed. Hands clenched at his sides, he forced the impulse down and struggled to stay calm. By the time he had regained control his face was hot from the morning light. Drawing the curtains closed he turned to find Alaric watching him closely.

"I saw a landslide once when I was a child," he said coolly, "The side of a mountain near where I grew up collapsed. It was terrifying watching something so permanent fall out of control with so much power."

"Do not fear, old friend. I am not yet fallen," Cyrus sighed as he sat opposite the other man, "Until I have regained my freedom there will be a struggle, but that shall pass."

Alaric nodded, not looking reassured.

"I managed to get us a flight early tonight," he said, changing the subject.

"But you are concerned about the cost," Cyrus guessed.

"Not if you aren't. I better go stop Meri before she invests too much time in her plan."

* * *

It was before dawn when Vanessa woke. She was still groggy since the nurse on duty had insisted on giving her something to make her sleep last night. Gingerly she ran her fingers over the wound on her chest. Through the dressing she could tell that it was almost gone. She took a deep breath and decided that her ribs were almost healed as well.

Carefully she slid her bedding aside and swung her legs over the side of the bed. Silencing the alarms on her monitor she disconnected everything but her IV and made her way to the bathroom, making sure not to wake Lilah as she went.

Pushing the door shut behind her, she squinted into the harsh light and saw that the bruises on her face were almost gone too. She knew that she should be grateful that her wounds were healing so fast, but all it did was prove to her that she wasn't normal after all; that there was still something of the demon within her. With a heavy sigh she grabbed her IV stand and exited the bathroom to come face to face with Lilah.

"What's wrong," she demanded.

"Nothing," Vanessa lied.

"Don't give me the teenage crap," Lilah said tersely, "There's been something bothering you since yesterday. Spill it."

Vanessa edged past her and sat on the edge of the bed, kicking her feet against the tile floor.

"I know I shouldn't be upset by how fast I've been healing," she began.

"But it makes you worry about what you are," Lilah finished for her.

"Yeah," Vanessa sighed, "I'm not a vampire anymore, but what am I?"

"My daughter," Lilah said emphatically, "Anything more than that I can't tell you, but that's what matters to me."

Vanessa reached out and pulled Lilah into a tight embrace. Tears burned at the edge of her eyes as searched for the right words.

"I'm sorry," she said at last, releasing her hold.

"Don't be," Lilah replied, smoothing Vanessa's hair with a smile. "There are plenty of adoptive mothers who have had worse baggage than this come with the deal."

Vanessa pulled back and gave Lilah a disbelieving stare.

"Okay, maybe not plenty," she amended, "but I bet no one else has quite as interesting of a background."

"Are you making fun of me?" Vanessa asked seriously.

"And what if I am?" Lilah shot back with a smile.

The serious mood broken, they talked about what they were going to do about school and Lilah's work. Their conversation drifted to the destruction at their house, which returned things to a solemn tone. By mid morning the doctor had decided that Vanessa could be released and the rest of the day was consumed with the paperwork surrounding that. It was only after they had checked into a hotel that Vanessa noticed a text from Meri waiting on her phone.

"They're going to be home tonight," she told Lilah with relief.

Chapter 26
Homecoming

Pacing in the back of the small cabin Cyrus was anxious to return home. His first foray out in centuries was very nearly a complete disaster. Urges he had thought long conquered pulled at him constantly. He shuddered to think at what would have happened if Meri and Alaric had come a day or two later. Now he felt the need to set right some matters that he had miss-stepped terribly on. Returning to the front of the cabin he rejoined his companions. Hands clasped before him in a demeanor of submission that was completely unknown to him he searched for the right words.

"I owe both of you considerably more than an apology, but I shall at least start with that," he said gravely, "Meri, you are correct that there is more to Vanessa's condition than I have been willing to admit. Perhaps if I had been willing to see that I would have been better prepared for all of this. I hope you can forgive me."

"Better late than never, I guess," she shrugged, "As long as you see it now we're square."

Something in her tone told Cyrus that despite what she said that he would hear more on this later. Instead of pushing the issue he merely nodded his acceptance. A chastising from Meri was a deserved penance all things considered.

"Alaric," he continued, "You have been telling me for some time that I should return to court and see how things have changed. I should have heeded your advice."

"The weight of the world shouldn't fall to one man's shoulders my friend," Alaric offered, "We'll just have to try and sort things out now."

"So what is our plan?" Meri asked.

"I would rather wait until we know where things stand at home before we plan a course of action," Cyrus replied.

"And see if Vanessa's safe," she added, her irritation clear.

"Yes I am concerned for her welfare, but I do not see why that is a matter of contention."

"It's not. Forget I said anything," she growled.

"What is bothering you, Meri?" Cyrus asked, taking a seat beside her.

"Nothing! I said forget it." She stood suddenly and stalked to the back of the plane.

Cyrus began to rise and Alaric put a hand on his shoulder, "Let me go talk to her."

He nodded and settled back into the seat. Resting his elbows on the arms of the seat his fingers formed a steeple before him. He could easily listen to the conversation at the back of the plane, but that wasn't his way. Instead he looked inward. Now more than ever he wondered if the world had moved too far beyond him. It was a self pitying line of thought he had never allowed himself to indulge in before, but knowing that his involvement was making the situation worse led him to consider it.

In the back of the plane Alaric eased himself into the seat next to Meri.

"Just piss off and leave me alone," she demanded.

"You know that's not going to happen."

"Fine, what do you want?"

"I just want to know what's wrong. This isn't like you," he said mildly.

"Oh because you're such a fucking expert on my problems," she hissed.

Alaric sat calmly giving her a patient look. She began to try and out wait him, but she had seen his interactions with Cyrus to know that he would still be sitting there staring at her when the plane landed. While she was more than stubborn enough to out wait him there was a part of her than wanted to talk; to share her burden with someone.

"I have visions. Some of the past, some of what could happen," she admitted in a quiet voice, not meeting his gaze.

"I know," he replied, "I don't envy you that either."

"Cyrus told you?"

193

"No. I've been magistrate for over three-hundred years. I have ways of finding out what's happening in my territory."

"Was," she corrected him, "You're past tense now."

"Thanks," he said sourly, "But I take it you've seen some things you don't like?"

"That's the understatement of the decade," she sighed, "I hate knowing this stuff. I never asked to be responsible for everyone."

"And…" he prompted.

"I don't think I'm going to make it through this. I really don't know if Cyrus will either," she continued, "And to be honest, it pisses me off that so much of this is to protect *her*."

"I've never really understood why he is so enamored of her either. But while she's certainly the biggest pain in the ass I've ever seen, I have to admit I've gotten used to having her around."

"That's what I'm talking about," Meri said accusingly, "Everybody that meets her seems to want to either kill her or protect her! There's something more going on there than we know."

Alaric leaned back staring into space thoughtfully for a few seconds.

"Have you said anything about this to Cyrus?" he asked.

"No," she scoffed, "He's blind when it comes to her."

"Yes he is," Alaric agreed, "but there may be something to what you're saying and I think maybe Cyrus needs to know." He paused and shifted to face her once more. "Is there anything else about what you've seen that you need to talk about?"

Meri knew he wasn't trying to get information out of her. He genuinely wanted to help. That was one of the things that frustrated her so much about him. In a sea of calculating callousness he was warm and sympathetic. That made his dispassionate application of the law so much more maddening to her since she knew he understood exactly how harsh he was being.

"There is a ton I'd love to tell you, but if I did then everything would change."

"If things are as dire as you say, maybe that would be a good thing," he offered.

"It never works like that," she sighed, "worse is the only option."

They sat in silence for a while before Meri shifted uncomfortably. "I'd like some space, if you wouldn't mind."

Dayflower

Alaric nodded and went back to the front of the cabin to chat with Cyrus. Neither were feeling very talkative though, each wrestling with the changes the last few days had brought them. Silence hung heavy for the rest of the flight until Meri informed them as they approached the airport that Vanessa and Lilah would meet them at Cyrus's house.

It was a surprise to Alaric that Derek was there as well when they arrived. As soon as they arrived Cyrus dropped his bag and went straight to Vanessa. Cupping her face in his hands he stared intently into her eyes. It was clear to everyone there that something passed between them that that the rest of them were not privy to. Once he was satisfied Cyrus released her and accepted her tight embrace with what grace he could manage.

"Sir, it's good to see you," Derek greeted Alaric, breaking the silence.

"You can drop the 'Sir.' I'm not magistrate anymore," Alaric said while accepting the strong handshake the younger man offered.

"For now," Derek countered, offering no further comment.

A flurry of conversation broke out with the silence having been broken. Cyrus, Vanessa, and Lilah formed a tight knot exchanging stories of what had transpired to each of them in the last few days. Likewise Derek and Alaric exchanged information. Meri stood apart from them all watching impassively. She was both jealous of the connections the others had and bitterly grateful for her lack.

Images swirled before her as the dynamics of the group opened a host of possibilities while closing others. She knew that whatever significance the tipping points before now had held, that this moment was greater. Looking at the two groups she had no idea where to focus her attention. More paths than she could follow spun out from this moment and she felt somewhat motion sick trying to sort through them all. What made her stomach clench in fear was how many of them ended in darkness.

"So what are we going to do about this Landina woman?" Vanessa demanded, cutting through the chatter.

"There is precious little I can do so long as that Stone holds my blood," Cyrus said gravely.

"How did she manage to take control of the Senate?" Lilah asked.

"I think she managed to manipulate Anton," Alaric offered, "There was a long spell where he wasn't active in our territories. When he came back he was much stronger and a lot of things had begun to change."

"So this is all my fault," Vanessa muttered.

"No!" Cyrus cut in sharply, "You did not create him intentionally. Not only that, but there were ample opportunities that I, or even Alaric early on, could have remedied the situation. The collection of misjudgments surrounding these events is large enough for us all."

"I get that she was using Vanessa as bait for you," Lilah said to Cyrus, "And I understand the power grab in the Senate. I just don't see what her end game is."

"She wants vampires to take over," Alaric answered.

"Essentially," Cyrus agreed, "This is an argument as old as our kind itself."

"I'm not saying I agree with the idea," Derek interjected, "But I can see where she's coming from. Why the tone of doom?"

"Because if people know about us they will hunt us," Vanessa answered quietly, barely speaking above a whisper. "And they will win. We would become extinct."

"How?" he argued.

Vanessa looked up at him with a heated glare. The rest of the group knew her background, what she had been through and held their silence. She stepped up to Derek until she had to crane her neck to look him in the eye. Her voice was cold and flat as she spoke, punctuating her words more than a shout could have.

"I have lived outside the rule of the magistrates," she declared, "I have scoffed at the rule of law they uphold and I have paid for that. The only reason we are not hunted like rabid dogs is by following the laws that men like him have made to preserve us." Heat filled her voice as she gestured at Cyrus. "So many of our kind think they are better than plain humans. Wait until they drag you into the light of day and pour holy water over you. See how great you are when you are outnumbered six to one."

"You've survived," he said hesitantly.

Vanessa laughed a bitter laugh. Tears wet the corners of her eyes as she stared him down.

"I wouldn't go down that road," Meri cut in. "You want to take a poll in this room of who would lay down their life to protect her versus who would do the same for you?"

Derek shook his head in response.

"I didn't think so," she continued, "I don't know why, but she isn't bound by the same rules you and I are."

"What do you mean?" Lilah asked.

Meri turned to face her. She was angry and hurt, but she struggled to keep herself under control. She knew that Lilah didn't deserve the brunt of her ire.

"Ask Alaric. Hell, ask Cyrus, how many hunters most vampires face and how many survive," she said coldly, "Then ask your little girl how many she's faced. I could only pray for her odds in Vegas."

"This is all beside the point," Cyrus said forcefully, "We are not here to argue about Vanessa's past. This is not a new idea. It has arisen before and has been answered. The Inquisition, the first crusade, the Roman purge. There is a reason that there are so few Elders about. There is a reason we hide."

"I'm sorry," Derek said, "I get it, but I can't help but think Landina must know all this too. What makes her think this will be any different?"

"Subtlety," Alaric answered simply, "Not an open vampire rule, but behind the scenes manipulation."

"Doesn't a lot of that already happen?" Lilah asked.

"Mainly it's just cover-up work and making problems go away. Nothing like what she has planned."

"So what do we do about it?"

"We wait," Cyrus stated, "We are not in a position to act boldly now. I am also not sure that her designs are exactly what we think they are. I suspect that this may be another ruse."

A lull developed in the conversation while everyone weighed what had already been said. Derek cleared his throat and shifted uncomfortably.

"I think this is my stop. Let me know if there's anything I can do," he offered.

"I'll walk with you," Alaric said, following the younger man to the door.

"We should be going too," Lilah added, "I have to deal with getting Vanessa cleared to go back to school tomorrow."

Cyrus saw Alaric and Derek out and returned to pull Lilah aside, "There is something I need to discuss with you before you leave."

Meri approached Vanessa as soon as the two were alone. There was an air of menace surrounding her that put Vanessa on edge. It was clear that it wasn't anger, but there was something dangerous about her.

"I'm going to break my cardinal rule here just because I don't see how telling you could make things any worse," she said in a harsh whisper, "Don't do whatever it is that you're thinking about."

"I'm not thinking about doing anything," Vanessa protested.

"Fine. Keep it that way. Just know that if you go off on your own Cyrus will die."

Vanessa wanted to think that Meri was just trying to scare her. Looking into her eyes she could see that wasn't what the woman was doing. Then she saw it; the danger was that of a trapped animal. Meri was terrified of whatever she had seen and Vanessa realized she would do anything to prevent it. She didn't try to imagine what that anything might include, but she knew where Meri's loyalty lay. Nodding her agreement, she stepped back slightly. Wordlessly Meri gave her a curt nod and left.

Alone, Vanessa walked to the great table in the center of the room. Something seemed off with Cyrus and she couldn't put her finger on exactly what it was. He *felt* different in her mind. Now that she wasn't lying to herself she had to admit that she could still feel her bond to him. He felt more like Clarius had, now that she thought about it. She wasn't sure what that meant, but it made her uneasy.

"Well, Little Flower," Cyrus said as he stepped up beside her, "I am glad to see that your roots run deep. From what Lilah tells me your thorns are still sharp as well."

"I guess," she shrugged. "I'm sorry you got hurt because of me."

"Do not blame yourself. My injuries are the result of Landina and her minions' schemes. If there is any blame to be taken for helping them along it would belong to me for my pride and inactivity."

She stepped in close and held him as tightly as she could. He was as solid as stone beneath his suit and when she looked into his eyes she saw the same brightness she always had. They visited for a while longer now that it was just the three of them despite Lilah's earlier desire to leave.

"It'll probably be a while before we can come back," Lilah said once she and Vanessa had left, "It was hard enough to sneak away for this trip."

Shadows from the streetlights played across the pair as they drove through the night. What little Lilah had salvaged from the house was in a hotel between her school and Lilah's work. Unable to go home, Vanessa wished she could just stay at Cyrus's. There was more than one reason she couldn't do that though.

"I know," Vanessa replied morosely.

"You okay Vee?"

"Cyrus has changed," she said flatly.

"He just went through a pretty big ordeal too. Give him time," Lilah soothed.

"Has it really been less than a week?" Vanessa asked suddenly.

"It feels like a lifetime doesn't it," Lilah agreed, "I would say I can't wait for things to get back to normal, but I'm not sure what normal is anymore."

Vanessa didn't say anything as she watched the city roll by outside. There wasn't really anything more for her to say.

Chapter 27
Coping

Weeks had passed since the meeting at Cyrus's house without a sign of Ivan or Landina. As the shock of everything began to fade Lilah and Vanessa began to chafe at the confines of their hotel room. Finally Vanessa called Derek for information. When he assured them that everything seemed quiet at the Night Court they decided to go home and try to salvage their lives.

Even after all of the time they had spent cleaning, Vanessa wasn't sure that the house looked appreciably better. Wiping the sweat from her forehead with the back of her arm she gave the living room a glaring look.

"Yes, I did send you the police report on the incident!" Lilah practically screeched into the phone.

Ever since they had returned home she had been locked into an ugly fight with the insurance company. Vanessa was glad that all she had to worry about was catching up her assignments.

"I would like your full name and a reference number for the recording of this call please," Lilah said, her voice suddenly very cold and even. "Yes. So that I can forward the information to my attorney. That's correct. Yes, it is. Thank you."

"What was that all about?" Vanessa asked.

"Mr. Stedman said that if we had any problems that he would help us out pro-Bono. Once the agent realized who my attorney was, he got a lot more helpful."

"What are they making such a big deal over anyhow?"

"The fact that it was a week from when the house was broken into before I got the police report," Lilah sighed.

Vanessa stood there with her mouth hanging open in disbelief.

"Exactly," Lilah said dryly.

Shaking her head Vanessa turned back to what she had been doing before Lilah's phone confrontation had drawn her attention. They had spent the last couple of days bagging all of the debris from Ivan's rampage through the house and staging it all in the living room. Now that the dumpster had arrived Vanessa prepared to start throwing it all out.

"I don't think that's a good idea, Vee," Lilah said, taking the bags from her.

"What?" Vanessa asked, confused.

"I just don't think you should be hauling things out."

"But I feel fine," she protested.

"I know, and I don't doubt that you're in better shape than I am," Lilah agreed, "But we still get reporters creeping around and I don't want any more questions raised if we can help it."

"This sucks," Vanessa pouted and threw herself onto the remains of the couch.

"I know," Lilah soothed, taking a seat on the arm of the couch.

"I wish things were like they used to be."

"Before Ivan did this," Lilah said with a gesture at the mess surrounding them, "or before you changed?"

"Before this," Vanessa answered sullenly, picking at where stuffing spilled out of a gash in the back of the couch.

When Vanessa had still been in the hospital following her assault on Ivan's stronghold Lilah had insisted that she be told everything. It wasn't easy or comfortable, but Vanessa had done so. She even shared the things that she had tried to deny to herself; her doubts and fears, the temptation presented by the container of her blood she had taken from Ivan. Only once since they had returned home had Lilah mentioned it until now.

"You've lived that life, Vee," she had said, sadness weighing on her voice, "I can't tell you what you should do. Only you can make that decision, and you do need to decide. But you have a home and mother here."

There was the unspoken "but" hidden in her words. She never said it, but Vanessa knew that if she were to go back to what she had been, became a vampire once more, she wouldn't be welcome here. Ivan and his thugs had managed to make sure of that.

"I don't want that," she said, her voice rough, "It was tempting when I thought that might help me save you, but that's not what I want."

Lilah eased herself down to sit beside her adopted daughter and pulled her close. Stroking her hair she struggled to find the right words.

"I'm sorry Vee. We haven't really talked about it, and I have to wonder if you don't regret giving all of that up. I saw what *they* are capable of..." Lilah trailed off, not finishing her thought.

"And it makes you feel powerless," Vanessa finished.

Lilah nodded. Her gaze swept across the ruined house they called home. Vanessa didn't need to ask to know what she was thinking. She had thought similar things herself. Facing the fact that there were real monsters in the darkness and knowing, not thinking but *knowing* what they could do, was frightening in a way nothing else she had experienced had been.

"Don't worry, I'll protect you," she said at last, a solemn expression on her face.

Lilah gave her a sober look, trying to decide if Vanessa was being serious or not. As a smirk broke at the corners of Vanessa's mouth Lilah sighed and smacked her with a cushion sending a spray of foam stuffing across the room. The pair burst into laughter, almost desperate in its intensity, as they tried in vain to pick the bits of stuffing from their hair. Almost as quickly as it had begun the outburst was over and they sat there looking at one another.

"I am serious, though," Vanessa said.

"I know."

"If it comes down to it, please promise me you'll leave me and get away," she pleaded.

"I will promise you no such thing!" Lilah protested heatedly.

"Lilah, I've had my time," Vanessa continued, cutting Lilah off, "Hell, I should have been dead a hundred times over. I can't bear the thought of anything more happening to you because of me."

Reaching out Lilah grasped Vanessa's hands in her own and squeezed.

"And I couldn't bear the thought of the girl I agreed to be a mother to being hurt or worse because I saved my own neck," she shot back. "It doesn't matter how long you've been around, you're still a girl in here," she continued, reaching out to touch Vanessa's heart. "You're my daughter and I'll be damned if I'm going to leave you to the likes of that lot."

The hug was as tight as it was sudden. Lilah smiled as she relaxed and returned the embrace. Until all of this had started Vanessa had never been overly prone to affection. The girl had always been appreciative, which Lilah was grateful for, but she had kept a certain amount of distance between them. Considering her past Lilah understood Vanessa's stand-offish behavior. If they could manage to put Ivan and Vanessa's vampiric past behind them it would almost be worth what they had been through for the way she had opened up.

"I'm sorry," Vanessa said as she drew away.

"Don't be," Lilah replied, patting Vanessa's arm. "We should get back at it, though."

They settled on Vanessa hauling the bags to the back door where Lilah would take over and drag them to the dumpster. She had to admit a small bit of jealousy at the way Vanessa had bounced back from her injuries and the unnatural stamina she still possessed. Aching after just a few trips she was tempted to let Vanessa take over hauling the bags out and take her chances with the media. In the end she decided that prudence was the wiser course after all and finished what she had started. She resolved to make Vanessa responsible for a lot more yard work in the future though.

That evening they settled down to a simple dinner together. The walls were still scarred and they had been forced to use the patio furniture indoors until they could replace what had been destroyed, but there was at least some semblance of normalcy to the house now.

"I wish I could talk to Cyrus," Vanessa mused as she picked at her dinner.

"Me too," Lilah replied, "But you know he's right. You'd be too obvious of a target going to him right now."

"I know. I'm just worried about him."

"Yeah," Lilah agreed, "God, that seems strange. Of everything in my life I never thought I'd have to worry about him."

Vanessa didn't reply, but Lilah could tell Vanessa was worrying as much if not more than she was. She tried to wait and see if there was going to be some response, but none was forthcoming.

"What's wrong, Vee?" she asked at last.

"It's my fault," Vanessa replied sullenly.

"I hate to burst your bubble," Lilah stated, "But Cyrus is beyond the definition of a grown man. He can make his own decisions and he certainly isn't your responsibility."

Vanessa wanted to argue, but they had held this conversation before and she knew there was no winning the argument with Lilah. That wouldn't have stopped her before, but right now the last thing she wanted was to push Lilah away. Instead she finished her dinner in silence and hoped that Cyrus was doing better than he had been when she had seen him last.

Cyrus's dark hands cut a stark contrast to the white limestone slab that made up the top of the table. Fighting urges he had thought long banished, he clenched his fingers tight on the edge of the stone until he felt the stone begin to give in his grip. Marshaling his willpower he forced himself to release the table. His hands formed fists at his side, shaking from the fury he fought to control. Only when he felt the cold touch of blood flowing across his fingers did he break the hold his hunger had on him.

Opening his hands he watched as the crescent shaped cuts in his palms closed almost instantly. Stepping into the kitchen to wash his hands he became aware that he was no longer alone in the house.

"What is it Meri?" he asked coldly.

"I just came to check on you," she replied as she stepped into the room with him.

"I am not a child that needs tended to."

"You're also not some untouchable demigod anymore either," she countered.

"Thank you for reminding me," he said acidly, "I had nearly forgotten."

"See that's what I mean," she said almost cheerfully as she hopped up to sit on the counter. She leaned forward to rest her forearms on her knees, letting her long red braid hang from her shoulder. "I think I like you more like this instead of being so reserved all the time."

He finished drying his hands and turned to face her. She could see the small tremble in his hands as he struggled with something. Since she and Alaric had brought him back from Ireland, Cyrus hadn't been the same. He was frequently in the grip of a burning rage and she knew that his hunger had returned. If she were to guess based on his behavior she was sure that it wanted to make up for lost time.

"Is there something I can do for you Meri?" he demanded.

"You can stop hiding in here and do something about this," she answered.

"I can not face Landina as long as she holds the Truth Stone."

"Fine, don't face her. Find Ivan, look for a solution to the problem some other way. You can't tell me that there aren't any books or scrolls in that warehouse of yours that could possibly have an answer," She badgered him, "Hell, I'd be happy to see you just try and break the geis yourself."

"It's too late for that," he replied quietly, "Maybe if I had done it at the very beginning, but now doing so would make me lose control."

Meri hopped down to stand directly before Cyrus. "You aren't exactly in control now."

"You don't know what I was like before."

"No, but I know what doing nothing is getting you. You need to get off..." she began.

Cyrus cut her off by grabbing her roughly and slamming her against the wall.

"STOP!" he roared.

The force of his compulsion hit her with the power of a falling mountain. Only her unique immunity to the ability saved her. Without it she was sure that a push that strong would have damaged her mind. As it was, a blinding pain shot through her head in the instant he had compelled her. The slow steady drip of blood from her nose onto Cyrus's hand broke the tension of the moment. He recoiled from what he had done and set her gently back on her feet. Without taking her eyes from his she reached over and took a napkin to stop the bleeding.

"I am sorry Meri," he said contritely. For the first time since she had known him she saw real shame in his eyes. It wasn't a comforting sight.

"Me too," she offered halfheartedly, "I pushed you to that. The thing is, I'm not the only one that's going to push you. And what you did just then would have destroyed almost anyone else."

Stepping away from him she kept her expression neutral as the bones he had broke slid back into place. Once she was able she tossed the napkin and cleaned her face. When she was done she looked up and he hadn't moved. Gently she laid her hand on his shoulder.

"I know why you won't let her come here," she said softly, "Not to protect her from them, but to protect her from you."

Cyrus nodded and met Meri's gaze.

"Do you really think I should try to break it?" he asked cautiously.

"No," she answered, "Not now. I do think you should go to the warehouse, though."

"I shall see if Derek is available tomorrow."

"Good. Now that that's settled, I'll let you get back to your brooding,"

He gave her a wry look that mirrored the Cyrus she knew. Smiling she turned to leave through the main library. On her way out she trailed her fingers across the top of his work table, noting a few fresh cracks in its surface. Since her back was to Cyrus she allowed herself the luxury of grimacing at what she saw.

A major tipping point was coming up very quickly. While her concern for Cyrus was very genuine, she really visited him tonight to eliminate some of the possible threads she saw before her. Her confrontation with him had shown her clearly what would happen if certain courses of action were taken.

It still maddened her that she couldn't share what she saw with anyone without sending her vision of the future skittering away like leaves on the wind. So it was left to her to try and make sense out of sometimes contradictory visions of what could happen to those around her. She knew that sending Cyrus to the warehouse was the right thing to do and urging him to break the hold Landina had on him would be disastrous. Now she only had another half dozen major problems to sort out. If she was lucky she might actually have another night or two to accomplish it. Too bad she wasn't feeling particularly lucky at the moment.

Chapter 28
Searching for Answers

Derek pulled his car to the curb in front of Cyrus's house with a certain amount of trepidation. The last time he had seen the man had been during the meeting after Cyrus and Alaric's return from Europe. It had been the only time he had seen Cyrus anything less than completely in control of himself. From what he understood this was the first time in recorded history, not just his memory.

That sudden shift made him feel uneasy. He had always excelled at reinforcing the foundations of power. In his life he had never run for public office, but he had worked hard on the campaigns of several men and women who had. He had always managed to be in the winning corner of such things.

With his new life it hadn't been hard to make his way into the workings of the Night Courts. His particular talents were just as useful now as they had been before. Whatever powers of damnation that had changed the vampires, they were still men and women first. Now he was forced to wonder if he had chosen the right side. His gut told him that it was the *right* side, but would it be the winning one?

He shoved his concerns aside and walked the familiar path to the door. Trying the knob he found it locked and was forced to knock. Moments later the door swung open to reveal Cyrus. His eyes looked haggard and for once his suit wasn't immaculate. For a fraction of a second Derek thought, *this must be what it feels like to see your parents naked*, before shoving the thought aside lest he smile.

"How are you feeling?" he asked hesitantly.

"Humbled."

Derek held his silence as he stepped into the main room. He wouldn't quite call it a living room with its racks of books lining the walls and filling the space radiating from the center work area.

As Cyrus closed the door Derek turned to face him, a questioning look on his face.

"The last few days have been most enlightening," Cyrus continued, "Somehow I became an almost mythical figure. I now realize that I had foolishly come to believe my own legends."

"'When pride cometh, then cometh shame: but with the lowly is wisdom,'" Derek offered.

"Proverbs; very apt. Shall we continue this conversation along the way?"

Derek nodded and waited as Cyrus smoothed his rumpled shirt and donned his jacket. The pair departed the house in silence, not continuing until Derek had brought them well underway.

"You seem a lot more at ease than the last time I saw you," Derek prompted.

"I was paid a visit by Meri shortly before I phoned you last night," Cyrus explained, "There are few things in this world that put a man in his place more soundly than a conversation with that woman."

"At least she didn't shoot you," Derek laughed.

"That may have been preferable," Cyrus replied wryly.

The conversation lulled for a time as they traveled. While he had never been there Derek was well aware of Cyrus's warehouse on the outskirts of the city. From before the existence of the United States an area surrounding Cyrus's home had been declared a neutral territory where the vampiric Senate held no sway. A similar space existed around the warehouse, though it was much less of an issue since few had any reason to approach it.

"Surely Meri isn't the only thing on your mind," Derek said at last.

"No... Much of my time has been spent considering my encounter with Landina,"

"And...?"

"I am nearly certain that her end goal is not the open vampiric rule that her toadies have espoused," Cyrus explained, "She has proven far too shrewd to fall into that folly. I think that she has used that as a tool to recruit pliable followers and possibly to try and draw me out."

"Why would she want to get you involved?"

"To accomplish exactly what she has done. To neutralize me."

"But you've been in exile for centuries."

Cyrus sighed heavily. Giving him a sidelong glance Derek saw that he was considering his next words. Long practiced in the art of patience he waited for Cyrus to continue.

"Myself not withstanding, who is the oldest of us you know?" Cyrus asked at last.

"Alaric."

"And how old is he?"

"I don't know exactly, but I'd say around eight-hundred."

"Very close. He is likely the eldest in this hemisphere. And, like myself, Landina has removed him from power," he said flatly, "There was not a single elder present in the Senate aside from her."

Derek pulled up to the gate for the warehouse and entered the numbers Cyrus gave him. A heavy silence ensued as the pair waited for the gate to open before Derek pulled in and parked the car. Now that they were stopped, he turned to face Cyrus. He knew that there was a larger point in here somewhere, but he was missing what the older man had been getting at. Not saying anything he gestured for Cyrus to continue, hoping he wouldn't have to explicitly ask what Cyrus had guessed.

"Landina managed to trap me as neatly as she pleased," Cyrus continued, "The woman is not only no fool, but is far shrewder than I would like. Open rule would be a ridiculous misstep. She has to know this. That can only mean that she has some other goal in mind and is deceiving her followers just as she did me."

"But what?" Derek asked.

"I cannot say, but whatever her intention is, it involves the removal of any of the Blood old enough to challenge her."

They exited the car and Derek stood there looking at the building with an unspoken curiosity. From what he could see it looked like nothing more than a two story self storage unit. Without a word Cyrus approached the building and entered a code into the keypad at the entrance. With a small beep and a green light the system admitted them into a small vestibule of solid concrete. Derek was sure that it would take much more strength than he possessed to breach these walls. He watched with awe as Cyrus grasped the anchors in the back wall and lifted the slab into a locking mechanism.

Once inside, Derek couldn't imagine how anyone other than Cyrus would be able to access this place. The exterior was merely a facade that hid the vault within. Thick concrete walls surrounded an interior vessel of heavy Lexan. The other detail he noticed was the complete lack of lighting inside the building. Even so he could see the two story structure that held a vast collection of racks and shelving.

Cyrus again brought them past a secure entrance. This time rather than electronics, the device was a complex clockwork puzzle. Derek tried to follow the rapid movements as Cyrus worked the device, but was soon lost. His interest was instantly broken as the door opened and cold air poured over them.

"This thing's a refrigerator?" he asked incredulously.

Cyrus gave him a patient look as he stepped into the vault. "Most texts are best preserved in cool, dry air. This storage unit keeps them at fifty degrees and forty percent humidity," he explained, "There are volumes here that exist nowhere else in the world. Are you bothered by the cold?"

"No. It was just surprising."

Derek followed Cyrus through the racks of books interspersed with cases of scrolls. Occasionally he saw individual books in glass cases set apart from their peers.

"Why is this encased?" he finally asked.

"Some of these were already deteriorating when I acquired them. They are sealed from oxygen to stop further decay," Cyrus answered absently.

"So why are we here?"

"To assuage Meri."

"Good enough," Derek nodded.

They continued to move slowly through the racks. Small tags showed the title, origin and age of each item they passed. Derek suspected that Cyrus was well aware of what each of these tomes was without even looking. As they continued and he saw more of the collection Derek began to feel like a child seeing the dates for the books before him. With a glance at his hands he smiled at his sudden forced perspective.

He was recently turned as such things were measured, less than a quarter century. He was still exhilarated at the fact that he looked as young now as he had then. Looking at Cyrus he knew that he too looked the same as he had the day he had been turned. The six millennia Cyrus had lived seemed an eternity to him, but he knew that there was a possibility, however remote, that he could still be walking the earth six-thousand years from now. It was a heady thing to contemplate.

"Interesting," Cyrus said, breaking Derek's reverie.

"What's that?"

"These scrolls are not in the correct order," Cyrus observed.

"And...?"

"I am not prone to conjecture, but I can only think someone else has been here."

"Is that possible?" Derek wondered.

"I have learned to accept that things however improbable may be possible," Cyrus mused, "This may be paranoia on my part, but I can only think Landina's hand is at work here."

"Why would she want to rifle through your scrolls?"

"I could not say. However, these scrolls detail the accounts of the staff of Moses after his passing. It was a holy relic of incredible power."

"Why would she even want that?" Derek wondered aloud, "It's not like she could use it."

"I have no doubt that as easily as she manipulated me that she could use a human toady like a puppet," Cyrus replied flatly. "I wonder if this is what I was meant to discover."

Derek shrugged to himself, feeling a bit out of his depth. He offered a hand when needed as Cyrus pulled the scrolls in question out and took them to a viewing table in the center of the structure. Most of them were enclosed in glass cases, identifying marks engraved on the bottom edge. They were incomprehensible to Derek, being written in either Aramaic or Greek as Cyrus explained.

The older man set the cases in a sequence that made no sense to Derek. While he could not read them it was easy to differentiate between the two languages. They seemed mixed at random as he looked at them.

It was clear that Cyrus was reading them as easily as he read the Times. Idly, Derek wondered how many languages the old man knew before deciding he didn't want to know. Minutes ticked into hours as Cyrus studied the fragments before him and Derek began to worry about the approaching dawn. At last Cyrus gestured for him to gather the cases and the pair put them back into storage in an order carefully dictated by Cyrus.

"So is this what Meri sent you here for?"

"Her pretext was for me to find a way around the Truth Stone," Cyrus answered, "But I am certain that there was more to it than that."

Cyrus spent a short while longer studying the various texts in the collection before selecting a few to study further at home. Sensing Derek's anxiety he gestured for them to leave. As they ventured back to the heart of the city curiosity ate at Derek until he was forced to speak.

"How could Landina's men have even gotten in there?" he asked.

"As much as I hate to admit it, her power over me with the Truth Stone is near complete. If she commanded me to tell her how to access those records and then to forget about it I imagine it would have happened."

"God. That's scary."

"Quite," Cyrus replied his voice as cold as ice.

They continued in silence for a good portion of the return trip until another question prompted Derek to speak.

"You said that Moses's staff was a powerful holy relic. Does that mean the stuff in the Bible was all real?"

Cyrus sighed heavily, looking at Derek as if he were weighing him.

"I cannot answer that question. While my time on this Earth has overlapped with many of those figures I was not in a place to meet them," he answered solemnly. "This is not the first time I have been asked such things. All I can tell you is that I have no memory of a flood covering the entire world, while there were great floods in isolated regions. I never met the son of a carpenter who preformed miracles, but I did hear people speak of such things."

Derek looked slightly disappointed. He drove wrapped in his own thoughts for a while before continuing the conversation.

"So if, for example, if Moses wasn't real, how could his staff be powerful? How is it that holy water burns us if it's not divine power at work?"

Cyrus ran a hand over his face. The questions Derek asked him to answer were not new to him, but they were one of the few things to make him feel every year of his age. It was exceptionally hard for him when people expected him to be able to explain the gods that were younger than he was.

Dayflower

"Religion is the oldest form of magic," he began, "and yes, magic is real. It is what powers the Sanctuaries, the Truth Stones, and other artifacts of our kind. How, besides 'magic' could you explain my longevity?"

He paused slightly, gathering his thoughts; Derek held his peace giving him the time he needed to continue.

"Just as we are the damned Children of the Night, our blood polluted by a demon there are the Fey whose blood is touched by the angels. Are the angels or demons Christian? No, they were here far longer than Christ; though he may have been one of them."

"Fairies are real?"

"I would refrain from using that term. They find it most offensive."

"But what if a vampire is atheist? If they don't believe, how does holy water work?" Derek demanded.

"The demon inside you believes," Cyrus answered, "And I've seen our kind burned as badly at the touch of a Lotus blossom as by any cross. There are more dangers out there than you know."

The last Cyrus said with a finality that made Derek reconsider further questions. Each wrapped in their own thoughts, the pair finished the drive home in silence.

Chapter 29
Tipping Points

Cyrus set the books he had brought from the warehouse on his worktable gently. While it was possible that he was missing something he was sure that they would not offer any solutions for his problem.

Knowing what he did about Meri and her gifts he was sure she had seen something that prompted her to suggest the visit, even if she didn't know exactly why he needed to go there. Almost as if his thoughts caused her to materialize he became aware that he wasn't alone in the house. He wasn't sure if he was relieved or disappointed to realize that it wasn't Meri after all.

"Hello, Alaric. Lurking in the shadows is not your usual forte."

"I didn't realize sitting here reading was classified as 'lurking,'" Alaric replied dryly. "I have news and was surprised to find you away."

"Unless you are here to tell me that Landina has suffered an untimely demise I seriously doubt that you have any news that is of interest to me."

Alaric rose from his chair to stand across the table from Cyrus. Leaning on the edge of the limestone slab, hands splayed on its polished surface, he still carried the air of command he had as magistrate.

"It may not be of interest to you, but it does concern you. I've been in contact with the other magistrates this side of the pond. While I did leave out your personal circumstances, I explained to them what we've learned."

He straightened and began to walk around the table to stand beside Cyrus; unconsciously rolling up the sleeves of his crisp blue Oxford shirt as he walked.

"They all said the same thing," he continued, "They don't like the way the Senate has gone and will break from it, but only on one condition."

Cyrus looked up at his friend at last. His eyes were older than Alaric had ever seen them. They looked tired, causing Alaric to frown.

"That I head the new body?" Cyrus guessed.

Alaric nodded soberly. "They also want me back in charge here. Graves is apparently rubbing some people the wrong way."

"I swore I was done with all of this. You should head the new body. I have been compromised." Cyrus paused and walked away, his feet carrying him without thought through the stacks of books. His head down, hands clasped behind him he thought as he walked. "Landina will try to destroy this new Senate. You know that as well as I."

"She'll try," Alaric said heatedly, "But we need backing to bring her down. If nothing else we can take one territory at a time just like she did."

"We? I cannot do this Alaric!"

"Goddammit Cyrus, we need you. I've had a taste of the new regime she is building. I don't want to live like that. I doubt you do either!"

The pair argued back and forth, tirelessly working over the same territory time and time again. Exhausted Cyrus realized that the dawn was rapidly approaching. He held up a hand in submission, cutting off Alaric's latest argument.

"I will consider it," he acquiesced, "If we can negate the Truth Stone."

"Fair enough." Alaric straightened himself, rolling his sleeves back down and reclaiming his jacket from the hook just inside the door. "Do you have any leads?"

"About that? No. I did find some subtle clues that lead me to believe she may be seeking the Staff of Moses."

Alaric gave Cyrus a disbelieving look. "Is that even real?"

"Oh I doubt that the genuine staff exists, but I am sure that there is a piece of wood that has been revered as a relic of that name out there somewhere."

"What would a fake relic gain her?"

"You know as well as I do that if enough people have revered it for long enough that it would have real power. Imagine the threats she could level at her opposition with that."

Dayflower

"Do you think she can find it?"

Cyrus made a sour face and shook his head.

"I do not know how long she was seeking it before she ensnared me and she has had several weeks since then to make use of the information she gained from my collection. I would like to say that it is unlikely, but she is clearly adept at finding things even I had thought lost."

Alaric nodded, at a loss for words, and slipped out the door. Cyrus crossed the room and locked the door behind his friend. As he wandered back to the table he considered the books before him. One was his own work; one of only three such volumes hand bound nearly a thousand years ago. Lifting it he thumbed gently though its pages.

It had been his first attempt to catalog all of the peculiar supernatural elements associated with his kind. He recalled a section on the Truth Stones which had prompted him to select it. While his memory was nearly eidetic there were so many things he had learned over his lifetime that it was inevitable that some things would slip through the cracks of time.

Rereading the words he had written so long ago he discovered a single passage that struck him with the force of a hammer blow. "*While I have not been able to test this, it has been passed onto me by our elders that a new application of a Truth Stone will preempt an earlier application.*" Cyrus reread the passage several times until it was burned into his mind. Such a simple thing that had seemed but a curiosity so long ago now meant everything to him. All he needed to do to escape Landina's grasp was find another Truth Stone.

His hands trembled with emotion as he eased the book back onto the stack before him. He paced around the main floor of his library. The next time he saw Meri he resolved to show her how much her guidance meant to him. Once he had regained his sense of calm he made his way into the kitchen and lifted the telephone from its cradle, dialing Alaric's number.

"I found it," he said simply to Alaric's voice mail, "I will accept your proposal if you can obtain a Truth Stone immediately."

He placed the phone back on the wall and walked slowly back to the library. Leaning heavily against the table he tried to clear his mind an imagine being in control once more. The demon snarled and revolted against the notion. Cyrus pushed it down savagely, his teeth grinding from the effort. Once he had regained his composure he decided to turn in, hoping for a better situation the next day.

Meri sat alone in her apartment, knees drawn to her chest as she stared out the window. She wished it was raining; a slow cold rain would suit her mood at the moment. Instead she was forced to make do with the harsh yellow glow of the sodium lights from the parking lot across the street reflected in the grime on her window. Somehow it wasn't the same.

Since this whole tableau had begun there had been one thing that she had tried to avoid, but as she continued to eliminate possibilities it had remained. No matter what she did far too many threads ended in darkness for her. While she couldn't know if that meant she would die or not since she was unable to see her own future, the sense of dread she felt made her expect the worst.

Her fingers twirled around a bloodstained bolt from Vanessa's crossbow that had somehow made its way into her things during the fight at B block. Its wooden shaft had been soaked in anointing oil, but the worst of it had been neutralized by the vampiric blood all over it. Even now it still felt hot in her hands; not enough to burn her, but uncomfortable to hold tightly.

Meri wondered why she felt responsible for everything that was happening. There was a certain amount of self interest involved since some of the possible outcomes were catastrophic. Aside from that she felt as though she owed Cyrus something and felt the need to protect Vanessa as well. That was the piece of the puzzle she didn't understand. She didn't particularly like the girl, and it wasn't like she would feel guilty if something were to happen. Ever since she had awakened to this new life guilt was something she just didn't feel. When she killed someone to feed it was like taking an ink pen from work; she knew that it was technically wrong, but it didn't bother her.

Somehow Vanessa bypassed whatever it was that had freed her from such things. She had tried to talk to Cyrus about this and he had stonewalled her, which was frustrating to say the least. She was convinced that just as she could see glimpses of the past and future, Vanessa made people want to protect her.

"OW!" Meri spat as the tip of the bolt sliced her finger.

Her finger flew to her mouth, her tongue running across the cut as it closed. Mixed with her blood was a tiny trace of the blood from the bolt. As it entered her system she was rocked by a vision that drove her awareness of anything else away.

She woke to find herself on the floor; blood covering her face where it had flowed from her nose and eyes. A dull throb echoed in her head and vertigo threatened to throw her back to the floor as she tried to climb unsteadily to her feet. Predawn light shone through the window making her stomach sink. There was no way she could act on what she had seen now. Fighting legs that tried to buckle with every step she sought refuge from the breaking dawn.

Safe within her bedroom she clutched her phone from the nightstand as she collapsed on the bed. With wooden fingers she typed what she could manage through the hazy red film over her vision. She struggled to stay awake long enough to get her message sent. As the darkness of sleep claimed her she hoped Alaric would have time to do what she couldn't.

Chapter 30
Falling Pieces

Her first day back at school was disconcerting for Vanessa. She felt fine, but everyone kept treating her like fragile china. As much as she wanted to tell everyone that she wasn't hurt anymore she had to remember Lilah's talk before she left that morning.

"According to what everyone has heard you were all but dead. I know what we went through doesn't compare to some of the things you have faced, but it would have been traumatic for anyone else. People will treat you as though you were hurt terribly because you were. Let them."

Worse than being forced to skip track practice was the fact that Miles wouldn't allow her to fight in his self defense classes. He set her a regimen of work on the heavy bag and some general exercises, but she couldn't participate in class. The frustration left a bitter taste in her mouth making the walk home an exercise in control. It was all she could do to keep from grinding her teeth as she walked.

Her senses suddenly came to life and she had enough time to think *"vampire"* and drop into her runner's stance before she felt the impact on her back. An arm like a steel bar slammed across her throat. Instantly, the muscle memory of Miles's teaching sprang into action. As the weight of her assailant hit her she shifted herself even lower, drawing him into leaning over her.

At the moment she felt his weight shift she shoved hard; straight up instead of forward. Her head slammed into his chin hard enough that silver spots swam before her eyes. A small sliver of something soft and wet bounced off her nose leaving a red smear in the edge of her vision as it fell. Her assailant growled in pain, his grip loosened slightly as she felt drips on the top of her head.

Dayflower

Using the opening she went limp and slid through his grip. Her arm tensed and Miles's words came to her; "*You practice pulling punches, you'll do it when it counts.*" That in mind she drove her elbow back with all of her strength, hitting his groin hard enough that her fingers numbed from the impact.

She hit the ground beginning to run, pausing when she heard him collapse. Spinning around she kicked her assailant in the face. As he recoiled she dropped down, her knee on his throat.

"Tell Ivan if he tries this again I'll castrate him before I kill him."

"Who da fug ith Ivan?" he asked, blood trickling through his lips.

"If you don't work for Ivan then who?" she demanded, leaning on his throat.

"Nobody. I wad juth tying to collecth the Blood Prithe."

"Fuck. That's all I need," she growled as she stood.

Once she was away from him she settled into an easy run that got her home quickly. She had been sorely tempted to tell him to pass the word that she wasn't an easy mark. The realization that he was unlikely to be vocal about the incident convinced her that it would have been a waste of time. And if her warning were to get out she was sure that future attempts would be much more difficult to handle. Either way this was all one more headache she wished she didn't have to deal with.

She hopped up the stairs to the porch two at a time and hit the front door, using it to stop her momentum. Taking a couple of breaths to slow herself from the run she swung the door open and stepped inside, tossing her backpack onto the ruined couch as she kicked the door closed.

"Hey Mom, I'm home," she yelled as she worked her way through the continued mess in the living room on her way to the kitchen.

Lilah stepped out into the hall with an anxious look on her face. That look changed to one of fear once she saw Vanessa.

"My God Vanessa, what happened?" she asked, sweeping a strand of blood soaked hair from Vanessa's face.

"Some vamp tried to collect on the Blood Price," Vanessa explained, "all of this blood is his."

She went to step around Lilah so that she could shower and froze. Something felt wrong. Looking back at Lilah she saw an unusual tension around her eyes and realized that Lilah had called her Vanessa, not Vee. She turned to Lilah and pulled her into a light hug, trying to sense anything that might be amiss. In that moment of silence she felt a familiar presence and realized that they weren't alone.

"Where is he?" she whispered into Lilah's ear.

Lilah looked meaningfully towards the kitchen as Vanessa stepped away.

"Run," she mouthed to Lilah as she put herself between Lilah and the kitchen door.

Lilah gripped her arm, shaking her head "no." Vanessa slid her hand into her pocket and held the nine on her phone down until she heard it beep. Then she slowly began to move towards the doorway. Before she had gone two steps Ivan stepped into the hallway with a revolver held loosely in his hand.

"Hello," he said casually, "You know I've had to do some serious thinking lately. No matter what anyone tries to do you manage to scrape through somehow. I figured out the secret."

"And what might that be?" Vanessa demanded.

"It's simple really. Everyone goes at you directly. That doesn't work. So I'm going to go after the ones you love." He punctuated his statement by leveling the revolver at Lilah's head.

"Do what you say or you'll kill her?"

"Oh no. I'm going to kill her one way or another; but if you don't do what I tell you, when I tell you to do it, I will turn her."

"You can't touch her. Graves declared her Familiar Blood," Vanessa said with a cocky smile.

Ivan's laugh was booming. He looked at Vanessa, grinning with genuine mirth. A sick feeling settled in Vanessa's stomach as her smile dissolved.

"You don't get it do you," he said, suddenly quiet. "You've got a Blood Price. I can tear out her throat and toss her on the steps of the Met and when I turn you in it'll be on you."

The cold smile on his face sent a chill through her and Lilah both. It was all Vanessa could do to keep from retching. She reeled at the notion of Lilah becoming his progeny and tried desperately to figure out what she could do. Ivan watched with satisfaction as what he had said sunk in. Reaching in his back pocket he produced a set of handcuffs that he tossed at Lilah.

"Put them on her."

"No," Lilah stated defiantly, "You can shoot me, I won't do it."

Dayflower

"That wasn't a request," Ivan sneered, "Put the cuffs on her."

Vanessa could feel the force of the compulsion Ivan leveled at Lilah. With a small whimper she stepped forward and snapped a cuff on one of Vanessa's wrists. Her movements were jerky as she resisted the compulsion, but she couldn't stop herself from obeying. When Lilah went to pull Vanessa's arms behind her to snap the other cuff in place Vanessa didn't resist. She hoped her attempt to call for help had worked. Almost as if he could read her mind Ivan stepped in front of her and stuck his hands in her pockets, pulling out her phone.

"And I'm not going to have you tracked by this little piece of work," he said as he hurled the phone through the front of their china hutch with a crash.

Flexing her wrist Vanessa was grateful to find that the cuffs were loose. Ivan had compelled Lilah to put the cuffs on, but the details were left to her. Vanessa felt a swell of pride at Lilah's ability to assert her own will. She knew from experience how hard most people found it to resist.

"Now I have a little business to take care of. Have a seat princess," Ivan said, shoving Vanessa towards the floor.

She twisted her arms behind her and managed to slip one hand free of the cuffs. Using the inertia of Ivan's shove she spun away from him swinging the end of the handcuffs still attached to her wrist against the side of his head. The blow made a cut along the side of his jaw that left a line of blood down his face as it healed.

With a snarl he brought the revolver up and smashed it into the side of her head, knocking Vanessa to her knees. Before she could rise he delivered a savage kick to her stomach that doubled her over in pain. All she could do was gasp for breath as he wrenched her arms behind her back and secured the handcuffs tight enough that her hands ached.

Ivan turned to Lilah just as she swung a floor lamp into the side of his head making him stagger to the side. With a speed Lilah couldn't believe he pulled the remnants of the lamp from her grasp and hurled it across the room. In a heartbeat he was on her, his teeth sinking into her neck.

"NO!" Vanessa shrieked as she struggled to get to her feet.

Before she managed to do anything the sound of sirens began to fill the air. In desperation she began to kick at Ivan hoping to draw his attention from Lilah. He lifted his head, dropping Lilah's limp body to the floor when he saw red and blue lights begin to fill the room.

"Damn you," he spat as he grabbed Vanessa, slinging her over his shoulder.

He tore out of the back door, which she now saw was a shattered ruin, and ran into the night. The city flew by as he ran reminding Vanessa in a twisted way of the night Clarius had carried her away from her parents so long ago.

Chapter 31
Court

The absolute darkness of the steel box Ivan had shoved her in made Vanessa wish she still had her vampiric sight. Only feeling the sunset gave her any idea how long she had been locked up here. She wished she knew what he was waiting for. There had been plenty of time the previous night for him to hand her over to the Court.

It was tempting to guess that he did it just to make her suffer more. While the cramped confines had caused her more than enough pain and humiliation she knew better than to think that was his reason. Ivan always liked to be more hand-on when it came to inflicting suffering.

She gave one more halfhearted kick at the lid of the box. The thick steel barely rang at her kick, much less suffered any damage. Likewise the cuffs still held her arms painfully behind her back. She had never bothered to try and break them; even at her strongest she had never been able to do something like that. If she had more room to move she could have at least managed to work her legs through to get her hands in front of her, but the box was too tight for her to move much at all.

A deafening rattle made her wince and wish she could cover her ears. Suddenly the lid to the box opened and she was hauled out roughly. Bright halogen lights burned her eyes as she blinked and tried to get some sense of where she was. Finally forced to look down by the light she got the answer in the familiar concrete floor beneath her. Blood stains still sat dark in places from her last visit here.

"Jesus," a voice she didn't recognize grunted with disgust, "Clean her up and put something else on her. Graves won't want her brought in like that."

Dayflower

Shortly after that she was hoisted in the air unable to do anything but burn in embarrassment as Ivan's goons ripped her jeans off and washed her off with frigid water from a hose. While she was still shivering and wet a pair of pajama pants decorated with princesses was shoved on her and tied tighter than was really comfortable.

As her eyes adjusted to the light she looked around and saw the gray contractor site tool box she had been locked in. Ivan sat on the rail at the top of the stairs watching as his men did his bidding; somehow she was positive that they were all his offspring.

The one holding her up dropped her to the floor followed by a rough shove in the direction of the stairs. Her legs rebelled at the sudden demand of walking and dumped her to the floor, her head bouncing painfully off of the bottom step. He simply grabbed her collar and dragged her up the stairs. Once again brought to her feet she winced as feeling returned to her limbs.

Ivan hopped lightly from the rail and forced her head up till their eyes met. Hate burned hot in Vanessa's chest as she glowered at his satisfied look. Smirking, he pulled a leash and collar from his jacket pocket. When he went to snap it around her neck Vanessa writhed violently and tried to bite him. Still smiling Ivan backhanded her hard enough that black spots swam in her vision. Trickles of blood from her nose and mouth joined that from her forehead.

"I just want to make it clear to you that even though everyone else seems interested in what you are, I don't give a shit," Ivan said, holding her head up. "And please try to escape. I could use some fun."

Vanessa lunged forward suddenly, driving the top of her head into Ivan's nose. She braced herself for the blow she was sure would come, but he just chuckled as he wiped the blood from his nose. Reaching in his pocket he pulled out what looked like a car alarm remote. His expression never changed as he hit the button and Vanessa collapsed to the floor screaming.

"Try something like that again and I hit the button. You run, I hit the button. You get the idea?"

"Fuck you," she spat, still struggling to rise.

"Mouth off..." Ivan said, his words trailing off as he pressed the remote again.

Dayflower

This time she was expecting it so she managed to stay upright. Still, her muscles tensed painfully and a growl escaped her throat despite her effort to stay silent. Once she was able to move again Ivan pulled her along behind him through the apartment building and into the parking lot. A battered old sedan sat waiting with the trunk open.

Soon they were moving through the night, not that Vanessa could see any of the passing city from within the trunk of the car. Determined to do something about her situation she kicked at the interior of the trunk liner over the tail lights until she heard them shatter. Before long the car was stopped just as she had hoped.

Small slivers of red and blue flashing light managed to penetrate her prison. Her heart pounded in her chest as she listened desperately for the officer to approach the car. The moment she could hear him outside the car she began to scream and rabbit kick the lid of the trunk. She couldn't make out the words, but the tone was clear. The officer had obviously heard her and was not pleased by what he heard. Her hope died as she heard Ivan slam his hand on the side of the car.

"You saw nothing wrong. We fixed the lights and you sent us on our way. Do you understand?"

"Yes sir. Thank you sir," the cop replied, his voice thick with the weight of Ivan's compulsion.

The flashing lights disappeared followed shortly by the sound of the squad car pulling away. Vanessa screamed as the collar shocked her again burning away any hope she still possessed. Her eyes burned with tears she refused to let fall for the rest of the trip. She wasn't surprised when Ivan activated the collar again before opening the trunk. With her background she couldn't blame him for expecting her to try something, no matter how much she hated him for doing it. Ivan seemed distrustful of her new passivity as they prepared to go. He wound the leash tight around his wrist as he led her up the familiar walk to the cemetery.

Just as she had every time she visited the place Vanessa couldn't help but think of the irony of the Night Court meeting on hallowed ground. As they entered the mausoleum that hid the entrance to the gymnasium sized chamber beneath she thought of when Alaric had ordered it built nearly two-hundred years ago. *"Let even the earth around us remind us each night of the danger we face even here lest we grow careless in our isolation,"* he had declared.

Dayflower

Even though the space was shrouded in darkness she could picture the thick stone pillars and arches that held back the burning soil that surrounded them. No light shone in the Night Court, and normally none was needed. Here and there she saw swaths a blue-white light where someone was using their cell phone. She wished desperately for a moment that she still had hers, even if it would do her little good.

She listened numbly as Magistrate Graves opened court. It was clear that Graves knew what was going to happen. Instead of simply opening court for the social vying and scheming that took place she read the full liturgy of the Senate's authority and asked for business to be brought before the court. Immediately Ivan stepped forward, dragging Vanessa along behind him.

"I, Ivan Nivikov, claim the Blood Price on Vanessa Miller," he bellowed loudly, shoving Vanessa out before him.

While she couldn't see anything it was hard to miss the collective gasp that filled the room. Silence held for several seconds as he pushed her forward away from the crowd and into the empty space before the dais. Her feet stumbled over an uneven spot in the tiled floor telling her that they were near the center of the room. Picturing the room in her mind she imagined Graves sitting on the dais in front of her. Normally a petitioner would approach the magistrate, but she knew Ivan would want the best vantage for the audience around them. Just as she had guessed she was jerked to a stop well short of Graves.

"Very well. Does anyone here speak for the damned?" Graves demanded.

"I am Alaric de Valois and I will stand for her," Alaric declared, shocking Vanessa and sending a buzz throughout the room.

"That is a bit surprising," Graves said over the murmurs, "From what I understand one of the charges she is facing is telling you to... How did she put it?"

"Yes she told me to shove my authority up my ass," Alaric answered coldly, "That was under my tenure and if I chose not to bring charges for the affront that is my business."

"Quite to the contrary, since there were serious doubts raised about how you handled this court many of your decisions are up for reconsideration."

Alaric came to stand beside Vanessa resting his hand on her shoulder. While she was grateful that he would stand for her she was just as surprised as everyone else. Guilt over how she had treated him added to the misery she already felt.

"Is Cyrus coming?" she whispered during a pause.

Before Alaric could answer a scream was torn from her as the collar knocked her to the floor with a shock harder than any she had yet received.

"Do that again and court be damned I will rip that smirk off of your head," Alaric warned Ivan. He leaned down to Vanessa, "Later," he told her in a whisper.

Ivan glared at Alaric with palpable hatred. Slowly he raised the hand holding the remote and pressed the button again wrenching another shriek from Vanessa. Alaric's hand shot out encompassing Ivan's and squeezed, shattering the remote. His other jabbed towards Ivan's face. Catching it Ivan pushed back, the pair grappling over Vanessa who remained crouched between them.

"I've been waiting to take you down a peg or two, old man," Ivan said through clenched teeth.

"That will be enough of that," Graves bellowed, silencing them.

The two men stepped apart, glares still being exchanged between them; Alaric reaching down to pull Vanessa to her feet. Guiding her face upward he placed a vial against her lips whispering for her to drink. She knew it was Cyrus's blood as it flowed over her tongue. Warmth flowed throughout her body wiping away the worst of the pain. Feeling even returned to her hands which had been numb for hours.

Opening her eyes she was relieved to find that she could see once more. Alaric moved to take the collar from her neck, but Ivan stopped him.

"Magistrate, considering the past record of the damned, I feel she should stay bound," he said loudly.

"I agree. Alaric, what can you possibly say in her defense?"

Letting his hands fall to his sides he drew himself up. The man who had been magistrate for so long was still clearly visible in his bearing. Many of the audience shifted under his gaze even now.

"Most of the charges against her are affronts to me, not you, your Honor. The most serious charge is the creation of the monster Anton. I maintain that she acquitted herself of that in his destruction by her own hand."

"I hope you realize how inadequate those arguments are," Graves replied coldly.

"As you say," Alaric nodded, "But I also think no one deserves to face the dawn without a voice in their defense."

Graves nodded thoughtfully before continuing. "Very well. I must say, though, that while your voice is... appreciated, it says something that he who is bound as her creator cared not to come speak on her behalf."

"Cyrus is indisposed and asked for me to speak in his stead."

Ivan chuckled, earning him a heated look from Alaric.

Graves rose from her seat and walked across the room to stand before Vanessa.

"While it brings me no pleasure to pronounce judgment on any of the Blood I can not feel as though this is anything but justice at work," she began before Ivan held up a hand interrupting her.

"During my capture of the damned, a woman named Lilah Monroe, declared Familiar Blood was killed. I am sure that will require action by you Honor and wished to make it known that this happened before my claiming of the Blood Price and I wish it included in my account."

Graves made a sour face as though Ivan's words left a bitter taste in her mouth. She looked at him with an ire nearly mirroring Alaric's.

"While I consider that to be a deliberate abuse of the law and as such find it sickening, I must admit that it is within the letter of the law. Consider it noted," she answered before turning her attention back to Vanessa. "As I was saying; custom would dictate you to stand before the dawn. Since all here know how futile that would be we must look to other options."

Vanessa's stomach knotted as she spoke. Even before the words were spoken she knew what fate she would face, her mind going back to the first time she had ever stood before the court.

"I hereby order the continuation of the execution of a child turned as ordered so long ago by my predecessor," Grave continued, confirming Vanessa's fears.

"Magistrate," Alaric said, stepping closer to her, "Vanessa was gifted with the age of an elder by Cyrus. She is exempt from that fate."

"No longer," Graves answered, "The Senate has ruled her life forfeit in any way the Court sees fit."

Dayflower

The two argued for hours with Alaric bringing up every legal argument he could, some of which seemed absurd even to Vanessa, and Magistrate Graves striking each one down. It was clear that he was stalling for time even though Vanessa couldn't begin to guess why. At last he had exhausted even the most flimsy pretexts to argue and the magistrate was clearly beyond the limits of her patience.

"Since there is no justification possibly left to argue for the preservation of the damned, her execution will commence. Ivan Nivikov, the price has been redeemed and all transgressions that lessen you before Us now weigh upon the damned."

At those words from the Magistrate Ivan nodded and retreated to rejoin the audience. A gesture from Graves sent two of her bailiffs to take possession of Vanessa while a third went to summon the executioner.

"Thank you for trying. I know you didn't owe me anything," Vanessa told Alaric, her voice rough. "And for what it's worth, I'm sorry I was such a pain in the ass."

"This is what it took to get an apology from you? Considering the circumstances I accept. Though hopefully this isn't over," Alaric said with a glance at his watch.

The bailiffs took hold of Vanessa lightly with meaningful glances at Alaric. He shook his head and placed a hand on Vanessa's cheek. "I'm sorry too, but according to the law she's right."

"I know."

Thoughts of one last attempt to escape ran through Vanessa's mind, but even when she had possessed all of her strength and speed she had failed to escape the court; she hadn't even been bound then. Her attention was drawn by a series of booms from the entrance. She saw now for the first time that the heavy steel doors were closed, an unbelievable departure from custom. For a moment she allowed herself to be hopeful, sure it was Cyrus. Her hopes were dashed by two words from the Magistrate.

"Ignore him."

They brought her forward to where the block had been placed over a tarp on the floor. The executioner stood nearby holding the same ax as last time. Strangely she wondered if it was the same man. Tears ran down Vanessa's cheeks as they pushed her to kneel before the block. She didn't resist either the tears or the bailiffs as they bent her over, placing her neck on the end of the log.

Dayflower

Her tears hit the tarp with a steady tic-tic-tic echoing the sound of Cyrus beating on the doors. The rest of the room was still in anticipation. Vanessa could hear the executioner raise his ax in the silence of the room. Focusing on her bond she closed her eyes filling her mind with the words *Goodbye Cyrus*.

With a grunt the executioner swung his blade as an exceptionally loud boom echoed through the court. Wind ruffled Vanessa's hair as she braced herself for the impact. She felt the blade bite the back of her neck and heard a hard "thunk." In shock she wondered that she didn't feel something more than the slight sting on the back of her neck. There was no life passing before her eyes or dark oblivion, only silence.

"I believe that will be all," a familiar voice said from above her. Then she felt the jostle of movement around her as those around her stepped away. "I am sorry, Little Flower," Cyrus continued, pulling her upright, "I did not expect the door to be barred against me."

"This is a touching repetition of history," Graves interjected, "But her sentence will stand according to the laws of the Senate."

"The Senate has become a pale mockery of the body it once was. I have decided this is a state of affairs that must end."

Cyrus turned from the dais and knelt, grasping the cuffs that bound Vanessa and pulled them apart. Once both hands were free he dropped the ruins to the floor and returned his attention to the Magistrate. He was not surprised to see Landina step up beside Graves.

"Good. Your presence simplifies many things," he commented calmly.

"Funny, I was about to say the same thing. Of course that was the point of dragging the brat in here, aside from the removal of an abomination."

Landina stepped from the dais and walked towards them. It was now plain that she carried the end of a shattered wooden rod, her hand clad in a gauntlet of hardened leather. Graves followed her down and several others stepped from the audience to form a ring around Cyrus, Vanessa, and Alaric.

"I hereby open this session of the Blood Senate," she declared loudly, "You three stand accused of attempting to break the power of this august body. How do you plea?"

Dayflower

Alaric stepped forward facing her, malice shining coldly in his eyes. "The territories here no longer recognize the rule of a Senate led by you."

"You no longer head this territory," Graves replied, "And I denounce your claim."

"The other Magistrates stand with us and by their authority I'll be taking my territory back."

Several of the gathered circle stepped forward and voiced their assent. Vanessa marveled at so many magistrates being present.

"That sounds like confession of guilt to me," Landina declared.

Alaric turned to face her, his mouth open to speak. The words never materialized as Landina swung forward swiftly and laid the staff on the side of his neck. Before he even had time to scream flames enveloped him turning him to motes of ash in a second. The entire room stood silent, stunned by what had just happened.

"And so begins the reign of the dark queen and the end of our democratic senate," Cyrus observed, disgust dripping from every word.

"Shut up and sit down you relic," Landina spat, "I may kill you someday when I tire of making you dance."

Cyrus strode towards her confidently, "Your hold is broken. Now if you recall I made you a promise," he said as he reached towards her.

Recoiling, Landina swung the staff at Cyrus, the jagged end aimed at his heart. Using the last of the power granted by the blood she had consumed Vanessa dove at the staff with every shred of speed she possessed. She caught the haft of it sideways under her arm, both hands gripping it. Her momentum carried the point away from Cyrus and spun Landina around.

Fire coursed through her at the staff's touch; searing agony wrenching a scream from her that tore at her throat. She felt as though her very bones were burning within her as light overwhelmed her. Then just as suddenly it was over.

All eyes in the room were on her as her scream died on her lips. Reacting on instinct she gave a hard pull on the staff. Though Landina was infinitely stronger, the gauntlet gave her a poor grip and the end slid through her fingers. Lashing out with the staff as if it was a sword Vanessa slashed the sharp end toward

Landina's face. The elder vampire dodged the swing easily and danced back away as Vanessa continued her attack. Her next step back was halted as she backed into Cyrus's immovable form. The dodge came up just short enough that Vanessa's swing grazed Lanina's cheek. At that slight touch she shared Alaric's fate, her ashes drifting down to cover Cyrus and Vanessa.

"That was not what I had in mind, but I think it a fitting enough end." Cyrus brushed himself somewhat futilely before turning to the audience around them. "This body will meet here tomorrow night. Any absent will be assumed to share Landina's folly. I guarantee that they will envy the woman her fate."

"Where's Ivan!" Vanessa snarled, still brandishing the staff.

The audience stared at her in mute disbelief. Long seconds passed as everyone was afraid to move. Cyrus placed a hand on Vanessa's shoulder and guided her to the door, the crowd parting before them.

"Everyone leave," he commanded.

As they filtered out he made it clear he was marking each face. His hand still rested on Vanessa who glowered at them as they passed. At last they were alone and he turned to her.

"Are you well?"

"I'm exhausted, but I feel fine. Are you okay?"

"I am improved. I have much lost ground to gain, but that shall happen in due course."

Vanessa nodded in understanding. Only then did she realize how tense she still was and forced herself to relax. Taking a deep breath she looked down, dreading the words she had to say.

"Cyrus, I think Lilah's gone," tears formed in her eyes as she talked, unable to look up at him. "Ivan killed her and it's my fault."

"Flower, we will talk of Lilah later. I am aware of what happened. Derek and Meri are with her."

"She's alive?"

"I said we will talk of her later. Can you still see in the darkness? Do you still feel our bond?"

Vanessa was stunned and confused by the sudden turn of his questions. She had to stop and think about what he was asking before she answered.

"I can see, but it's different. I can still feel you, but it's not like it was. Why? Does that mean something?"

"We shall see," he answered, leading her out of the chamber through the ruined door. "There is still much to be done before we worry about that though."

Chapter 32
The Precipice

The walk back to Cyrus's was long and left them arriving there shortly before dawn. Vanessa had tried to suggest they take a cab or something to speed the trip, but Cyrus refused saying he had too much to think through before they got there. Especially upsetting to Vanessa was the way he refused to talk about Lilah, though it was clear he knew something. Finally as they entered, him locking the door behind them, she lost her patience.

"Cyrus, stop putting me off. Where's Lilah?" Vanessa demanded.

Cyrus heaved a weighty sigh and put his hands on Vanessa's shoulders. A frown turned the corners of his mouth as he sighed a second time. Vanessa's stomach sank as she began to expect the worst.

"I have done something that I swore I would never do, Little Flower, but you currently hold the ability to undo it," he said gravely with a gesture toward the staff.

"No..." she whispered, tears beginning to form in the corners of her eyes.

"That is why I was detained. Derek's connections informed him that something had transpired at your house. He contacted Alaric and I about Lilah's condition. By the time I reached the hospital she was fading. I tried to give her my blood, but..."

"But it can't heal blood loss," Vanessa interrupted.

"Yes. So I tried to bond her as a familiar in the hope that it would give her enough strength," he continued, his face dark. "It did not. The only hope she has left is the fact that I did give her enough to turn her."

He slid his hands up to cup Vanessa's chin, tipping her face up to meet his eyes. The look he gave her felt as though he were looking through her into her soul. Her grip tightened on the rough surface of the staff still hanging in her grip. She understood what Cyrus had meant about undoing what he had done. Nodding, she pulled away and held herself against a chill she suddenly felt.

"She was your mother. While I knew her longer, you knew her in a way I never could. It is unfair of me to place this burden upon you, but the loss is yours."

She spun around, hot angry tears wetting her cheeks. Cyrus didn't retreat from her glare, but lowered his head in remorse. She was furious at him for forcing her to make this choice, at Ivan for having taken her mother away, and at vampires in general for all of the pain she had been through. For a precarious moment thoughts of vengeance filled her mind. After centuries of being the hunted she finally understood what drove the hunters. It was tempting to succumb to that cold rage. Hatred tried to slide into the hole Lilah had left in her heart.

Looking down at the staff sitting in her hands she knew she had the tools to accomplish it if that was the path she chose. She realized she was standing in the heart of one of Meri's tipping points. Gripping the staff she considered how easy it would be to fall; to let the rage in. Cyrus stood there impassively watching her struggle, surely knowing the kinds of thoughts she entertained.

"Is that what she would want for you?" was all he said.

Vanessa shook her head.

"She won't be the same will she?" she asked after a long pause.

"No she will not. She will still be Lilah, but she will be changed."

"She won't be my mom anymore," she murmured.

It wasn't a question and Cyrus didn't answer. Stepping up to her he embraced her, carefully avoiding the staff. They stood like that for several minutes, her tears soaking into his shirt leaving a mask of her sorrow on him. Once she was done she stepped away wiping her eyes.

"Where is she?"

Wordlessly Cyrus guided her to the stairs. She walked ahead of him already knowing that they were going to his room. When she stepped through the door she saw Lilah on the bed. Her pale blond hair was spilled out across the pillow and her hands were clasped on her breast. Were it not for the horrible wound on her throat she could have been asleep. Derek rose from the chair he had been holding vigil from and stepped over beside Cyrus.

"Cyrus, it's Meri..." he began in a whisper, stopping at Cyrus's raised hand.

"You know she told me once that she used to fantasize about convincing you to turn her when she was young," Vanessa said softly, "But that now that she was older the idea of eternal life seemed like more of a burden. I wonder if her soul will find rest now, or if she is already damned."

"I have walked this earth longer than most gods have existed. I find it hard to believe someone with a heart as good as her would be turned away from any heaven I have heard of," Cyrus answered. "As far as my blood damning her; I have opened the door, she has not yet passed through it."

Gently Vanessa lifted Lilah's hands and placed the staff in her grip. There was no sound, no light. Only the fact that Lilah's skin surrendered its last hint of color to the gray pallor of death showed that anything had changed. Running her finger down Lilah's cheek the words "I love you" fell soundlessly from her lips. She turned from the bed and scrubbed her eyes with the heel of her palms.

"I kinda thought there would be more..." she said, her words trailing off.

"That is often the way of the world."

"Did I do the right thing, letting her go?"

"Do you honestly believe that this is what she would have preferred?" Cyrus asked, waiting for her to nod. "Then you did."

Exhausted, both mentally and physically, Vanessa left them for the solitude of her own room. Closing the door she took her violin from its case and began to play Lilah's favorite piece.

"Is she alright?" Derek asked in a low voice.

"No. She has suffered a hurt so large she has yet to find the true depth of her pain. We should continue this upstairs."

He turned, leading them up the stairs to the main room. Passing through the stacks of books Cyrus felt uneasy. He also doubted if his actions had been the right ones. Many he had already decided were not. His inactivity had cost him so much. For the first time he weighed the cost he, and others at his behest, had paid protecting Vanessa and entertained a moment of doubt.

"What happened tonight?" Derek continued as soon as Cyrus stopped.

"The long work of repairing the damage done by my idleness was begun," Cyrus replied, "And at a terrible price. What were you going to say about Meri?"

Derek grimaced, glancing at his phone one last time before sticking it in his pocket.

"She went out after Ivan alone. That was hours ago and I can't reach her."

"Unfortunately in my current condition it is too close to dawn for anything to be done about it tonight. We can only hope she knows what she is doing."

"I'll see about having someone come for Lilah," Derek offered contritely.

"Yes. Please do. Have them place the staff on the table here," he answered, coming to lean on his work table.

"I should go, I need to catch up to Alaric too."

"I am sorry to say that Alaric is lost."

"What happened?" Derek gasped, coming to stand next to Cyrus.

"Landina had found a way to hold the staff and used it to kill Alaric when he defied her. She was attempting to strike me with it as well when Vanessa foolishly interceded."

"Foolishly? We couldn't afford to lose you too."

"Landina's blow would never have touched me. One of the benefits of my age, I suppose, is speed equal to my strength."

Derek nodded and left leaving Cyrus to wonder if Meri was going to be added to his losses.

Meri sat on the couch impatiently waiting. She tried not to think about the first time she had seen this room. There was a certain symmetry to thinking things may end in the same place they had started. She couldn't see what happened after this. It was possible that it was simply because she couldn't see her own future, but her gut told her that it was more than that.

It was tempting to pace or go to the front of the abandoned theater, but she knew her only hope of taking care of Ivan was to catch him by surprise. All of the things that could ruin that for her ran through her mind. The bond would betray her if he cared to think about it, likewise he could easily sense her presence once he was close. She just hoped that by the time he was close enough for that it would be too late.

Dayflower

Her anxiety mounted as the minutes ticked by. Whatever was going to happen at court should be over by now and dawn was rapidly approaching. She wasn't prone to doubting her visions, but she was beginning to wonder if she had been wrong when she had seen him come here. She had managed to skirt disaster on so many tipping points this night. Disaster was still in the cards if things went wrong with Lilah, but she had done all she could there. What she knew for certain was that Ivan going free would be almost as bad as Landina.

For the third time she checked the Sig and her taser. On impulse she moved from the couch to behind the door. Before she had settled in the door exploded in a cloud of splinters. Ivan was in the room before the shards of the door had landed, pistol in hand. He fired as he moved, bullets cutting an arc through the room right where Meri had just been sitting.

Not hesitating, Meri opened fire on Ivan's back. The first round caught him just below the shoulder blade, but he rolled to the side moving under the remaining shots. Meri tried to follow him with the gun, but he was faster. Before she could pull away he grabbed her ankle, gripping it so tightly that she felt bones crack under the pressure. She growled like a feral cat, firing as her leg buckled under her. The bullets found their mark, but Ivan shrugged off the wounds and lurched to his feet.

Desperate, Meri fired the taser hoping to immobilize him. He roared as he grabbed the wires out of the air and ripped them from the face of the gun. Blood trickled from the corners of his mouth and soaked his shirt from half a dozen holes in his chest as he stood over her, his face a mask of rage.

"Now I will break you," he wheezed, lunging for her.

As she raised the Sig to fire again he slapped her hand aside with enough force to shatter the bones in her hand. With one hand he gripped her throat and lifted her from the floor. She struggled to fight back, but she couldn't reach past his shoulder. Almost casually he caught her injured arm and twisted cruelly until her shoulder snapped. A scream escaped her through clenched teeth.

Visions swam behind her eyes overlaying everything she saw. She knew she was in the heart of a crucial moment and she could feel it slipping away from her. Not knowing what else she could do she gripped Ivan's arm in her good hand and focused on all of the pain and rage she felt. She gathered all of the darkness she held inside and for the first time willed it outward. Every ounce of fear and despair she had felt or seen since she had been reborn poured out of her into Ivan. He screamed at her, blood flying from his lips and hit her hard enough that she tasted blood. All it did was add to the torrent pouring back into him.

After what seemed an eternity he dropped her and staggered back. His eyes were the solid red of blood and a soundless howl twisted his face. Meri watched from where he had dropped her to the floor as he slowly collapsed in front of her. Exhaustion made her feel as though her limbs were made of lead. When she tried to rise her leg still buckled under her. She could feel the sunrise on the horizon, robbing her of what little strength she had left. Glancing through the ruined door she was grateful for the long shadows of the tall buildings around them.

"Whatever happened to fast healing," she croaked, her throat still raw from Ivan's grip on it.

Crawling to his body she knew she had pushed her reserves to the limit. She had never used her ability that way before and wondered if that had something to do with her slow recovery. Not to mention the fact that she was anxious about how long it would keep Ivan down.

Using her good arm and leg she dragged him inch by inch through the ruined theater towards the door. Her head was in agony and she had to fight to keep her eyes open as the sky lightened outside. By the time she had him to the front entrance sunlight was beginning to filter through the opening.

Heedless of the stabbing pain in her head she reached out for any impressions she could find. While everything was hazy she saw enough to know that she had to make sure Ivan was finished for good. Grimacing, she resumed her trek. By the time she had him to the sidewalk her skin was peeling away like scorched paper. The pain was unimaginable, but she tried to find satisfaction in the fact that Ivan was burned worse than she was.

It was all she could do to get him clear of the building and into full light. Once that was done she scrambled to return to the protection of the theater. She could move faster now that she wasn't pulling him along, but her progress was still slow. All she could do was roll to the side once she was past the doorway before everything went black.

Chapter 33
Aftermath

"Is she going to make it?" Vanessa asked, peering past Cyrus and Derek at Meri's burned form.

They stood in Cyrus's bedroom where Meri was situated on a hospital bed beside Cyrus's own. While there were no monitors or other medical devices there was an IV stand laden with bags of blood feeding her.

"I can not say," Cyrus answered, "I have never seen one of us burned so badly that had not succumbed to the light. The fact that she is has survived so far is encouraging."

"Can't you give her some of your blood? I mean she'd heal faster, right?"

"Yes she would, but that would create a bond between us that I do not want to inflict upon her without her permission."

Vanessa gave him a sour look and slipped out of the room. The men could hear the heavy thuds of her taking the stairs two at a time followed shortly by the impact of her falling into one of the armchairs. Cyrus winced at the commotion.

"Thank you for finding her and bringing her to me," he said to Derek once the noise had died down.

"I'm just glad my guys managed to reach me in time. From what I could see of the scene I'm fairly sure Ivan won't be an issue anymore."

"Are you certain that is who the remains belonged to?"

"As certain as we can be. There was an ugly fight inside. The forensics guys found a pistol they matched to prints that a few of us knew were Ivan's. Not to mention I can't think of anyone else she would hate enough to drag into sunlight like that."

"True," Cyrus agreed. "We should leave her to rest. There is something I wish to discuss with you."

Dayflower

"What's that?" Derek prompted as they made their way upstairs to join Vanessa.

Once they were at the top Cyrus took a seat and steepled his fingers before him. True to habit he gathered his thoughts for several minutes before speaking. When he finally dropped his hands he gave Derek an appraising look.

"How would you feel about assuming the mantle of Magistrate?"

"What? No, I'm way too young for that," Derek protested.

"Landina was right about one thing. It is time for some of the old customs to fall. We have been tied to age and station for too long. That is what led us to the situation we were in with her. If she had gotten her way I am sure that we would now have a monarchy instead of the Senate."

"That's what you think she was up to? This whole nightmare was so she could play queen!" Vanessa spat.

"Basically, yes. It is the only solution that makes sense."

"But why drag us into it all like she did?"

"She had already manipulated Anton into removing most of the other elders. I have yet to determine exactly how she accomplished that, but I have spoken with some contacts I maintain in Europe and they verified my suspicions there. I was the last big threat to her power. As for you, my Little Flower, aside from being bait for my involvement; you have unfortunately made a lot of the Blood unhappy over the years. Eliminating you would have served as a great token to gain acceptance here."

"That's all fine, but if we don't go by age, what will we do?" Derek interjected.

"It is time that ability is paramount. Alaric already relied upon you and your ties to the human authorities to accomplish much of what he needed done. It only makes sense for you to take his place. Unfortunately I will be placed in a position much like we prevented Landina from taking to see these changes through."

Cyrus rose and began to pace around the room, hands behind his back.

"I helped found the Senate and write the laws we follow so I feel no hypocrisy in ruling until you and your new peers manage to create a new order that will force my obsolescence," he concluded.

Derek shoved himself away from the table and crossed the room to grab his jacket from the hook by the door. "Speaking of that, you'll have a forced audience waiting on you soon," he reminded the older man.

"True. Go ahead, I will be along shortly."

After Derek left Cyrus busied himself preparing to go. Vanessa grasped his arm and turned him to face her. While she wasn't crying her eyes were bloodshot and damp. Cyrus reached out and laid a hand on her cheek.

"What is it, Flower?"

"What about me? Us? I don't know what to do, what I am."

Cyrus set down the ancient tome he had been holding and brought her to sit across from him.

"I tried to remove you from this life, this world of darkness, and I was wrong in doing so. Meri was right before and I have been blind when it comes to you. I wanted you to have what you wished so badly that I refused to see the truth. We have paid a heavy toll for that. You will have a home here if you wish it until you are old enough in the human world to care for yourself," he began.

"Please Cyrus, don't dodge me this time," she cut in, "Lilah told me that Meri had guessed I was a therian, what does that mean?"

He clasped her hands in his and looked at her in that searching way he had.

"A therian is what happens when a vampire undergoes a full transference. It is what you nearly became the first time you saw Jason, and is what he was after you turned him."

"But I'm nothing like that."

"Sometimes, rarely mind you, the demon will overwhelm the soul of the person turned, but will hide within them. They are incredibly powerful, but also terribly susceptible to the things that harm us. Usually they will only surface during the new moon so that there is no light to harm them. They are the source of tales you hear of werewolves, and like in the stories they rarely survive more than a lunar cycle or two before they are hunted and destroyed."

"So if I'm not that, what am I?" she pleaded.

"When you turned Jason I had warned you that the balance had to be perfect. Some of the demon remained within you making you a shadow of what you were. In some ways you were a Familiar to yourself. I was blind not to see it."

Dayflower

"But what about now?" she interrupted, "I still feel you, but everything is different. I don't feel like my old self is still in there somewhere like I did."

"The staff burned the demon out of you. That part of you is gone. As for the rest?" Cyrus paused, wringing his hands together, "This is only the conjecture of an old man, but I believe that you have lived too long in the shadow of the supernatural to be untouched by it. You are something new."

"What if you're wrong? What if the vampire is still in me?"

Cyrus reached out and lifted a lock of Vanessa's hair from her shoulder and held it before her. With his other hand he brought her fingers up beside it.

"The demon denies change. If it still held you then this would not have happened," he said as he rolled the hair with his thumb. She saw now that the normally raven hair she had all of her existence was shot through with strands of white. "Likewise your nails are already longer than they were. You may not be 'normal' as you put it, but you are not of the Blood any longer."

Releasing her he rose, reclaiming the items he had been holding. Moving to the door her turned back to see her looking at her hands, shock clear on her face.

"What happens now?" she asked her voice flat and hollow.

"That is something we will find out together," Cyrus returned to rest a reassuring hand on her shoulder before continuing, "Only this time we shall make the journey with our eyes open."

Vanessa nodded. Still unsure of the answers he had given her, but aware that she would get no better she squeezed his hand and released him.

"I will not be long, Little Flower. Please try to stay out of mischief while I am away," he said with a smile before slipping through the door.

Relatively alone in the house she tried to absorb what Cyrus had told her. Was she really free from her vampiric life at last? In a daze she went down to the bathroom and looked at herself in the mirror under the harsh light of the vanity. There *were* white hairs mixed with her black. She also saw a gold tint to her eyes that had never been there before. Something had changed; she had to admit that much. Only time would tell if it was a good change.

Listless she wandered into her room and threw herself onto the bed and looked around the small space. This had been home to her for more years than any other, yet it felt a little colder now knowing that Lilah was gone. The whole world did. This room didn't have the same feeling of *rightness* it had once held, but it was still home.

A glint of silver caught her eye drawing her to her feet. Nearly hidden behind her violin case was a thermos. *The* thermos. As if approaching a poisonous snake she reached in and pulled it out. Only Cyrus could have placed it there; or Meri she amended.

She unscrewed the stopper and peered in at the crimson liquid. With a shiver she looked away and replaced the stopper and cap. Now she was forced to wonder if Cyrus was leaving another choice for her or if Meri had seen something important. Putting it back she tried not to think about it. There were already more things in her mind than she had room for. Any one of them could suffocate her if she let them.

As she gazed thoughtlessly though the plexiglass case at her violin she removed the instrument almost before she knew what she was doing. Carefully she cradled it and the bow in her arms and made her way to Cyrus's room. It was hard to look at Meri as badly hurt as she was, but she refused to look away.

"I know you don't like me that much," she whispered, "But I hate to think of you being alone down here. I've been thinking and I think you're right. All I've ever done is let people take care of me or run from things. Now everyone's been hurt and while Cyrus says it isn't my fault I know a lot of this wouldn't have happened if I had done things differently. Maybe it's time for me to grow up and start taking care of myself."

She paused, looking at the floor. For a time she tried to find something more to say and failed. After checking the tuning on the violin she looked at Meri again.

"I don't know if you like classical music, but that's all I know. Maybe if it bugs you you'll wake up and tell me to knock it off."

And then she played.

About the author

Cameron likes his quiet country life with his wife, 2 kids, dogs, and cat.

Almost all of his spare time is spent in some artistic endeavor be it writing, working at the forge as an artisan blacksmith, weaving, or one of the other creative pursuits he follows.

Now that Vanessa has had her say it's time for more stories to come to light.

35726428R00139